Glory on Mars

Colonization Book I

Kate Rauner

Table of Contents

About This Book

Welcome to the first book in my On Mars series. Real-life settlers may travel to Mars in our lifetimes - what will a colony be like?

In these stories, Earth-born and Mars-born settlers struggle to survive the challenges of a hostile planet and threats from Earth as they build a new society. Will they survive?

I have two kinds of readers. Some of you want me to "just get on with it." I hope the story moves along well enough for you to enjoy.

Some of you ask for more details. You'll enjoy the Bonuses. These vignettes enhance the story but aren't essential to the plot. There are no spoilers in the bonuses, so you may read them before you start the story, after you finish, or never. This is, after all, your book. - *Kate* -

Epigraph

"Humanity is destined to explore, settle, and expand outward into the universe." Buzz Aldrin, second man to walk on the Moon

Tharsis Quadrangle

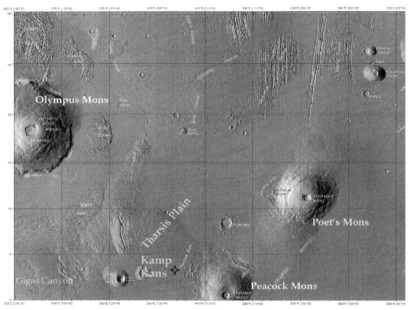

Olympus Mons

Tharsis Plain

Poet's Mons

Kamp Kans

Gigas Canyon

Peacock Mons

Tharsis, MC·9
Mercator Projection

Chapter One: Incident

THE SEASIDE RESORT of Noordwijk was a strange place to train for a mission to the barren deserts of Mars, but Colony Mars had its tidy headquarters north of the Dutch city, inland from the deep dunes of the beach. Sightseers hurried through the visitors' center to join guided tours of a Martian colony mockup and settler-candidates stopped between austere buildings to admire the summer flowers that replaced spring tulips.

Emma was about to start her last English-language tour when her link beeped an incoming message - the tone for "urgent". One family was still coming up the ramp, two young boys ricocheting among signs diagramming the mockup of the colony. Emma turned discreetly to one side and tapped her headset.

Emma didn't check her contact lens for metadata - that was the mission lead's voice in her ear. "There's a mission problem. Come to the control room as soon as duties allow."

A chill ran through Emma. Maybe her launch date had slipped. Maybe they'd miss the window entirely and she'd remain on Earth, temporarily reprieved. Why was that the first thought that came to her? Must be pre-launch jitters.

Emma was about to fly on Settler Mission Three and her journey depended on a narrow launch window. Balancing the planets' orbital dance with fuel requirements, Colony Mars could launch a mission every twenty-six months. If they missed it, there'd be a twenty-six month delay. But Emma excelled at focusing on the task at hand, so she turned her attention back to her tour group.

"If we're all ready? My name is Emma Winters and I'm a Martian settler. In twelve days, Colony Mars will launch me

1

and three crewmates into orbit to board our transport ship. I'll be your guide today through this replica of the Kamp Kans colony habitat or nederzetting, as our Dutch founders call it."

"Wow," one of the bouncy boys said. He was clearly a fan, dressed in a rugby shirt from the gift shop, striped in rusty red and sky blue just like Emma's uniform. "Are you really going to Mars and never coming back?"

"Yup. This is my last day in Holland."

She watched everyone's eyes widen at that. Public outreach, like this tour, was part of every settler's training, right up to their final day at headquarters. Personal contact kept public interest and donations high.

The urgent message tugged at her thoughts and she pushed it away again.

"Why don't one of you young men open the door and we'll begin." She gestured towards the white metal hatchway.

The younger boy hopped forward, stopping just before he ran into the door. "Hey!"

"You have to open it manually, dummy," his brother said. He looked back at Emma proudly. "All the nederzetting's doors are manual."

"That's right," Emma said with a practiced smile. The tour always started with the surprise of a manual door.

"Colony Mars uses the latest technology for some things, like construction, communications, and power generation. But technology requires lots of support - spare parts and maintenance. There are only eight people on Mars now; twelve when my mission gets there. Human beings are flexible. Our hands can replace dozens of servomechanisms."

The boy scowled at her skeptically.

Emma held up a pencil she carried especially for this bit. "Even simple tools are complex to manufacture. The wood for this pencil is logged in Oregon, in America. The graphite in the center is mined in Sri Lanka. Zinc and copper from Africa for the cap, and the eraser combines Italian pumice with Canadian rapeseed oil."

She waggled the pencil at the crowd. "I haven't mentioned the machines needed to produce it, or the thousands of workers and piles of parts at every step. On Mars, we use low tech wherever we can."

Emma spun the wheel-shaped handle, and stepped to one side as she heaved the door open. "Even 'no tech'. These hinges will still be working a hundred years from now."

She pushed the urgent message firmly out of her mind as the group stepped and stumbled over the door frame.

***

The quickest route to Mission Control was through the visitors' center. From the lobby, tourists turned right to enter the museum and gift shop under a banner in four languages.

Mars is ons geschenk aan de toekomst
Marso estas nia donaco al la estonteco
Mars est notre cadeau pour l'avenir
Mars is our gift to the future

Instead, Emma stepped behind the lobby's welcome desk. Rather than the usual cheery greeting, the attendant nodded grimly. Alarmed, Emma laid her hand on the scanner, a door concealed in the wall clicked open, and she hopped on the walkalator to the Mars-Earth Exchange building.

She could see the MEX antenna farm from the glass corridor. Today a group from the nearby European Space Agency's Technology Center stood at the base of the main dish - their visit had been the day's news at breakfast - but she was too distracted to wonder if they'd award another grant to Colony Mars.

She entered at the back of a stadium-style control room, behind two dozen stations, each arranged like an individual cockpit, and scanned the room for Filip Krast, the stocky MEX mission control lead. The front row, on the lowest level, was fully occupied as always by controllers running the satellite systems that orbited Mars - communications, tracking, weather, and solar power. On the second level technicians were installing upgrades for Emma's Settler Three mission.

Filip hurried across the top level, past the special projects stations, and ushered Emma to a glass-walled cubicle against the back wall.

"There's been a... an incident at Kamp," he said. "This isn't easy to watch." He steered her to a video console in the corner and hit playback. "There's been a death."

Emma sat up straight and felt her fingers go cold.

On the vid, the colony's doctor, Ingra, was stepping through a door in the habitat module. The lights were dimmed and the audio feed was silent except for the hum of life support systems - it was pre-dawn at the settlement. She crossed to the airlock, slowly rotated the door handle, and hopped through.

Filip tapped the console, switching to the playback from inside the airlock.

Ingra sealed the door and looked up at the imager. "By the time this transmission reaches Earth, I'll be gone. I can't stay here any longer. There's a huge old oak tree beyond that little crater. No one can see it, but I know it's there. I'm going home. Forgive me." She walked past the surface survival suits hanging on the wall and reached for the airlock control panel.

Emma felt a knot tighten in her stomach. "She can't get out without a suit, can she? The airlock pumps are slow; she'll pass out before the pressure is low enough for her to open the outer door, right?"

Filip pointed back to the screen.

Ingra stepped to the outer door. With a pull and twist, she opened the emergency decompression valve. Red lights began to flash and ice fog clouded the imager lens. Ingra fumbled with the outer door and it opened. With her last lungful of air, she pulled the door open and disappeared into the darkness.

Chapter Two: Explorers

EMMA LOOKED UP, not quite believing what she'd seen. Filip shook his head. "We sent alarms from here as soon as she entered the airlock, but she was gone before anyone received our transmission. With the outer door open, this airlock is disabled. Two of the settlers have already suited up and gone out the other way - to retrieve her body.

"You're the last of your crew to view this," he said gently. "The others are in the settlers' lounge. If you'll wait there, we'll keep you posted."

The lounge was at the opposite side of the building, down the main hall. Murals would one day cover the walls with a panel for each mission, but there were only six missions sketched out so far, with only Settler Missions One and Two completed in full color. Emma walked past pictures of the early robotic missions, the satellite system with its orbiting power station, and the squad of construction robots on the Martian surface. She stopped at the Settler One panel, *The Pioneers*, to look at portraits of the first crew. Ingra's face was smiling and confident. The first four settlers had lived in their ship, its modules repurposed on Mars' surface, for two years while building the large plaza and utilities spine.

Settler Two's panel, *The Builders*, depicted four more smiling portraits above a diagram of the growing habitat. Their transport ship had also been disassembled and ferried to the surface. All the ships would be cannibalized this way. There was no going back to Earth.

I don't understand, Emma thought as she gazed at the panel. Sure, the first two years were tough when they only had the three modules from their transport ship as habitat. But the second transport added three more modules and they constructed the plaza bay, pressurizing it with air harvested from the wisp-thin Martian atmosphere. Things were looking up.

She reached up to the diagram and touched the airlock Ingra had used. That airlock was probably still open to the frozen Martian atmosphere. Dust is drifting in, she thought idly. It will be hard to clean the airlock seals.

She jumped when her headset beeped with an incoming message.

"Hi Emma. It's Malcolm. Have you heard about Ingra? Are you okay?"

His face, projected into Emma's left eye on her contact link, was pinched with worry.

"Malcolm, you shouldn't contact me in real-time."

Malcolm and the rest of the Settler Four crew were nearing the end of an isolation evaluation, sealed inside a mock-up of a transport ship's habitat module. Anyone who came out early would lose their place on the mission.

"I'm sorry I can't be there with you," he said.

It was like Malcolm to risk a direct message. But then, he was a charmer and claimed he could talk his way out of anything. At a party, he was always in the middle of the crowd, offering jokes and compliments. They'd spent a long weekend together once - he'd planned everything and she had fun.

She walked past her own portrait - *Settler Three, The Explorers* - to the Settler Four panel, stood so his image in her eye overlaid his portrait, and hugged herself. "But we can't talk like this. Send a time-lagged message. And don't worry about me. I'll be with my mission crew."

***

Emma walked into the settlers' lounge, past a table to a circle of sleekly upholstered chairs pulled close together. Liz Brown jumped up. She had her hair pulled back in a streaked blond pony-tail, which emphasized her long face. Liz's eyes were red and, as they hugged, tears formed in Emma's eyes, too.

She'd never lived outside the United States before joining Colony Mars so Liz, a Canadian, felt like a friend from home. Emma had cross-trained as Liz's back-up farmer and they made a good team.

Emma sank into the empty chair next to Liz. On her other side, James Moore gave her a wan smile. The son of a diplomatic family, he'd lived all over the world and was generally irrepressible.

It was strange to see a sober expression on James' face. "Do you think they'll delay our launch?" None of them were especially close to Ingra - she'd left Earth before they arrived at Colony Mars' headquarters - so James was probably more worried for the mission.

Claude Krueger leaned over to them to speak softly. "I think that will depend on the other settlers on Mars." He was the oldest member of the S-3 crew - a field lithologist and looked the part, squarely built with callused hands. Claude was German, but had been teaching in California when he applied to Colony Mars.

Emma glanced around the room. The S-4 crew was, of course, in their isolation evaluation. Candidates for S-5 clustered together on the opposite side of the room. One of them gave Emma an uncertain nod. Settlers had a say in selecting subsequent crews, and they didn't know how to react to Ingra's suicide in front of the S-3 crew.

"Suicide. Could it be anything else?" Claude asked.

"I don't know." Liz had talked with Ingra more than the rest of them. She took medic training and they often messaged *back and forth. "She sounded delusional on the vid. She was hallucinating."

"She's Kamp's psychologist," Claude said. "I don't see how this could happen."

Liz sighed. "Doctors make lousy patients. Being a psychologist, she'd be able to fake her own routine psych evals."

"Well, this may be ghoulish," James said. But her death's sure increased interest in the colony."

Emma's eyes snapped up to the Earth Scan sphere spinning in the far corner of the room at the ceiling.

The most sophisticated artificial intelligence used by Colony Mars didn't run life support on Mars or pilot spaceships; it tracked their public presence on Earth. Earth Scan collected trillions of inputs worldwide, compiled reports, and projected a holographic sphere, a snapshot of how billions of people viewed the colony project.

The sphere was swollen to double its usual size, reflecting increased views. Color coded like a main sequence star, the sphere had intensified to blue from the usual yellow. Inside the translucent sphere, a silver hoop spun to show the rate of earnings from premium content, donations, and merchandise. It was twirling.

"MEX cut the live feed when they realized what was happening," James said. "And I guess the premium subscribers have been howling. They released the vid a few minutes ago."

"Hell," Emma said. "They released the entire video? What if her family sees it?"

Emma's link interrupted her with another message from Malcolm. She answered in a whisper, as if talking out loud would draw more attention to his breach of protocol.

Malcolm didn't sound worried. "I talked to one of the women on my crew. She'll trade places with you, so you can fly with me."

"That won't work. The robotic rovers and walkabouts are already packed in the cargo module. And I'm the mission roboticist. I've got to go."

"I don't want you in danger. Ingra was the colony's psychologist, for god's sake, and she killed herself. It's not safe until the experts figure out what's going wrong."

Emma huffed. "I'm not going to kill myself."

"Of course not. But what about the others, the colonists already on Mars? What if another one goes crazy?"

"The colony's Artificial Intelligence can run psych evals for psychologists on Earth."

"It's just that, I'm worried for you. I love you, Emma. I don't want anything to happen to you."

His intensity transfixed her. It had drawn her to him originally and a tingle ran down her spine. But they hadn't spent enough time together to talk about love.

"I'm signing off, Mal. My crew's waiting for me."

"You can't go." There was a cold edge to his voice.

Emma's feelings shifted abruptly. His concern had been touching, but he had no right to tell her what to do.

She'd been talking softly, but now pulled out her pocket pad to type a private reply. *I'm not volunteering to give up my spot on S-3.*

The words looked harsh on her screen. He was, after all, worried about her with good reason. Critics predicted psychological issues would destroy the colony. That's why Colony Mars decided evals by Kamp's AI weren't enough and included a psychologist among the settlers. Ingra's evaluations of individuals were, of course, confidential, but Emma read all her summary reports. There was insomnia among the settlers, fatigue, loss of appetite, and trouble focusing. None of that sounded fatal, but Ingra was dead.

Don't worry about me. I'm with a good crew and I can take care of myself. You need to take care of yourself. Talk to your mission counselor.

"Malcolm," she said in response to Liz's raised eyebrow. "He's flipping out."

"He was a lot of fun at that candidate meet-and-greet party." Her forehead wrinkled with concern. "I didn't know you were still seeing him?"

"I'm not, not really. We've each had so much training, different duty schedules..."

"He should talk to his counselor if he's upset."

"That's what I'm telling him." Emma read the pad again and hit send.

When the public information officer walked in, he had more details, but no more insight. "I've received a few suggestions to change your mission," he said. "But there's not enough time to explore what unintended consequences could arise. And no one wants to miss a launch window. So the *Explorers Mission* is still a go."

James must have been holding his breath. He heaved out a sigh in relief, Liz and Claude nodded, and Emma ignored the tightness in her stomach.

"But if any of you want to drop out..." the officer said. "I'll try to place you on another flight, but I can't make any guarantees."

"I'm ready to go," Claude said and the others nodded resolutely.

Emma's back straightened and her jaw set. "I'm not dropping out."

"I knew you'd all feel that way." He smiled grimly.

Emma sat with her crewmates the rest of the day, abandoning plans for a final walk along the shore. They followed reports from Kamp, watched as Ingra's body was carried beyond the colony's construction zone for burial, and as the airlock was cleaned and closed. Colony Mars issued a formal statement and began planning a memorial service. Emma was sorry they'd miss the ceremony, but not sorry she'd miss the subtle fund-raising that would, no doubt, be embedded in the eulogies.

The launch window wouldn't wait and she had to pack - they all did. The crew's flight to Spaceport America would leave Rotterdam airport the next day.

Then on to Mars.

Chapter Three: Spaceport

SPACEPORT AMERICA'S main terminal squatted like a huge horseshoe crab shoved into New Mexico's desert floor. Dry mountains rose in the distance and roads crisscrossed a sandy plain to launch pads, past low scrubby trees raising gray-green leaves to the blue sky. It was the end of the rainy season and birds flitted across the landscape, searching for ripening seeds.

The reception party was canceled after Ingra's death, but a banner still hung at their arrival gate: *Welcome Colony Mars Settler 3 Explorers*.

Ground-support teams met them, accompanied by spaceport officials. They'd spend two nights in the spaceport's elegant hotel before shuttling out to the launch site.

Emma carried two duffle bags to her room. Settlers took few personal possessions with them and she dropped that small bag on the closet floor. The second bag held what she'd need for her time at the spaceport. She'd leave it behind.

The room was huge. The bed alone was larger than her room on Mars would be, where she'd have a bunk in one of the repurposed ship modules. Kamp's dormitory bay wouldn't be built for years.

She activated her link and made a voice contact. "Hi Mom. I'm at the spaceport."

Her mother had vacillated between congratulations and tears throughout Emma's training. Today it was tears.

"I can't believe you're really going," she said with a sniffle. "Living on Mars! It doesn't seem real. What are you going to *do* every day?"

"Mom, didn't you read the Colony Mars mission site?" She'd tried to explain a dozen times. Her mother never paid attention for long.

"Yes. Well, some of it. What's this about you eating worms? Sounds dreadful."

"It's practical. The first two missions have been living on space rations while they build the basic settlement bays. There's room to plant gardens now and, yes, raise mealworms for protein. Fish, too, if that sounds better to you. But the exciting part is the exploration robots. We're taking the rovers and walkabout suits from Dad's company."

Colony Mars engineers had argued for simple surface buggies, but her father could be eloquent. He'd convinced management that rovers fully integrated with the colony's AI would be more flexible and safer. And if the high-tech interface failed, Emma could strip it out and go back to manual operation.

"You and your Dad are like two peas in a pod on this robot thing." Her mother laughed through her sniffles. "I never could follow the conversations you had, even when you were a little girl."

According to her mother, her father's early business ventures all failed. But he started a robotics company about the time she was born and it took off. Mom wasn't interested in robotics or business and Emma couldn't remember a time when her father wasn't working long hours. It was no surprise that her parents divorced shortly after she started college.

It was her father who got Emma interested in engineering, in robotics, and in Mars. After she finished her engineering degree, he gave her a job on his contracts for the colony - much more exciting than tweaking designs on domestic bots, which is what new-hires usually did. All his talk about destiny in space inspired her to apply. That, and the chance to personally test the robots on the Martian surface.

Emma's enthusiasm bubbled up as she talked about the walkabouts. "The adjustable seals on the walkabouts were a real challenge. I had to..."

"It sounds very interesting, dear. I'm sure your father's thrilled, though I haven't heard from him lately."

Emma sighed. She should know better. Mom could only listen to technical talk for so long.

"I've arrived at my maker-space, so I've got to go. I'm going to miss you so much." Her mother smiled through tears. "I'm proud of you and so happy you're following your dream."

Emma flopped across the coral and turquoise bedspread as the link closed. Her mother never shared her zeal for engineering - Emma was her father's child in that way. He'd encouraged her, though mostly from a distance, answering her messages late at night from his lab or while traveling. She'd treasured every message he sent and saved them all. Sometimes it was hard to tell where his passion stopped and hers began. Emma hoped she was following her dream.

***

Emma expected to have the next morning to herself, but as she dressed her link beeped, summoning her to a meeting, immediately. She'd already pulled on a tee-shirt and old jeans - comfortable old jeans she'd leave behind. She decided not to change and headed for the room noted in the message, trying to ignore her growling stomach.

The room was a top floor suite and, as she lifted her hand to knock, the door opened. She didn't recognize the man who tipped his head politely, but he was dressed in khakis and a Colony Mars blue ground-support shirt.

He waved her inside. "Please come in. Your crewmates will be here shortly."

Emma stepped into a large sitting room and looked past the upholstered chairs to a splendid breakfast buffet across the room.

"Please, help yourself," he said.

She was starting on a plate of fluffy scrambled eggs when her crewmates arrived and happily filled plates for themselves.

"I don't know what this meeting's about," James said, spearing a perfect strawberry and holding it up. "But I approve."

The doorman bustled around, pouring coffee for each of them and offering a carafe of warm cream.

He turned, holding the coffee pot balanced against a crisp white napkin. "Good morning, Mademoiselle."

A slight, elderly lady in a formal business suit quietly entered from the suite's next room.

"Mademoiselle Lambert, may I present Claude Krueger, Liz Brown, James Moore, and Emma Winters." He nodded at each of them in turn. "Ladies and gentlemen, Mademoiselle Amelia Lambert."

Claude leaped to his feet and the others followed. Mlle Lambert was Colony Mars' benefactor, a wealthy reclusive patron whom no one, as far as Emma knew, ever met.

Mlle Lambert stepped forward and shook Claude's outstretched hand, shook hands with Liz and James, and turned to Emma.

"I've looked forward to meeting you, Doctor Winters. I've known your father for many years."

"My pleasure," Emma said uncertainly.

Damn, she thought. Does everyone know my father?

"Jason, champagne for my guests, please. Then take something for yourself and relax."

The doorman pulled an ice bucket and bottle from under the buffet tablecloth and popped the cork. He conjured crystal flutes and served Mlle Lambert, then Emma and the other settlers before retreating out of sight. Emma didn't think he relaxed.

"I might inquire how you like your rooms," Mlle Lambert said after a sip. "But I imagine you are more interested in why I asked you here."

"Why, yes, mademoiselle," Claude said. He recovered his manners faster than the others. "It's a great honor..."

"Rather a great surprise, don't you think?" Mlle Lambert's eyes sparkled over a mischievous smile. "I have a special request. I thought I'd deliver it in person.

"You probably know the settlers at Kamp have cut off their live video feeds. The colony's artificial intelligence system is recording everything, but the settlers have voted to limit the feed to Earth. Right now, we have access to one imager in the plaza bay, the most public portion of the nederzetting."

"It's understandable, isn't it?" Liz asked. "They want privacy after Ingra's death."

Mlle Lambert pulled a pad from her pocket, laid it flat on the table, and called up Earth Scan's 3-D image. A miniature sphere glowed and spun above the pad.

She tapped the pad again and a bar chart, like a handful of pencils, floated in mid-air. "Understandable, *oui*. But it does not help us enlist public support. It does not help with fundraising."

She ran a finger along each axis. "Here are donations, here's time. People are frustrated when they can't see the settlers, can't hear their reactions. They lose interest and that reduces donations.

"Colony Mars plans to keep sending settlers forever, but in practice, we can only send missions as long as we have funding. My people use Kamp's feeds to produce weekly infotainments. Access to live feeds is a perk for our premium subscribers.

"I can fund Colony Mars for a time," Mlle Lambert said. "Sale of my Tuscan estate, for example, bought your transport ship. But it's my hope that Colony Mars will continue to send settlers long after I am gone."

She closed the chart display. "I am a determined woman. All the women in my family are willful. When we choose to accomplish something, we succeed, and that is the attitude needed to colonize Mars. Technology may keep you alive, but attitude will allow you to thrive."

"Perhaps you understand the situation," Mlle Lambert said. "Once you join Kamp Kans on Mars, perhaps you will favor the video feeds."

Liz and James nodded and Claude frowned. The little speech reminded Emma of her father, but she didn't need more inspiration.

"I don't think the first thing I want to do is start an argument with the other settlers," Emma said.

"Very wise," Mlle Lambert said. "Keep in mind the colony is not yet self-sustaining. We will launch ships through mission seven, one every twenty-five months - then we must skip a few years, so ships don't arrive at the height of Mars' storm season. After that... we shall see. By then, perhaps there will be enough resources on Mars for the colony to survive without us."

"Mission seven. We'll have twenty-eight settlers on Mars by then," Claude said.

"Twenty-seven." Liz corrected him quietly.

Mlle Lambert sipped her champagne for a moment. "Twenty-seven are not enough settlers to satisfy the experts, as you know. But, with luck, perhaps enough for humanity to have a permanent home on Mars."

She rose from her chair. "Of course you must do what you feel is right. But it would be a very sad thing to be both the first and the last humans on Mars."

Jason appeared and opened the door behind her.

"Please enjoy your breakfast," she said. "A human foothold on Mars has been my lifelong dream, and you are making it come true. You have my gratitude."

She gave them each a nod, turning to Emma last.

"Your father never mentioned me, did he?"

"I'm afraid I don't remember..."

"Quite right. Good luck Doctor Winters." Mlle Lambert stepped through the door and Jason followed her. There was the soft click of a lock turning.

"Well, I'll be..." Claude continued to stare at the closed door.

"She seems to like you," James said to Emma. "What do you think of this business with the vid feeds?"

"It's close to eight months before we enter Mars orbit. Maybe things will sort themselves out," Emma said. She walked back to the buffet and picked up a wedge of watermelon. "It's seedless, Liz."

"Too bad. We don't have any watermelon seeds with us."

They were leaving so much behind.

I'll have to request that watermelon seeds be added to the next mission, Emma thought.

Chapter Four: Farewell

THAT EVENING, Emma dressed for the farewell event in a standard settler's uniform: a rust and blue striped rugby shirt over khaki cargo pants. The versions she'd wear on the spaceship and at Kamp Kans were stain-free, self-cleaning fabrics knit from fibers infused with a slippery film.

At least I won't be doing laundry for years to come, she thought, and sadly rubbed the soft cotton shirt between her fingers.

Emma didn't usually worry about how she looked. In robotics labs, fashion consisted of colorful frames on safety glasses. Outside the lab, Colony Mars had been dressing her for a couple years. But for the journey to Mars, she'd cropped her hair short and the severe cut didn't enhance her square, pale face. Tonight was a party, so she tried to fluff her hair out around her ears but didn't bother with makeup - there'd be none on Mars.

There was just one last duty before the farewell party, a final media conference in the convention wing of the hotel.

She was walking down the hall with the rest of the crew when her link beeped.

"Huh, it's Dad," she said to Liz. "I'll be along in a minute."

Her father's face appeared over the link. He usually wore a solemn expression, but tonight he looked grim.

"I'm starting a new line of asteroid mining bots," he said. "I need a group leader. I'd like that leader to be you. Your own lab, and of course you'll pick your own team. We'll start with a research-oriented budget..."

"What? Dad." She interrupted him. "What are you talking about? I'm on my way to Mars. I'm at Spaceport America now."

"I know that," he said. "But you can do more for the company on Earth than on Mars. Would you rather take over the future Colony Mars contracts? I want you to stay."

Emma stopped dead in the hallway.

"What? You encouraged me to go. What about all those speeches you made? What we learn will benefit humanity - the lure of the unknown - the noble experiment to inspire future generations - that exploration is in our DNA. What about the benefits to the company by ensuring our bots are part of a scientific breakthrough?"

"It's not just the company." He wore an odd, strained expression. "To survive you've got to maintain a bubble of Earth on Mars. If that bubble bursts, you'll die."

Emma snorted. "You've seen the technical specs..."

"No one knows the technology better than I do." He took a deep breath. "I'll miss you, hon."

"We never see each other anyway." She waved her hands in exasperation. "We can trade messages - just like always, every couple months." Emma felt inexplicably angry.

"You don't have to give up Mars. I've got contracts right here at home for future missions. Take your pick."

"Look, Dad. I'm going. Nothing changes between us."

"I'll miss our dinners together when I'm in town." He sounded hurt.

"You want me to give up a dream for dinner once a year?"

Liz glanced over a shoulder at her. Emma took a deep breath and calmed the shrillness in her voice.

"Dad, you've got pre-launch jitters. Everything we've planned over the past few years - me and you - it'll all be good, you'll see."

She hurried to catch up with the crew and whispered to Liz what her father said.

"His wavering is natural," Liz said. "It's hard to say goodbye. But we're lucky. We'll have contact with our families, and all our favorite book and picture files. That's more than most immigrants had throughout history."

"Did it give you second thoughts? Saying goodbye, I mean?"

"I've cried, but - no. Mars or bust." Liz shook her fist with a thumbs-up.

"What about Ingra? You have medic training. Do you think someone else will go crazy?"

Liz shook her head. "Who knows? But it's worth the risk. Expanding the spiral of creation is the purpose of life."

Emma retreated to her own thoughts. Liz belonged to SolSeed, dedicated to seeing life take root among the stars, as she'd often said. Mars was humanity's first step and Liz wasn't worried about personal deprivations. Emma didn't have a cosmic purpose to comfort her.

In the small conference room, Colony Mars functionaries ushered the crew to seats at a long table. Logo-festooned banners hung from the table and two staff psychologists were already seated. A dozen folding chairs faced the table, all empty. Emma was used to these internet press meetings. As each journalist was tapped by the coordinator, their hologram would pop up in a seat and a question would be read into her ear in English, out of synch with the lip movements of whatever language the questioner spoke.

Most questions tonight were about Ingra's suicide and Emma was happy the psychologists answered those. They offered assurance that the colony would survive - serious answers tinged with optimism.

A dark woman popped up in the front row. "My viewers wonder, how is this colony different from the space missions we're used to, from the European Space Agency or from NASA?"

The public information officer answered, but Emma could imagine Filip Krast nodding for all the mission controllers.

"Letting the settlers manage their own lives in space, accepting that we're not in charge anymore. It's as hard as any engineering challenge."

Finally there was a familiar question, one asked all the time.

The image of a pale man with sagging jowls appeared on their left. The crew turned their heads. It was easier to be engaging if they pretended he was really there.

"Why go to Mars?" he asked. "You'll be the most isolated humans who ever lived. Why, especially, do you want to live the rest of your lives there? I'd like to hear from each of you... Miz Brown?"

"Earth's a fragile orb. Something catastrophic could happen, natural or manmade. I'll be making life multi-planetary."

James couldn't resist adding something. "If dinosaurs had a space program, they wouldn't be extinct."

"Noble, but, Miz Brown, is there nothing personal?"

"There's the opportunity for transcendence, to grow spiritually, and gain a greater appreciation of life."

Claude got a faraway look whenever he answered this question. "To gain new knowledge."

The jowly man was persistent. "How about creating wealth? An entire world of untapped resources? You're a geologist - isn't that what you do?"

"Geo means Earth, so I'm a lithologist now. I study rocks on Mars." Claude shook his head.

"And - no. One reason that people are fascinated by Mars is that it's beyond our current culture. Earth can't make a profit from it. It makes no economic sense. We go for science."

James was their most popular spokesman. He kept a little speech ready. "Humanity evolved in Africa - so why aren't we all still there? I think it's because of what we are - what we do. We wander. We explore.

"Half a millennium ago, Europeans set out to conquer the Earth for gold, glory, and god. Well, Claude wants to study Martian rocks - that will be our Martian gold.

"Liz is called to carry life to a barren world, a sacred obligation to god.

"But me and Emma..." Here he turned to her. "We're in it for the glory. The pure, glorious idiocy of the challenge."

Emma smiled into the room's cameras, ignoring the tension in her body. "Yeah, my walkabout bots are so unconventional, I couldn't find anyone else willing to pilot them on Mars."

That got a laugh, as always. But it was a relief when the conference ended.

They walked straight down the carpeted hall to a large ballroom. Emma paused at the door to look around. There were spaceport officials and Colony Mars executives glad-handing significant donors. The ground-support team members were milling around quietly, easy to pick out in shirts striped with two shades of blue instead of the settlers' blue and red.

A Colony Mars official gestured the crew to join him, grabbed a microphone, and the crowd quieted. After a short eulogy to Ingra, he called for a minute of silence.

When the minute passed, he raised his fist defiantly. "Ingra's sacrifice is not in vain. On to Mars."

"On to Mars!" The crowd shouted back to him and the party began.

Someone pushed a flute of champagne into Emma's hand. She abandoned her usual restraint, had a second glass of champagne, and switched to tangy margaritas when waiters brought out platters of cheese-stuffed jalapenos.

"Settlers, we need you at the front of the room." The climax of the evening was coming. An officious looking man in a suit waved his hand solemnly and the crowd parted, letting Emma walk to the front of the room with her crewmates.

"These are the final Colony Mars contracts," the man said. For an oddly archaic effect he held long paper pages over his head. Liz pushed forward to sign first and the rest of the crew queued behind her. Emma scribbled her name awkwardly with a pen. She understood there was no chance of returning from Mars, understood her survival was not guaranteed, and relinquished her right to sue Colony Mars for any reason.

"Okay everyone. Gather round." The support team lead hopped up on a chair and swayed precariously. "It's time for the electronics swap."

Unexpectedly, Emma felt a wave of panic battle the tequila in her bloodstream. She'd had phones and tablets, games and links for as long as she could remember. But batteries were a luxury on Mars, used only for necessary applications. All her earthly devices would be left behind.

One by one, with laughing and back-slapping, the crew of Settler Three relinquished their devices. Contact lenses were popped out and pads were dropped into a box.

"We don't leave our intrepid settlers out of touch," the support lead shouted over the crowd. He passed Emma a hand-sized pad.

With a cord. An electric power cord. And then he handed her an extension cord.

Emma stared at them. Of course, she used corded pads in training, but the permanence of surrendering her own devices left her hollow inside. She wandered towards the edge of the crowd, to the ballroom wall, and plugged into an outlet.

Her pad powered up immediately and, already set to Emma's account, popped open a message.

"Hey! I've got a message from Kamp," she called out. People nearby turned towards her and the room quieted when they saw her puzzled face.

"They want a cat," Emma said.

"What?" The support lead tumbled off his chair in confusion.

"They want us to bring them a cat." Emma held up the pad, hitting the end of the power cord.

"You mean a pet-bot?" someone asked.

"No. A real, live cat. They say they've arranged for a kitten to be delivered to our ship from Lunar Base."

Fuzzy with margaritas, Emma was perplexed. Maybe the settlers on Mars were going crazy. But a cat would be more life on Mars and, somewhere in the crowd, she was sure Liz was smiling.

***

Emma slipped out of the party and wandered to a hotel coffee shop. Real coffee with real cream was something she'd miss and she didn't trust the stuff they'd brew at the launch facility. This could be her last chance.

She chose a small table in the far corner of the room. As she nursed her cup, Claude Krueger came in. She wasn't sure she wanted any company and certainly not another settler. But he spotted her, carried his coffee with exaggerated care, and sat at her table.

"Hi, Claude." Emma forced a smile. "Enjoying your last night?"

"They're all so damn happy in there." He gestured vaguely down the hall. "They're not going to Mars. You and me. James and Liz. We're going. I don't even know most of those people."

"The party's not really for us. It's a Colony Mars event. Didn't you take your vacation last month with family?"

He didn't seem to hear her.

"Wanna see a picture of my wife?" He fumbled in his pocket and laid out his pad, then swore. "I forgot. This thing needs to be plugged in."

Emma leaned forward, realizing she'd been wrong - she did want to talk.

"Do you ever have second thoughts? Regrets?"

"Second thoughts, no. Regrets..." He slurped at his coffee and wiped a hand across his mouth. "I've had regrets since I filled out my application. I had a good life." He fingered the pad.

"So why did you apply?"

"For a chance to go to Mars!" He sat back in the chair and spread his hands helplessly. "How could anyone ignore the opportunity? I've taught classes on Martian lithology, designed experiments to determine its mineralogy. If I had the chance and passed it up, how could I live with myself?"

24

"I helped develop the rovers and walkabouts we're taking," Emma said. "That's what gives our mission its name - the Explorers. That's what I'm going for."

Claude waved his hand dismissively. "Tools. Just fancy versions of my rock hammer. It's the rocks. The damn, blasted rocks, that are important."

"Claude, you're drunk. You should go to bed."

Without another word, he snapped the lid on his cup, pocketed the pad, and tottered out of the shop.

He's right, Emma thought. Who could pass up the chance to go to Mars? She felt a tingle in her gut, maybe thrill or maybe fear.

I've got grit, she thought as she watched the barista serving another late-night customer. It's my best feature. When I say I'm gonna do something, I do it. I got top grades in school because I've got grit and that made Mom and Dad proud of me. I got my PhD because I've got grit, and my advisor was impressed. Now I'm going to Mars for the rest of my life because I've got grit. It's the opportunity of a lifetime.

She stared at the coffee counter. Next to the pad where people tapped their links to pay was a jar with a few coins.

Whenever she dithered over a decision, her mother told her to flip a coin. You'll be relieved at the result or disappointed, she'd say, and either way that tells you how you really feel.

"I'm borrowing a coin," she said to the barista. "Just for a minute."

She tipped the jar, fished out the largest coin, set its edge against the counter, and gave it a spin. As the spin turned to a wobble, she whispered.

"Heads for Mars, tails for Earth."

The coin fell and she knew. The tightness inside her vanished. Emma was going to Mars.

Chapter Five: Mass Driver

THE NEXT MORNING, slightly nauseous and head aching, Emma boarded a spaceport sand coach with James and Claude, leaving Liz behind for a day of intensive veterinarian training. The coach set out eastward across a broad desert valley. After a while, Emma looked up, then over her shoulder. The spaceport was hidden by a colorless slope behind them.

"Have you followed the cat debate?" James asked. "They've been at it all night."

He used the coach's link to play some messages out loud. It seemed the colonists had been talking to Lunar Base for weeks, ever since the Loonies announced a litter of kittens was on the way - kittens to be born on the Moon and raised at the Collins Space Dock. Emma roused herself enough to wonder why the settlers kept it a secret from MEX.

Colony Mars engineers, quite reasonably, balked at adding an element to their mission at the last minute, especially a live animal. But Lunar Base had a complete proposal ready. They'd provide everything, including a plan for feeding a cat long-term on Mars. After Ingra's extraordinary suicide, the psychologists were inclined to approve whatever the colonists requested. The added mass of the cat's supplies was well within the transport ship's margin of error for fuel, so the engineers didn't object. So a cat was formally added to their mission.

The coach bounced and Emma squinted out a wide window.

"Where are we?" she asked the driver.

The coach ran on autodrive, so the driver wasn't actually driving. Spaceport never left clients without a real live human escort and he rode with his seat swiveled to face the crew.

"Jornada del Muerto," he called out cheerfully. "Named by the Spanish who first explored this desert. The Journey of Death."

Claude roused himself to grumble. "Hopefully not prophetic."

"It's a long ride," Emma said with a sigh.

"We're this far from the terminal so the space ramp could be built up onto the mountains, to take advantage of the angle for launch," the driver said. "The spaceplane launches over a restricted area, the White Sands military base, so if you crash on take-off, you won't kill anyone."

"I'd feel terrible if I crashed on someone," James said. He was recovering and sounded chipper.

"We'll go under the launch track in a little bit," the driver said. "Do you know how many loops you'll make before they shoot you up the ramp? Never tried it myself. I'm told the ship builds up a lot of g-force."

Emma shuddered at the thought, settled back into her seat, and closed her eyes. James chattered with the driver but she was silently grateful for a smooth road the rest of the way.

She opened her eyes again when the coach stopped. Sloping concrete walls supported a heavy metal track ahead of them, above a narrow shadowed tunnel.

"See the electromagnets mounted on the sides?" The driver said, pointing. "They accelerate the spaceplane."

On the other side of the tunnel, the track stretched into the distance around them. The center of the huge circle was filled with heliostatic tracking mirrors focused on a central receiver tower - power for the mass driver magnets. On the loop's opposite side, towards the mountains and the space ramp, was the launch building - an entirely utilitarian, squat, flat-roofed structure of unpainted concrete. They'd be isolated in the east wing along with the medical staff. A separate building on the west side, equally ugly, housed the ground team on duty. They'd had their own, non-alcoholic party last night and were back at work. The relief team would arrive in a few days.

Filip from MEX greeted them.

"I wondered why I didn't see you at the party," James said as he hopped down.

"I'm not much for parties, especially when there's a control room to see instead."

"Your control room's in Holland," Claude said with a frown.

"My team has preparations well in hand, and Lunar Base handles the transport ship while it's in Collins Dock. MEX doesn't take over until you're ready to break orbit, so I'll be back at MEX in plenty of time."

Filip grew solemn. "This is my last chance to shake hands with each of you."

Emma straightened up, sensing a ceremony not listed in Colony Mars' media kit.

"It's been an honor working with you. Good luck from me, the team, and posterity." He clasped each of their hands tightly before holding open the door and waving them towards the isolation wing.

***

The crew started final launch preparations immediately. Emma's first appointment was for her pre-flight physical. The doctor was a tiny, birdlike woman.

"Take off your shirt, please," she said after introductions, and looked slightly over Emma's shoulder, reading from her contact lens link.

"Your contraceptive chip is in your upper left arm."

It didn't sound like a question, but Emma answered, fingering the spot.

"You have your personal device to deactivate the chip when you choose." Again, not a question, but the device was in her personal duffle bag. "Colony Mars has the code on file for you, should you lose your device."

The doctor now looked at her and, somewhat abruptly, smiled.

"If you would stand here, and place your arm in the gauntlet tray..." The doctor closed the lid and Emma felt pressure build along her forearm.

"Stand still, please. This will take a moment. A little more..." The doctor looked over Emma's shoulder again. "Party last night, I see. But you're cleared for launch."

The gauntlet popped open and Emma rubbed her arm. It was covered with hundreds of barely-visible red dots.

"If that redness isn't gone by morning, call me. I'm right here in quarantine with you. This is the last readout you'll receive until the Settler Four mission delivers full hospital diagnostics to the colony."

Emma nodded.

"That's only two years away and there's no reason for a healthy young adult to have a full diagnostic more often than every five years." She took a plastic case out of the drawer next to her.

"This is your lacertossum medichip, which will tweak your own hormone production to improve bone density and muscle tone."

She turned the case towards Emma to display her name across the top. "Emma Winters, correct? Your upper right arm this time, I think. I'll just deaden the area..." She used a thin needle to inject analgesic at a half-dozen points- enough drug to visibly swell a spot on Emma's arm.

"This has to go in deep enough to ensure capillaries will grow into the chip..."

Emma looked away until the doctor pressed a bandage over the area.

"The chip doesn't relieve you of your exercise obligation," she said as Emma pulled her shirt on. "But avoid lifting anything heavy with that arm for a couple days."

Emma hurried off to a briefing on feline care shoehorned into her schedule. She'd never paid much attention to Lunar Base news before, but now learned a few of the Loonies spent their spare time figuring out how to keep cats on the Moon and had been happy to donate a kitten.

The final week before leaving Earth was filled with briefings and medical tests. Emma fell into her bunk each night too tired to think, thankfully asleep before she hit the mattress.

Chapter Six: Goodbye Earth

ON THE MORNING of the first launch attempt the crew was awake before dawn. New Mexico's rainy monsoon season was over, so weather wasn't a big risk for an August launch, but the ground team carefully reviewed the forecast. The morning was clear and all systems were ready.

Emma dropped her small personal duffle bag at the edge of the embarkation stairs. Red lights outlined the launch building so her eyes adjusted quickly to the lingering darkness and stars shown despite the eastern sky lightening to gray.

James dropped his own bag next to her. "I hope you enjoyed your last opportunity to use toilet paper. It's a perfect morning, so we're sure to launch."

Emma could only work up a faint smile. "I never thought about it much before, but I'm going to miss the stars."

"Yup, atmosphere's too dusty for much stargazing on Mars," James said as he rocked impatiently on his feet. "And there's no full Moon to swoon over, either. Just a couple little rocks zipping by overhead."

Ridiculous to notice the stars, Emma thought. I've never spent much time looking at the sky.

Ground teams were loading the spaceplane - half the seats had been removed to allow for their cargo. Emma watched as they moved canisters of fish and mealworms, each in its own life support unit, and packs of sturdy young plants. Food for the body is food for the soul, as Liz would say. Last on board were cases of seeds packed in nitrogen.

The transport ship that would take them to Mars had blasted into Earth orbit months ago atop heavy-lift rockets. Today the crew and the rest of the live cargo would follow. An atmospheric ferry overhung the track above them, blocking a view of the spaceplane on top.

After a final briefing, the settlers, dressed in their uniform of cargo pants and striped shirts, walked up the stairs, waved back at the cameras mounted on the launch building, and stepped through the spaceplane's hatch. The pilot welcomed them like they were tourists. He had nothing to do until the ferry released the plane at the top of the atmosphere, so he busied himself ensuring his passengers were comfortably strapped in. Emma felt the tingle in her gut grow as the ferry pilots called out their checklist over the comm system.

Just hang on, Emma thought to herself, letting her breath out slowly. Nothing to do but hang on.

The hatch was sealed, the stairs retracted, and the craft began slowly accelerating. They each had a window and Emma watched as they circled the ring until the increasing speed forced her to relax back into her seat. There wasn't the slightest bump when the craft transferred to the launch ramp tracks. The ground dropped away.

The ferry fired its onboard boosters and vibrations shook the ship. With a terrifying thrill, Emma wondered if something had gone wrong, but the ship settled into a steady rumble beneath her and she loosened her grip on the armrests.

The pilots kept up a running commentary as they tacked through bands of strong winds. They skirted the jet stream near the top of the troposphere and continued up to the edge of space. The curve of the Earth stood out distinctly and the sky was black. At maximum velocity, Emma's weight disappeared and only the harness straps squeezed her torso.

Emma was glued to her window when the pilot announced separation. The ferry clamps disengaged, thrusters fired, and Emma felt the seat drop under her. After a moment to clear the ferry, the plane pilot engaged his ion engines, and the force of acceleration pushed Emma back into her seat.

It wasn't long before the engines cut out and they were weightless again, cruising towards the Collins Space Dock. The dock was located at a Lagrangian point, a spot where the gravity of the Earth and Moon balance, where their transport ship was effectively parked. The Moon was a disk faintly illuminated by Earthshine and thinly rimmed by a crescent of light.

The pilot announced they were free to leave their seats.

Liz pulled herself close to the window looking down on Earth, turned to view the Moon, and back to Earth. White clouds swirled over a dark ocean as the edge of a continent appeared on the curve of the planet.

"I've never felt closer to God," Liz whispered.

Within an hour they spotted the ship with the enormous Moon, now half illuminated by the Sun, hanging beyond.

Settler Three didn't look much like a spaceship. The heavy-lift rockets and aerodynamic nosecone had been stripped away and sent back to Earth, leaving a cylinder. The solar collectors below the habitat module were still in their stowed position and three small engines with individual tanks hung on the aft end, fueled with hydrogen and oxygen mined from ice at the lunar poles, ready for the journey to Mars. Airlock cylinders had been welded on by the Collins teams and protruded at regular intervals. Once in Mars orbit the ship would disassemble and each module would land to become part of the settlement, connected at those airlocks.

It looks like something I made in kindergarten from cardboard tubes, Emma thought as she pressed against her window.

The spaceplane slowed and rolled, putting the ship out of view. Finally a shudder ran through the cabin as the pilot locked the docking clamps and the Collins dockhands opened the hatch.

Emma floated slowly through, crinkling her nose at her first whiff of the ship's air, like hot metal, a smell picked up from ions in space and brought in on the dockhands' gear.

James slid past her like a swimmer under water. "This is the coolest sensation I've ever had - better than the simulator pools. Hey, you look a little green."

Emma smiled at him but continued her slow progress with one hand on the hull. She'd passed the motion-sickness screening. They all had. There was no relief in zero-g and it could be debilitating, even fatal if vomiting led to dehydration and unbalanced electrolytes.

Vomiting was not the thing to think about right now. Emma gripped a vent cover and let a spell of dizziness pass. She firmly ignored the white plastic bags in her pockets and pointedly looked away from James spinning in a slow roll.

"Ship: I'm Emma. Activate my transponder."

"Welcome aboard, Emma." The transport ship's artificial intelligence had a vaguely feminine voice. Each settler announced their presence.

Emma had trained in an identical habitat module. She could cross the living quarters in eight steps on Earth, though steps didn't mean anything in zero-g. She released her grip on the vent, kept her feet aimed at the gray deck, and let the air current move her gently away. An oval table was mounted left of center, so it was a straight shot across to the second airlock where the Collins team's shuttle was docked. To her right were cocoon-like bunks and to her left, the galley. Macronutrient cylinders stood against the hull there, floor to ceiling, and there was a food printer to extrude the nutrients into different shapes with, hopefully, appealing textures. In front of the galley, exercise equipment was bolted to the floor.

An Earth Scan sphere floated at the ceiling, glowing green. The settlers' arrival was streaming live, another reason to avoid thinking about her stomach.

Emma clung to a chair at the central table to survey her new home. The habitat module was configured for its ultimate use in Mars' gravity, so floor and ceiling, up and down had meaning. The airlocks entered on the lower level, the living space. Above was the life support level with sanitary facilities. Wiring, ducts, and all the electronics were installed in the cylinder's hull, hidden behind panels for the most part. The exceptions were sets of three small LED lights, each below a finned black heat sink protruding from the hull. They provided supplemental cooling for the individual servers behind panels - specialized, fault-tolerant, with a very low failure rate - the physical brain of the ship's AI. Emma maneuvered in a slow circle, checking their status. No red lights glowed, which was good. In half or more, the center green light blinked a slow on-off rhythm. Those were installed spare capacity on stand-by. The rest were in use as the solid green lights indicated.

Watching her crewmates explore the habitat, Emma appreciated the effort Colony Mars made to balance their skills. Emma came to Colony Mars with a degree in robotics, and she also knew a lot about all the systems in the exploration rovers. That gave her a passable knowledge of life support, control systems, and comms applicable to the ship and the colony, too. As a lithologist, Claude would prospect for raw materials vital to their survival on Mars, but was cross-trained in life support, including all the utility installations required as the nederzetting expanded. James had primary knowledge of communications and the satellite systems orbiting Mars as well as AI administration.

Emma was cross-trained in biodynamics, the system of farming that was Liz's specialty. Liz further cross-trained in medicine. They all had first aid training, of course, but Liz could perform basic surgery. One of her most important tasks would be to ensure they kept up with psych evaluations - since Ingra's suicide those were scheduled monthly. The AI could remind them of the schedule but Liz was the human being who would, if necessary, cajole them into compliance.

Emma reached one arm towards the bunks to guide herself and stowed her personal bag. She could touch both elbows against the inside wall of her compartment, but at least she'd have a modicum of privacy. She zipped it closed leaving everything she owned inside. It was a wild, liberating, scary thought.

Chapter Seven: The Cat

OCKHANDS in yellow coveralls glided back and forth from the spaceplane, bringing in cargo.

"Was there any trouble with the knarr?" Emma asked a nearby woman. She was feeling steadier already and balanced against her bunk with fingertips as she gestured towards the habitat floor. "The cargo module, I mean."

She'd seen original Scandinavia knarrs on a trip to Demark, to museums preserving graceful wooden cargo boats from the Viking era. It seemed a grand term to apply to the can attached below them, studded with airlocks and packed with supplies, and with their exploration vehicles.

"We don't have access to the knarr during the flight." Emma was worried about her rovers and walkabouts. "If anything shifts, we'll be out of luck."

"Everything's fine, ma'am," the dockhand said. "The cargo's packed so tight I doubt you could slip in to check even if there was a hatchway through the deck."

As the spaceplane was unloaded, Emma followed a deckhand with the fish canister *up* to the life support level. With his help, she hooked it into the water recycling system while Liz unpacked seedling pots and slotted each plant into special lighted cabinets.

There were herbs, barely sprouted, to give gardening on Mars a head start. And fist-sized banana root corms kept cool to slow their growth. There wasn't enough space for full sized banana trees.

Emma floated down the ladder head-first to watch the dockhands stow their seeds. They tossed the hard-sided cases from hand to hand. The last man stood on the ceiling with his toes braced under stowage brackets.

Another dockhand glided in from the Collins' shuttle. In one hand he held a large yellow duffle bag and in the other a small pet carrier with mesh sides. The carrier meowed insistently.

"Here's your cat," he said. "We picked a rusty colored kitten for a rusty colored world. Better not let him out until all the airlocks are sealed. He's a hellion." He grinned proudly. "We put a transponder on his collar for you. Ship - this is the cat."

"Welcome aboard, Cat."

Liz pushed off and bounced into him.

"Oops, sorry," she said as he steadied them both against a handhold.

"How old is he?" She took the carrier and peered inside.

"Eleven weeks. He was born on the Moon and he's been on the dock platform with us for a couple weeks now, so he's used to zero-g."

Two more dockhands drifted in behind him, carrying large sacks against their chests.

"Here's your cat food. There's about six months worth of dry food for use on Mars, double bagged so the little tike can't claw the sacks open. In space you'll have to rehydrate these squeeze packets. Inject water here." He fished a packet from a sack and pointed. "Squeeze the food out here. The cat knows how it works."

The dockhand with the dry food kicked off towards the ceiling to stow the sack. He hung there as more sacks tumbled up to him from someone in the airlock.

"You better show me how the zero-g litter box works," Emma said, swinging away from the life support hatch to let another dockhand through. "I see it's already plumbed into the air system on the vacuum side."

"What's that?" Liz asked as yet more cat supplies arrived, this time a stack of stiff knobby fabric squares floated in through the airlock.

"These go on blank spots on the hull," the cat man said. "He needs places to grip with his claws and to scratch. Sorry the color doesn't match your hull, but we didn't have time to bring up anything else from Earth."

"Damn cat has a bigger gear allotment than I do," James said as the dockhands glued the squares around the hull, leaving it crudely checker-boarded with green on beige. "Tell me again why we're taking this creature."

"Because Ingra is dead and who's going to say 'no' to the survivors?" Claude looked as dubious as James sounded.

"Cats are a wonderful diversion," the cat man said. "You'll be pleased to have him. Space is deadly dull most of the time."

"I'm already pleased," Liz said.

Emma was fairly sure James feigned annoyance, and she hoped the cat man was right. Psychologists had warned her it would be a tedious journey so any diversion was welcome.

Once everything was stowed, the Collins Dock team wished them luck, said good-bye to the cat, and double-checked the airlock seals as they left. The spaceplane and the Collins shuttle undocked with a few clunks.

There wasn't anything else to do. Settlers were passengers. The ship's AI system and controllers at MEX would pilot them to Mars.

"Hold this so I can unzip it," Liz said to Emma. The meowing stopped and a small striped head poked out. Liz cooed and inside the Earth Scan sphere at the ceiling the silver earnings hoop spun happily.

"He's awfully small." James held out a finger for the cat to sniff.

"He's only a kitten. Besides, there are limited resources in space so Loonies breed small cats. They don't expect him to be more than half the size of typical house cat, full grown."

Suddenly the cat rocketed out of the carrier, sending Emma floating backwards. He bounced off the hull like a ping-pong ball, flailed his legs towards a fabric square, and clung there. He was an orange tabby with closely spaced tiger stripes, white paws, and a wild look in his yellow eyes.

"We should be named the biophilia mission," Liz said. "Life-loving. There's a theory, you know, that human beings need to be surrounded by nature to thrive, that we understand that on an intuitive level. The cat, the fish, and the plants we're bringing should raise morale."

She shook her head sadly. "Too late for Ingra."

The cat shot across the module.

"Kittens can fly, even on Earth," Emma said. "This guy will be quite an acrobat in zero-g."

***

Since the weather had cooperated and the spaceplane took off on the first scheduled attempt, they had a week before the transport ship would leave orbit. They elected to immediately go on a standard Martian day - a sol - twenty-four hours, thirty-nine minutes and thirty-five seconds long. MEX was staffed full-time while their ship was in flight, so allowing daybreak to drift through the Earth day was manageable.

"Time to adapt our circadian rhythms to a Martian day," Liz said. "Ship, initiate our light therapy routine."

"Done, Liz," the ship said pleasantly.

"You've all experienced this in training," Liz said. "So it should be easy. The ship will shift the module's light level at the end of our day."

"I know what the experts say," James said. "Make the light bluer in the evening to reset our body-clocks. I'm not sure I need that. I never had trouble staying awake into the night."

Liz shook her head. "I bet you overslept the next morning. Without light therapy, the extra-long day on Mars is like a little jet-lag every day."

"We'll be living inside a sealed habitat. Who cares if our body-clocks are out of synch with the Sun?"

"I care, once we start prospecting," Claude said. "If the colony stays on Earth time, habitat-morning and surface-morning won't line up. I want full days to work."

"Just as importantly, you're going to be a Martian." Liz was exasperated by James' contrariness.

James raised his hands in surrender. "I'm not objecting. Let's add the extra forty minutes every day to the cocktail hour."

Emma suppressed a laugh at the disapproval on Claude's face. "The extra minutes will be productive time, once we get to Mars," she said. "But maybe James has a good idea for Saturdays."

"Every day is Saturday now." He gave her a wink.

He was right, since they didn't have any work to do while MEX waited for the perfect instant to break orbit. Emma practiced maneuvering in zero-g and began to enjoy gliding magically up and down the ladder. James preferred superhero leaps which often ended in tumbling crashes.

"Look there," he said to Emma with a nudge as they both clung to the ladder after one spectacular save. Claude was turning somersaults above the table, towing the cat in a wide circle as it clung to his arm.

"In zero-g, even a serious old curmudgeon will play."

Emma giggled.

They spent a lot of time on the net link to Earth - from orbit the transmission delay was barely noticeable. Emma still occasionally felt a sensation of falling and had to suppress the urge to flail around looking for *down*.

When MEX announced they were ready to break orbit, the crew tipped their bunks to the proper orientation for acceleration and strapped in. Liz cajoled the kitten back into his carrier and held it next to her.

As they waited, Emma plugged her pad into the bunk outlet and found a message from her mother, wishing a safe journey.

She must have checked the mission site for our departure time, Emma thought with a smile.

"Ready guys?" Filip Krast's voice rang through the module, cheerful and confident. "Here we go." And the engines fired.

Colony Mars used a standard transfer orbit for their missions. The ship was already in a high Earth orbit so a relatively small amount of thrust was needed. Even so, after a few days in zero-g the acceleration was uncomfortable.

Vibrations rumbled through the ship and into the bunks, and the constant hum from life support seemed to push harder against Emma's ears. The kitten yowled and Liz made comforting shushing sounds. The engines continued and Emma couldn't hold her breath any longer. She closed her eyes, breathing out slowly, practicing her meditation routine. The minutes ticked by.

Then it was over. The engines cut out and zero-g returned. A small shift indicated thrusters had aimed the tail of the ship towards the Sun, so the packed knarr module would provide extra shielding against solar radiation. The trajectory would stretch their orbit into a long ellipse where, mid-course, a short engine burn would send them to Mars.

Emma floated loosely against the straps. Liz unzipped the cat carrier and the kitten rocketed out and up to the life support deck.

James shocked them with a shout. "Breakaway! Come and get me, Earth. You can't, can you? Cause I'm a spaceman. I'm a god."

"You're Wodanaz, the crazy lord from mythology." Claude shot out his bunk and caught James around the waist. They tumbled together, laughing.

Emma snagged Liz under one arm and launched towards the spinning men.

"Ow, ow." James laughed as they bounced him into the hull.

Emma wanted to run and jump, but there was nowhere to go. After a few somersaults in the restored zero-g, following Colony Mars' recommendations seemed the only thing to do. They gathered in front of the galley imager, floating arm-in-arm in semblance of standing together, grinning like fools, and took turns describing the start of their journey. At MEX, controllers reviewed the ship's diagnostics and quietly confirmed they were on course to Mars.

"We've got enough vid," Filip said. "You can turn off the live stream. Thanks, guys."

Claude plugged in his pad. "I've got a personal message. Mind if I play it on the main screen?"

The others turned to their own pads, offering him what little privacy they could, but he caught Emma's eye.

"I wanted to show you my wife, Emma," Claude said. "Come watch."

He opened a vid of a slender lady dressed in a red parka, standing on a windy shore.

"That's my wife," he said. His face was impassive, but tears spread a sheen of moisture across his face.

The vid must have been taken from a boat. The camera pulled away from the lady and, as she grew small on the screen, she waved. Claude cleared his throat and wiped his face.

"We're going to stay married," he said. "There're benefits from Colony Mars for a spouse, and she deserves them."

"It must be hard to leave her behind," Emma said.

"Since I was selected, we've been like kids. Sophia moved back to Germany, and every day I had off we met somewhere, every place in the world we said we wanted to visit. It's been great." He wiped his face again as the vid ended and the screen went blank.

Chapter Eight: Journey

THE JOURNEY was not fun. Emma knew she wasn't the only one to think so, because the Earth Scan sphere, which continued to float at the habitat ceiling, shrunk and glowed a sedate orange.

Emma expected a lot of things would set her teeth on edge. There was the constant hum of life support pumps and compressors, more noticeable than the ventilation systems in earthly office buildings. There was vibration, a tremor always present, that she noticed whenever she touched fingertips against a surface. There was the repetitive sound of the flexion machine; since MEX scheduled each of them for two hours of exercise every day, the machine was in use half the time she was awake. But mostly, she was sealed in a can with three other human beings, which was deeply annoying.

Meditation helped her manage. Every afternoon the crew meditated together, which was supposed to build a community bond. Emma would open an eye to peek at the others. James preferred to place himself, cross-legged, upside down in relation to everyone else. He often had a sly smile on his face as he floated in classic lotus position, a novice achieving the yogic levitation that eluded gurus on Earth.

Emma paid careful attention to her exercises, her sleep schedule, and her meals. Every day experts sent an evaluation of her recreational time on the net, looking for any negative psychological patterns, and biometrics right down to analysis of her breathing rate.

But MEX didn't have access to everything. Personal messages remained private and the AI relayed them automatically without any interference from MEX controllers. Too much surveillance, psychologists noted, led to paranoia.

***

The settlers weren't employees anymore and their salaries stopped when they left Earth orbit. But even though the AI flew the ship, they weren't simply passengers either. The ship needed maintenance.

Emma volunteered to monitor the life support systems. Every day she towed herself up the ladder to spend an hour listening for any changes in the hums and whirs, touching equipment cases to feel their vibrations, torquing fittings, changing filters, and confirming the AI's readings.

She heard the rattle in a fan before the ship reported the problem and pulled its shroud off.

Every piece of equipment generated heat and, in zero-g, the hot air hung motionless. Without fans, everything would overheat and eventually burn out.

I wonder if I can repack bearings in zero-g? Emma thought as she flipped off the fan. Until she found out, there was a cabinet of spares and her training included replacements. Emma sang happily to herself while she worked.

Fans didn't solve all their air circulation problems.

As Liz observed, wherever human beings go they take billions of microbes with them, and even organisms that are beneficial to life can damage sealed systems. Once a week they opened all the hull panels to release any damp stagnant air and spray biocide if anything started to grow. Colony Mars put as much development into waste handling as it did into rockets and engines. Nothing was actually wasted, so they had to compact or compost everything and carry it on to Mars. They rotated responsibility for cleaning the sanitary unit in life support.

"Just think," James said as he pulled himself up the ladder hand-over-hand for his turn. "Colony Mars spent billions to turn me into a toilet attendant."

"They couldn't have picked a better person for the job," Claude said.

They grinned at each other.

Emma chuckled. James had a knack for cheering everyone up, even Claude when he had a gloomy spell.

***

Meals were the designated communal time, when conversation was encouraged. As recommended, Emma respected her crewmates' privacy, but sometimes news couldn't wait.

Liz, I got a message from Malcolm, Emma texted across the module. Claude was exercising and wouldn't notice, but James sat at the table, deeply involved in something on his pad, and she didn't want to disturb him.

Rather than text back, Liz raised an eyebrow from across the module.

S-4 isolation eval is done and Malcolm washed out - dropped as a settler.

Liz drifted over to Emma and they turned their backs to the imagers. Emma glanced up at the Earth Scan sphere which had brightened to a golden yellow this morning. Perhaps MEX had released a new infotainment on S-4's final crew selection.

"Oh, Emma." The white noise that filled the habitat easily concealed Liz's whisper. She reached for Emma's arm with a sympathetic touch. "You were counting on him following you on the next mission. Are you okay?"

Liz meant well, but annoyance bubbled up. She liked Malcolm, sure, everyone did. But she'd succeed on her own.

Emma looked down at Malcolm's text message.

I took your advice and talked to my mission counselor. You shouldn't have told me to do that, because she never liked me. All I did was show some concern for Ingra's death and she flunked me out. It's so unfair. I registered a protest but the mission leader's just as bad. It's all over for me - the dream of Mars. They took it away.

But I can still take care of you. There's a controller job open on the satellite team. As a failed settler I have priority for a MEX job and I'm fully qualified. It's miserable consolation, but took it. I'll be here.

45

She hesitated to show Liz the message. It gave her a little shiver as she reread the words. He was upset so some bitterness was understandable. He did care for her, Emma felt certain. "He says he's got a job as a MEX controller for the Mars satellite systems."

"That's a big team. There must be fifty guys managing the satellites between communications, GPS, weather, and the power station. They don't talk to the settlers much, though."

"It's okay, really."

Liz gave Emma a hug and pushed off, drifting back across the module.

Actually, it's fine, Emma admitted to herself.

Chapter Nine: Onboard

JAMES HAD NO TROUBLE filling his days. He was finishing a PhD thesis, which occupied him for endless hours, headphones on, sometimes typing, sometimes scrawling on his screen with a stylus. He bolted a chair to the deck facing into his open bunk to make a study carrel and running a fan so the carbon dioxide he exhaled wouldn't build up around his head.

"What's your thesis topic again?" Emma asked at lunchtime conversation.

"It's sort of abstract." He sounded apologetic. "It's a theory of quantum cohomology. Kinda hard to explain without the math equations. Actually, with my implants deactivated, it's hard for me to follow, too."

"You have cerebral implants? Wow. But why are they deactivated? I thought those were biologically powered." Emma stopped, embarrassed. "Sorry. I know enhancements are private."

"It's okay." James smiled, tight lipped. "We're going to be closer than family. Batteries aren't the problem. It's a lack of technical support - calibrations and periodic rebalancing of my brain chemistry. None of the necessary equipment will be sent to Mars until Settler Mission Fifteen at the earliest."

"That's, like, twenty-five years from now."

"Settling on Mars is like going backwards in time." James sighed with resignation.

"Not that it matters. University's not the world I'm competing in now." But he frowned.

Emma supposed losing a mental edge so suddenly would hurt. Liz, sitting on his other side, must have seen that, too, because she gave his arm a pat. "You're giving up a lot of technology in return for the privilege of spreading life to a dead world."

"I get to keep my high-tech, my robotics," Emma said. "Liz, you get the low tech, unless we need a medic."

Claude snorted. "With the equipment Liz has, it's like being treated by witchdoctors. No offense..."

Liz laughed. She was hard to offend. "I like gardening. Manual labor is low tech, sure, but it's a timeless connection to our ancestors. The high-tech is in the seeds - we have the best biological stock."

"Hey, I'm learning to be a pilot." James' good humor quickly rebounded. "This ship has a simulator."

"That sounds more like you than quantum whatevers, anyway," Liz said.

"Kamp has two jumpships and two pilots, but they want to train backups. It's not too hard - the AI does most of the work." He grinned wickedly. "The simulator lets me nosedive into some spectacular crashes."

"So that's what your shouting's been about," Emma said. "Somehow, I doubt crashing will get you behind real controls anytime soon."

"What are you up to, Claude?" Emma asked politely.

"I set up a net site for geology students at my old university." He transferred his pad image to the main screen.

"Have you got them submitting papers to you?" James asked.

"I offered my services as editor. I like to keep track of their research."

"What's this?" James pointed to a sidebar of links.

"Proposals for deploying the prospecting drill we're carrying. I'm considering their suggestions. Kamp Kans will need to mine metals if we're going to survive."

James sniggered. "It looks to me like you're assigning homework. You can't be anyone's favorite professor."

Claude rapped his pad in irritation and the main screen went blank.

"Just kidding, professor." James affected an innocent expression that made Emma laugh despite herself.

Claude's brows knit together above a scowl. "This is my technical outlet. I'm a Martian lithologist, but I'll spend my first year on survival projects - pulling cables and laying pipes in the new settlement bays."

"I think it's wonderful to stay in touch with past students," Liz said with a thin lipped frown at James.

"I understand Claude's frustration," Emma said. "I have to help Liz get the mealworms and gardens established before I'm scheduled to deploy our exploration bots. When I got a degree in robotic engineering, I didn't expect to become a subsistence farmer."

"Farming's a great job. Panspermia in reverse," Liz said with a smile. "Maybe life came to Earth from the stars, so it's fair for Earth to spread life out to the stars."

"Mars isn't very far out," James said.

"It's a start."

"You never worry about contaminating Mars with Earth life," Emma said. There were still groups agitating to stop colonization of Mars for that very reason. "What if we kill off Martian life?"

"If there's any life on Mars, it's dying today. If we find it, we'll nurture it. Settlement will be good for Mars."

"Liz will set a heater on some patch of ice and have red trees towering over us in no time." James meant it as a joke, but he'd reminded them of Ingra hallucinating oak trees as she stumbled out the airlock to her death.

The main screen suddenly activated, repeating the last entertainment they'd watched.

"Ship, did you turn that on?" Claude asked.

"Yes, Claude."

"Why?"

"A settler requested the screen be turned on."

The kitten was clinging to the bottom of the frame, batting at the screen with one paw.

49

"That's kinda scary," James said. "The ship takes orders from a cat."

"Ship, don't open any airlocks for the cat, understood?"

"Don't worry," the AI said. "I know that he is a cat. I have modeled his access as 'human toddler'. Besides, airlock operation is manual."

***

The kitten was a great distraction and MEX asked for more vids of his antics. Liz found her pad would project a red dot of laser light for him to chase. He found all the spots in the habitat where he could get a grip with his claws, and would streak wildly around the module or launch across the room, legs stretched out and toes spread wide.

They took turns feeding him from small tubes of food rehydrated to mush. He'd grip the hand holding a tube with his front claws, and lick at a little blob as it squeezed out. They had to be careful giving him water, which could crawl around in zero-g like something alive. Feeding was a slow business, but the cat liked the attention and purred lustily throughout. Soon everyone's hands were laced with fine pink streaks from his claws.

One morning, James' shouts woke Emma. She hurriedly squirmed into her clothes and unzipped her bunk.

Flakes of something floated in the habitat, like a beige snow storm. She pulled the neck of her shirt over her nose to avoid breathing in...

"What is this stuff?"

"It's just wheat bran," Liz said through the hands she held over her face. "We have compressed sacks of it for mealworm bedding. It's stowed at the ceiling." She pulled herself towards the storage brackets.

An orange blur rocketed past. The cat.

"Looks like the cat tore open a sack."

50

Emma heaved a sigh. The tingle of fear in her stomach subsided. There was nothing to worry about. Well, there was one thing. "This is going to plug the air filters."

"I'll take the filter off..." James said.

"No, wait. Then the bran will get sucked into the compressors. I've got an idea." She swam up the ladder to life support.

"Hey, Settler Three. What's going on?" Filip called over the module link. The transmission lag was becoming annoying.

"It's okay. Just a bag of wheat bran broke open, that's all," Liz said.

Emma returned with some large squares of plush filter medium in light frames.

"Brush off as much bran as you can, and then put a clean filter in front. Like this." Emma slid the new filter up as she brushed bran off the one installed in the hull. Airflow held it in place as bran collected on the surface.

"We just keep changing the filters until we collect all the bran. We'll need bags, and - where's that vacuum cleaner?"

Liz floated over, passing out dust masks from the medical kit. They drifted in the swirling bran storm, waiting for the filters to collect enough to vacuum off. The cat clung with his back claws to a fabric square on the hull, wildly swiping at flakes floating by.

James pointed to the Earth Scan sphere, now brightened to yellow. "The little beggar is upstaging me."

They spent all day cleaning. Even though it got tedious after a while, Emma welcomed the break in routine.

***

Holidays also broke the routine and brightened the Earth Scan sphere. Oktoberfest was international, so everyone enjoyed that. They celebrated Canadian Thanksgiving for Liz and Halloween for James.

There weren't any candles on board, of course, but Claude dimmed the module lights and looped a vid on the main screen of children singing and carrying Martinmas lanterns through a forest.

"Why lanterns?" Emma asked.

"Sunset is earlier as winter comes, so children carry lanterns to the neighbors."

"I prefer Halloween," James said. "Then I get candy."

Emma expected Claude to grumble at James, but he looked lost in thought.

"Let's eat," she said brightly.

While cylinders of macronutrients couldn't provide much holiday cheer, even extruded into funny shapes by the food printer, there were a few treats in the galley cabinets - dried fruit, chocolate, textured cheese, and some squeeze tubes of wine and beer.

"Beer loses something in a squeeze tube," Claude said sadly. "I can't watch bubbles rise or smell the brew properly."

"I can't smell anything anyway," Emma said. "My head's all stuffed up and achy. I feel like I'm hanging upside down."

"As your medic," Liz said, "all I can suggest is grin and bear it. You'll feel better when you get some gravity under your feet."

"I know what you need," James said. He maneuvered up to the ceiling and unfastened a few bungee cords.

"Hey," Claude said. "Those hold cargo in place."

"Oh, relax, Professor. The cargo's not going anywhere." He pushed off from the ceiling and landed next to Emma.

"I bungee myself against my bunk wall at night. Try it. You can snuggle into the sleeping bag. You'll feel better after a good sleep." He grinned at Claude. "It improves your mood, too. Want to try, Professor?"

Claude scowled.

"Well, I'm going to," Emma said, taking the bungees. "The closer we get to the course correction, the less patience I have with this trip."

Chapter Ten: Mid-Point

SHORTLY AFTER American Thanksgiving the mid-point engine burn approached. The ship was still in an enormously elliptical orbit around Earth and had to increase velocity to transfer to a Mars orbit. If the engines didn't fire, their ship would start a long fall back to Earth. Malcolm reminded her of that in another message.

"He said, this is my chance to return to Earth," she whispered to Liz. "He wants me to tell MEX to call off the burn - let the ship fall back to Earth."

"Does MEX know he's saying these things?" Liz asked. "I bet they wouldn't appreciate Malcolm trying to sabotage the mission.

Liz spoke with a cautiously neutral tone psychologists used, but her eyes narrowed. "You don't want to go back, do you?"

Emma's back straightened and her shoulders squared. The journey was going well and she was happy - there was no reason to abort the orbital transfer.

"No. I'm going to Mars. I've told him so."

"Good," Liz said, relaxing into a smile. "I know how to take your mind off Malcolm. I want to neuter the kitten now, so he'll heal before the engine burn. You can help me set up the surgical kit after lunch."

She told Claude and James over fake-pasta shaped like stars. "Guys, it's time for my big medical procedure. I need to pull one of the downdraft panels from life support to use here on the table."

"Okay," James said. "But I don't see why you have to neuter the poor little fellow. He'll be the only cat in the world. It's not like he'll make babies by himself."

"He'll be a better citizen. It'll keep him cuddly and prevent any objectionable male behaviors."

"Don't look at me when you say that." James kicked out of his chair and up to the ceiling in mock distress.

"Don't worry, James," Liz said. "You're safe. A colony wouldn't make much sense without children, would it?"

Emma laughed with the others, but her fingers rubbed the spot on her upper arm where her contraceptive chip was embedded. She couldn't feel it, but it was there, reliably tweaking hormone production until she shut it off with the little device in her duffle bag. That was one personal electronic device she got to keep. But Colony Mars hadn't scheduled the first Martian pregnancy for another five years. That allowed time for S-4, the Doctors' Mission, to arrive with a test batch of frozen embryos.

S-4 would have been Malcolm's mission, Emma thought dryly. He'd cross-trained as a physician's assistant, but Colony Mars replaced him with a full-fledged doctor who had a psych specialty. A replacement for Malcolm and for Ingra.

All the research said Colony Mars' chosen cryochamber design was impervious to the dangers of space flight, but with abundant of caution, S-4 would confirm the embryo viability and set up a medical bay. And after the Doctors would come Settler Five, the Kinderen mission.

S-5 was the only all-female mission, a chance to jump-start the settlement's first generation. Colony Mars never used the term "breeders" in their PR - it was too harsh, too clinical. They preferred to keep the public's attention focused on the future children. That's why, they explained once when Emma asked, S-5 was the Kinderen Mission and not the Mothers' Mission.

Colony Mars was scheduled to announce finalists for the S-5 crew and, ironically, the cat would be neutered that same afternoon. Liz used a specially prepared surgical kit and he recovered quickly. James sagely observed that his behavior remained as objectionable as ever.

***

The ship's AI announced the engine burn an hour in advance and, tracking his transponder, helped Liz and Emma find the cat wedged between some pipes in a particularly warm spot in life support. He protested as Emma pulled him out, stuffed him into the carrier Liz held waiting, and sucked at the scratches on her hand.

They tipped the bunks into acceleration position and strapped in. Emma's hair had grown long enough to put back and she twisted on a stretch-tie. They were secure far enough in advance for James to complain about the wait before the AI began the final countdown.

Despite being ready for acceleration, Emma could hardly breathe through the burn. The cat meowed pitifully. Emma was beginning to worry the ship would send them into the asteroid belt when the pressure evaporated and she sucked in a deep, shaky breath.

"The course correction is completed," the AI announced. "Engine performance was within parameters."

Emma glanced at the Earth Scan sphere, which was a soft orange. Apparently news of the successful burn hadn't registered on Earth yet.

"Yee ha!" James pulled his straps loose. "Next stop Mars."

Chapter Eleven: Arrival

SHORTLY AFTER the mid-course correction, a video transmission arrived from Mars. The vid showed the seven settlers watching a screen displaying an animation of the Settler Three ship. Engines on the animation fired, the blast lasting much less time than Emma remembered, and then cut off. An orbital diagram superimposed over the image showing a curved path catching up to the red dot indicating Mars. The settlers cheered, hugged, and spun around to face the imager.

"You are now closer to Mars than to Earth." A man in the center of the group shouted and waved. "More Martian than Earther."

Daan von Berg would stand out even if he wasn't waving. He was fairly tall like most Dutch men, with blue eyes and a dirty blond mop of hair. He was a *builder*, as the S-2 crew was designated, and Emma had met him and his crewmates on Earth.

She also knew Luis, the dark wiry Belgian who piloted Jumpship Two, Melina from Greece, and Sanni from Finland who stood in the background. Settler One's crew, the Pioneers, she recognized from messaging. Ingra had been a Pioneer and now three remained.

"In a time-honored tradition of once before, we declare a holiday for each settler mission's mid-course correction," Daan said. He raised his cup.

"To quote the poet - Where never lark or even eagle flew,

"With silent, lifting mind you tread

"The high untrespassed sanctity of space."

A little thrill ran through Emma.

"It's a Christmas present eight days early for us," James said back to the screen. Emma and Liz passed out squeeze bulbs of wine as the message was transmitted to Mars and a reply came back.

"Days!" The Belgian scoffed. "You sound like an Earther. This is sol three thirty-two of jaar one hundred six. Though why we use an old NASA numbering instead of starting over at jaar zero, I'll never understand."

"Jaar one! Starting over at jaar one," someone called. People argued how to number the first year with passion. Maybe that's good, Emma thought - we need something safe to argue over, since we must cooperate to survive.

"And that's why we stick with jaar one-oh-six," Daan said with a laugh.

"Forgive me," James said, bowing to the screen as he braced on the table. "I'm only half Martian this sol."

Minutes passed again.

"I'm sure the 'American Mission' knows best," said Ruby, a Polynesian Kiwi from New Zealand, the jumpship pilot from the S-1 Pioneers. "Coming to show us how to run Kamp."

"Come on, Ruby," Daan said, his mouth ticked up at one corner. "This is a party."

Emma turned away. "Where did that come from?" she whispered.

"Liz is Canadian," Claude said indignantly, straight into the imager. "And I'm German."

"Shtart schpeaken vith a zicker accent," James said. "Zo people know."

Claude glared at him.

"Joke, Herr Professor. It's a joke."

"Be pleasant everyone," Liz said, looking down and running a hand across her mouth as she whispered.

James turned back to the imager with his grin intact.

"Okay, so New Year's Eve for us Martians isn't two weeks away. It's only mid-jaar for Mars and our next New Year's is..." James calculated in his head. "Ten months... Can we use months when Deimos orbits once a sol and Phobos three times faster?

The year - 'scuse me, the jaar - on Mars starts on the northern spring equinox, orbital designation Ell Sub Ess Zero degrees... sol zero..."

James wrote with a finger in the air in exaggerated sweeps. "Over three hundred sols away. That's a long time without a holiday. When's the next party?"

They waited quietly through the transmission lag, sipping from their wine bulbs.

"We still use months." Asynchronous communications were hard to keep track of. Daan's response was from a few comments back.

"And weeks. They're just too handy to drop. Seven sols a week, four weeks a month, twenty-three months a jaar, plus one short month..." Daan stopped, listening again.

Ruby stood behind him, arms folded across her chest. Emma thought someone was cajoling her from off-screen.

"You'll like month twenty-four," Daan said. "We figure the last, odd-ball week to be three and a half sols of festival before we reset the calendar at Elle Sub Es Zero. It'll be easier to talk when you drop into orbit. For now, congratulations on the engine burn."

The two groups of settlers went back to their separate parties.

***

"I've been wasting time," Emma said the next sol at breakfast. "I should be viewing the Mars feeds, not Earth net entertainments."

"We all read Kamp's daily summary," Liz said.

"Not the same thing at all." Emma shook her head. "I should know more than an Earthside fan. For example, each bay is constructed with a pond. That's for independent water storage in case one pond leaks, and they're all part of the recycling system, but we'll also use them to raise fish. Which pond should we start with? It's an engineering question as much as a farming question."

"I see what you mean," Liz said.

"Maybe we've all gotten numb on this trip," Claude said. "It's time to be proactive. I'm going to pull up the wiring status in Kamp's Spine." He unwrapped his feet from the chair legs and drifted to a hull outlet to plug in his pad. He floated there, one foot hooked under a handhold, as he scrolled through the records.

"I'll send my jumpship simulations to Ruby and Luis and get their evaluations," James said.

Emma opened the detailed Kamp logs, but didn't look at fish ponds first. The settlers were well ahead of Colony Mars' building schedule and she studied how they'd optimized the construction robot squad.

Kamp Kans was sited on the Tharsis Plain, near the equator, because the surface there was covered with a thick layer of fine-grained regolith - sand that proved easy to scoop up and fabricate into stone building blocks. They were recovering water at a decent pace, harvesting a pint or two from each cubic meter of regolith. But warming the heavy-walled bays took longer than expected. They were still very cold, and the ponds were still filled with ice.

"Look here," Emma said. "The greenhouse bay is colder than a Canadian winter."

"Yeah, I saw that. I'll have to keep all the live cargo in a habitat module until the bay warms up."

"But the bananas are already pot-bound, aren't they? And the fish will be so big they'll be gill-to-gill in that transport canister."

"You've got an idea, don't you?" Liz asked.

"Not really my idea. The habitat simulation team in Holland suggested they leave parts of the nederzetting dark and consolidate the heaters they have into the greenhouse."

Liz bunched her eyebrows. The settlers' reluctance to follow Colony Mars' recommendation was perplexing.

"I'm going to work it out directly," Emma said. "Settler to settler, without mentioning Earth."

She fretted over crafting a text message, and finally sent an upbeat text to all the settlers.

Daan answered. *I'm involved with the utilities right now, along with Melina and Sanni,* he sent. *Melina says she wants a meal of real food as soon as you can grow it. So what do you want us to do?*

Emma replied. *The empty fuel module that's attached to the Spine is ready to use, right?*

Every bit of each ship was cannibalized and incorporated into the settlement. That included an empty tank, as big as a ship's habitat module, which had fueled the heavy-lift rockets. It now connected the Spine to a stone bay. *I see you've vented it clean and the greenhouse bay attached to it is complete. If you close it off from the rest of the nederzetting, it should be easy to warm up. Pull enough lights and heaters from other areas to achieve the optimum environment.*

By the end of the sol, they had worked out a plan to let Liz start growing her plants, fish, and mealworms as soon as she landed. Emma smiled with satisfaction. She'd already proved herself useful and discovered Daan was fun to work with.

***

Their efforts grew more urgent as the transport ship coasted closer to Mars. Emma counted down the sols until MEX and the ship's AI maneuvered them into Mars orbit, pacing the solar power station. They were right on schedule and well before the planet's storm season. The crew could have tapped into the Martian satellite imagers at any point in their journey, but knowing they orbited the planet made the habitat screen feel like a window.

MEX used the classic, twentieth-century Mars charting system that divided the planet into thirty quadrangles. Claude transferred to an image over the Tharsis quad.

Olympus Mons was easy to spot. It was the largest volcano on Mars and marked the western edge of the bulging Tharsis Plain. The volcano was clearly visible from orbit, and ragged white clouds streamed from its peak. Southeast of Olympus was a string of three more massive volcanoes. The center peak, right on the equator, was Peacock Mons, and off its flank, still invisible at this magnification, sat the tiny handful of habitable structures that made up Kamp Kans.

Emma's fingers went cold and she held her breath. The enormity of it hit her. She was orbiting Mars. Home would never be closer than sixty million kilometers away. But Earth wasn't home anymore. She'd traded that warm, wet, beautiful world for the rusty sands below.

"Zoom in on Kamp," Claude said, and the ship's AI obediently brought Kamp into focus.

"*Onze nederzetting*," Claude said. "Our settlement."

"Camp Opportunity," Liz said thoughtfully, calling the settlement by its English name. "Sometime we'll have to track down the Opportunity rover and bring it to its namesake. It's south of the equator someplace, isn't it?"

"Yes, but almost halfway around the planet," Claude said.

"It would make a nice sculpture for the center of the plaza bay," James said, grinning. "Turned it into a fountain or something. I could bring it back with a jumpship."

The Earth Scan sphere was spinning, large and green, as they eagerly examined Kamp Kans.

A mound of protective regolith sand covered the modules from the Settler One ship, now strung together via their airlocks in a row at the south end of the settlement. Only the first ship's power receiver was visible at that end.

The Pioneers had lived in those three modules while they constructed the adjoining Plaza. Running north from Plaza was the Spine, a long narrow structure that would house utilities and interconnect future bays - three bays were already complete and their barrel-arched roofs protruded from the dunes. Settler Two's habitat module was attached at the north tip with a second power receiver.

Detached and off to one side was a large bay for the construction bot squad, where they could be taken for repairs or to hunker down during sand storms.

As they admired their new home, Emma's pad, which floated at the end of its power cord, beeped. She reeled it in, tugging it away from the cat.

Emma gave Liz an aggravated look to tell her it was Malcolm.

She looked at the text, something about refueling from the base on Phobos to return to Earth.

That wasn't even possible, Emma thought. Phobos Base was designed to refuel jumpships during satellite maintenance, and the little moon barely had enough water ice in its regolith for that. It would take months and months to manufacture fuel for the transport - but then, it would be well over a year before there might be a launch window to Earth. There was extra food in the nutrient cylinders, but not that much - Emma was sure. Could Malcolm be serious?

That joke's not funny, Mal, she texted back.

A second message came in - there hadn't been time for her response to reach Earth.

"What's MEX want?" James asked, recognizing the beep tone.

"Nothing, just a friend of mine." Emma didn't read the text out loud.

Don't let them disassemble the ship. I'll be back on shift after the weekend to convince people here.

Emma rapped the message closed in annoyance. She hoped no one at MEX saw what he sent. She didn't want to be singled out because of his weird message. Thankfully, everyone was too enthralled with the view of Kamp to bother about the message further.

"I'm receiving a transmission from Earth," the ship's AI announced. "Lead Controller Filip Krast sends your schedule for disembarking."

Claude frowned at his pad. "We're scheduled to rest for three days before landing."

"It's more like MEX is scheduled to rest, so their controllers will be sharp," Emma said.

"Hurry up and wait, as always," James said. He tapped out a sentence on his pad and held it angled away from the imagers for the others to read.

Let's ask Kamp what they think.

"Ship, can you give me a private channel to Kamp?" he asked out loud.

"Standard channels are recommended for all communications."

"I thought so." James held up his pad again.

Tonight.

Chapter Twelve: Disassembly

"YOU DON'T NEED a big conspiracy," Emma said to James at supper. "We're free agents now." Colony Mars controlled all the operations on Earth, but insisted they merely advised the settlers once they arrived at Mars. Perhaps they could coerce obedience by threatening to stop future missions or restrict the communications link, but coercion would violate their own vision of an independent, self-sustaining colony, and certainly wouldn't improve fundraising.

"You don't know how to be a rebel," James said. "Day shift is over on Earth, so no experts to talk us out of what we want to do. You're all with me, right? Anyone want to cool your heels in orbit for three days? Okay Ship, open the Kamp channel."

James cleared his throat. "Hi guys. We don't need a three-sol rest up here. Are you ready to bring us down in the morning?"

In a few exchanges, they planned the landing. Emma glanced up at the Earth Scan sphere. It would be half an hour before it reflected any earthly reaction to the change in plan. As James predicted, MEX controllers on the night shift offered no argument that changed their minds.

***

The crew woke before the Sun rose over the Tharsis Plain and secured everything in the galley. They sent a message to MEX to confirm the ship's telemetry was being received. By the time a quick breakfast was finished, the response came back: all systems nominal.

"Let's get into our suits," James said when the ship's AI announced that both Kamp jumpships had taken off.

Colony Mars provided one suit for each of them. The suits were designed for use on the Martian surface but they would provide some protection if a jumpship lost pressure, so suits were a safety protocol requirement. Emma opened her bunk, slid away the back panel, and pulled hers out. It was designed for short jaunts outside Kamp, azure blue for visibility against the red Martian sand. She struggled into the surface suit, leaving her helmet off for now.

Ruby and Luis piloted the jumpships and docked at airlocks on opposite sides of the habitat. Claude and Liz opened the inner doors and Luis entered first. They collided against each other in a group hug, the cat clambering across their backs, meowing for attention.

Ruby entered, holding her helmet to her chest, precluding any hugs. Her black eyes were set in a wide brown face and, Emma thought enviously, she retained her color even after years living shielded from sunlight. Straight black hair, knotted in a bun, didn't soften her expression a bit.

"What a singular aroma you've created in here." Ruby wrinkled her nose. "Sort of a mix of antiseptic and garbage."

"No one's fault - it's space funk," said Luis, who ducked his head with a laugh.

"Are your eyes stinging?" Liz asked, laughing back. "I don't smell it anymore."

"Let's get all your gear stowed in Ruby's ship," Luis said. "I'm taking your habitat module to Phobos Base, so don't leave anything you want behind."

Emma pulled the fish canister out of life support first. The tiny fingerlings were full grown now without any extra room, so she started the external filter system to keep the water oxygenated and pH neutral. Next came the mealworms which had barely changed in their chilled container, and the box of lunar cat food.

Liz carefully closed the plants inside individual plastic sleeves while Emma uninstalled the litter box. She hoped the cat would continue to use it on Mars. Claude passed along cases of seeds and the rest of their gear.

Liz lured the cat with a packet of food and unceremoniously shoved him into the carrier.

"Here Emma," she said, adding the carrier to the duffle bag straps looped over her arms. "Ruby already took my surgical kit to the jumpship. Luis wants you to go with Ruby and all the live cargo. He'll take the rest of us."

"Ship," Claude said. "Close the Earth Scan display now." The spinning sphere disappeared. "Have you linked up with the Kamp AI?"

"Yes, Claude. Our merger was successful. I'm part of the nederzetting."

"You all can log in with Governor now," Ruby said. She paused and looked around. "The ship's imagers are streaming live, aren't they?"

She turned to look straight into the closest one but didn't smile.

"It's a bit of a joke, naming our Artificial Intelligence 'Governor.' We're a self-directed group and this colony will never have a governor, so there's no chance of confusing the name when we call the AI."

Emma swung the carrier up, not sure which sensor the AI was using to read their transponder codes. "Hi, Governor. I'm Emma. And this is the cat."

"Welcome to Mars, Emma. Welcome, Cat."

The others logged in and Governor greeted them.

"It's time to blow this ship apart," James said happily.

Emma snagged her helmet with her fingertips and followed Ruby to Jumpship One. From S-3's airlock she entered the smaller jumpship airlock, mid-cabin between the life support systems and a passenger compartment with four seats in two rows.

The rear seats were quite conventional. The pilot and co-pilot seats were somatic exoskeleton control systems. They stood like rigid chains of overlapping metallic scales the width of a spread hand, supported just below the shoulder blade by a pillar bolted to the floor. If Ruby took over from Governor, she'd control the ship with her whole body.

They strapped the cat carrier in one seat, the plant cabinet in a second, and stowed the rest of the cargo wherever there was empty space. Ruby waved Emma to the co-pilot seat.

If Ruby was trying to make her uncomfortable, she failed. Emma used a similar system in the limbs of her walkabout exploration suits. She propelled herself with fingertips along the ceiling of the cabin to her seat, slipped into the five point harness, pushed her back against the scales and tightened the straps. As her hands slid into the control gloves and the seat sprang to life, conforming to her back and arms. She wiggled her legs against the scales that ran down the back of her thighs and calves and curled around her heel to support her feet.

"Don't worry about your movements," Ruby said. "I've got the jumper set to accept only my commands."

Emma pulled her hands loose to seal her helmet in the shoulder ring, twisting it till it clicked. She gave a little tug upwards to check and was proud of how well she handled that until her nose began to twitch. "I'm going to sneeze."

"Oh, hell, woman. Tip your head forward and sneeze into your chest or you'll splatter the visor."

Her advice came just in time. Emma half-swallowed the sneeze, then tilted her head back and sniffed vigorously for a while.

Ruby activated her seat - her movements would control attitude and speed as intuitively as walking. During the high-g portion of descent the AI would take over and stretch the seats out to support them, but otherwise it would follow Ruby's lead.

Ruby undocked and the jumpship floated away from the transport with a puff of its engines.

Unlike the transport, the jumpship had windows. The cabin sat on one side of a square frame big enough to surround a ship module, with an engine at each corner. The jumpship was a sky crane.

"I'm clear," Ruby said over the jumpship channel. "Ready for disassembly."

"I've got everyone else with me," Luis said. "Go ahead Governor."

Emma got her last look at S-3 as a spacecraft, a white cylinder studded with protruding airlocks and skirted with photon collectors. Puffs of gas jetted out at the module bulkheads as the frangible nuts detonated, connecting struts folded back, and the modules drifted apart. The photon collectors uncoupled and floated away. In a few minutes, the ship was an expanding formation of individual components.

"Perfect separation." Luis' voice sounded inside Emma's helmet. Someone, probably James, was chattering in the background.

Ruby couldn't help but smile with satisfaction. "It's quite a sight, isn't it?"

"You grab collectors three and four," Luis said. "I'll take one and two."

Ruby unfolded the jumpship's articulated grappling arms and pulled her hands from the control gloves to let the AI grab the fragile photon collectors.

As the jumpships approached the orbiting power station, Emma had a good view of the satellite that powered Kamp Kans. It was an elegant solution to the limitations of solar power on the surface. The orbiting station was always in sunlight, in a stationary Clarke orbit above Kamp. It beamed energy down to receivers that converted microwaves to electricity. Settler Three and every transport ship that followed would add their collectors to the orbiting station. Kamp Kans was short of many things, but there was plenty of power.

From the angle of their approach, Emma couldn't see the satellite's central generators, but the deeply colored, iridescent collectors spread out before her. Ruby maneuvered the jumpship to the end of a long cylindrical strut. A robot crawled around the strut and into view, one of two long, multi-limbed tool boxes that maintained the power station. Ruby passed the collectors one at a time to the bot, and across the shimmering station Luis was doing the same with his load.

Ruby relaxed in her seat. "The bots will weld those collectors into place, wire them up, and we'll have more power to draw on."

"You did a great job," Emma said.

Ruby snorted without reply and modified their trajectory. The jumpship caught up to the S-3 modules in less than an hour.

The modules had drifted quite far apart.

"Right behind you." That was Luis' voice.

"You go first," Ruby said over the ship channel. "Luis is very good at this. I like to watch," she added without glancing at Emma.

Jumpship Two maneuvered to the habitat module, reached out its arms, and grabbed the lifting lugs at the forward end.

"This'll take a few hours. See you later," Luis said as he towed the module away, accelerating to match the speedy little moon when Phobos caught up with him.

"Thanks, Ruby," Emma said. Psychologists had trained her on how to form relationships so she grasped for something positive to say. "I appreciate getting such a good view."

"We're taking the empty fuel module down," Ruby said, ignoring her attempt. "Luis will drop the habitat module on Phobos. The bots there built a pad for it. You know there's a squad of construction robots on the moon, don't you?"

Of course I do, Emma thought with irritation. But she mumbled some thanks out loud, which sounded stupid.

"Once he sets the habitat in place and the construction bots hook up the Phobos power station, we'll have a handy little maintenance base." In addition to maintenance, Phobos Base was a lifeboat of sorts for Kamp Kans, an evacuation base in an emergency. Emma knew that, but thought saying it out loud might be unlucky.

"Time for us to grab the empty fuel module."

Emma had viewed simulations, but watching Ruby capture the module was still fascinating. She matched the jumpship's attitude to the forward bulkhead of the module, deftly closed the grapplers' fingers around its lugs, and reoriented so the module hung in the center of the jumpship's square frame. The engines pivoted and they slowly lost altitude.

Emma watched the Tharsis volcanoes pass under them as the jumpship made a complete orbit before slowing over

Peacock Mons. Nothing could be more desolate than the drifted, pock-marked surface. She tried to imagine the entire plain enveloped in a massive haboob sand storm with even the mountain tops lost.

The ship shivered with the effort of descent and she lost sight of the ground from her window. Emma was alternately pushed down and released as the engines fired on and off, adjusting their descent. She gripped the armrests tightly and exhaled slowly. Dust blew up around the windows as Ruby set the module on its waiting pad against the long Spine of the nederzetting, disengaged, and rose up again.

"We're docking at the south modules," Ruby said over the vibration of the engines. The jumpship settled on a large pad and docked.

"Bingo!" Ruby said. "You can take your helmet off now. We're home."

Chapter Thirteen: Jumpship Down

EMMA PULLED off her helmet and the cat's yowls assaulted her ears. She started to push her legs down to stand, but fell back. "I feel dizzy."

"Gravity," Ruby said. "But then, you'd know that, wouldn't you?"

She unbuckled the cat carrier and passed it to Emma.

Emma wasn't looking forward to carrying the cat's few extra pounds. Mars gravity was only two fifths that of Earth, but it was crushing her now. She was not, however, about to let Ruby hear her complain. What was that woman's problem? She slipped out of the harness and levered herself slowly from the seat.

Dust still hung thickly around the ship, but Emma could see a module's hull through the cabin windows. The jumpship rested against a retaining wall, docked to an airlock on the module's upper level.

Anyone coming in from the surface through the lower level airlock would have to vacuum off dust and doff their suit before entering the module. Surface dust was irritating to people and damaging to seals and filters. But Emma and Ruby were clean and continued straight through.

A cheer sounded as Emma stepped out of the airlock and the cat went suddenly silent. Settlers greeted them, alternately giving Emma hugs and propping her up as she toppled under their enthusiasm.

"Here, sit down." Someone pushed a chair towards her. Emma looked up thankfully and saw it was Daan.

"You remember Melina and Sanni," he said, gesturing to the two women from Settler Two. "But I bet you want to meet our stars."

A distinctive Ulster accent interrupted. "That's rubbish, mate."

Daan was right. The two Pioneer Brits were easily the most famous of the settlers, so well-known by their nick-names of Yin and Yang that no one used their real names anymore. They were both from the same city in England, and if Emma closed her eyes she could barely tell their voices apart. Both were tall and thin, but there was no trouble knowing Yin from Yang.

Yin was the darkest black man she'd ever met, while Yang had pale milky skin and washed out blond hair. Despite their common city, they didn't know each other before joining Colony Mars but quickly became inseparable. Upbeat and chatty, responsible for fabricating and constructing the Kamp settlement bays, they remained public favorites, however modest they might be.

Emma pushed against the chair arms and stood to shake hands.

"Do sit down, love, before you fall over," Yin said, turning the handshake into a hug that lowered her back into the chair. Yang produced a second chair to set the cat carrier on and unzipped the flap. "Here's our new star."

The cat pushed his head out cautiously.

"There, there, baby." Sanni scooped him up. "I've messaged with Lunar Base on how to adapt him back to gravity." She cooed to the cat in baby talk.

"Where's his personal bag?" Melina asked. "The Loonies promised to pack a special cushion with his things."

At least Emma could help here. "It's the yellow one. I left it in the jumpship."

"I'll find it," Melina said, hopping into the airlock.

"What's his name?" Sanni asked.

"We didn't name him," Emma said. "Thought we'd wait until we got here."

"He's the only cat in the world," Daan said. "He doesn't need a name." He reached out a hand to pet the cat, but hesitated. "Can I hurt him?"

"Stroke him along the side, like this, while he's recovering. Poor little guy," Sanni said, carefully adjusting how she supported him. "He's been in zero-g almost since he left his momma. I've read all the Lunar Base reports. He's got a medical chip implant that the Loonies developed especially for cats, did you know that?"

Emma had to creep down the ladder to the docking module's lower level, and rest again in a chair. Daan pointed out the lower airlock to her, where three bright blue surface suits hung, ready for a ground-level exit. After a few minutes rest, everyone walked through the interior airlock to the adjacent habitat module from Settler One. There was a table in the center, just like in S-3's habitat, and six door flaps to tiny private rooms reconfigured for use in gravity.

"I'll help Emma with her suit," Melina said. "Daan, why don't you get her some water?"

Taking the suit off was easier than putting it on. They slipped off the thermal layer, peeled down the compression layer, and tied the sleeves around Emma's waist so the shoulder ring balanced on the knot.

"It's best to keep some pressure on your lower body until you're ready to lie down," Melina said. "So the blood doesn't pool in your legs."

Someone produced Emma's personal bag and she pulled on her striped shirt. Daan gallantly offered a cup.

"Ah," she said. "Water that stays in a cup. Thanks."

"I can't take credit for the gravity," Daan said. "Or blame, for that matter."

Emma looked up at him. His wavy blond hair bounced around his head as he smiled. She quickly took another sip.

The settlers unloaded the jumpship, interrupting themselves to talk with Emma or get snacks at the habitat's food printer. The gathering felt like a party. Ruby checked on Luis' progress from time to time. He dropped the S-3 habitat on Phobos and picked up the knarr cargo module from orbit. He'd arrive shortly.

Governor spoke over the habitat audio channel. "Jumpship Two is descending."

"Luis will drop the knarr at the end of the north string of modules," Ruby said. "Governor, north imager on screen, and put his channel on audio."

"...my approach," Luis said. "Looking good."

The screen showed a cloud of beige dust obscuring the dark shape of the module as Luis lowered it towards the ground.

"What the... Shit."

The jumpship channel went silent.

"Jumpship Two has experienced an engine shutdown. I am receiving no signal," Governor said in its usual mild tone.

For a heartbeat, no one spoke.

Then Ruby, still in her surface suit, grabbed her helmet and dashed towards Jumper One. Everyone else ran the other way, out the Plaza airlock, and a cold draft flooded the module through the open door.

"Governor, what's happening?" Emma stood up slowly, gripping the chair.

"The S-3 knarr is lying on its side. Jumpship Two was at a thirty-degree attitude when I lost telemetry. Jumpship One was at a ninety degree attitude when I lost telemetry."

"Wait. What?" Emma said. "Jumper One?"

"That's right." Ruby stepped in from the docking module. "My ship's buggered, too. Totally off-line." She crossed the habitat in one kangaroo-hop and disappeared through the opposite airlock.

Emma followed Ruby with a slow, shuffling walk. She pulled the first airlock door closed behind her and opened the second to the Plaza.

Cold air caught in her throat and Emma coughed and shivered. The bay was dark with a few puddles of light along its length. She bumped into something waist-high - the fish pond, filled with a mound of ice. With one hand on the pond wall as a guide, Emma walked the length of the bay.

Above eye level were tiny green lights, some solid, some blinking slowly. In the darkness they glowed brightly.

White light tumbled in at the Plaza's far end through an archway to the Spine. Emma continued through the Spine, only vaguely aware of the throbbing equipment around her.

To her right another airlock stood open. Shivering violently, Emma was pulled the door closed behind her to shut out the cold. This was in the north habitat module where Daan and Melina were pulling on survival suits.

"Yin and Yang are suiting up in the airlock while it pumps down, and they've called the construction bots." Ruby stepped into the habitat.

She caught sight of Emma.

"Did you bring the surgical kit?"

"No. Aye..." Emma's words slurred. Her lips and tongue felt sluggish and heavy.

"Idiot." Ruby pushed past her.

Emma staggered to the table where Daan and Melina were halfway into their suits. She suddenly felt sick. If she tilted her head, it was like she was falling end over end.

Her friends were in trouble and the best she could do was clench her jaw and not puke on the table.

"Hey, just sit still," Daan paused to help her into a chair. "You can't fight gravity."

Chapter Fourteen: Burial

EMMA CLOSED her eyes and concentrated on getting her spinning head under control. Around her, people scrambled, then quiet returned, then a frigid gust and another scramble. She heard Ruby's voice calling to use the upper level airlock. After what seemed forever, a door closed and the cold draft stopped. Emma opened her eyes to find Sanni rummaging at the module's galley.

"Everyone else is outside," Sanni said. She sat across from Emma with the cat in one arm and a cup in her other hand. "Governor, put the north feed on the main screen. I want to monitor all the settler channels."

Emma didn't chance twisting her head towards the screen. Audio from outside was confusing. Sounds of heavy breathing, occasional grunts and half-understood commands jumbled together. Then Yang's voice rose above the rest - or maybe it was Yin.

"I've got the hatch open."

"What happened?"

"That's Liz's voice," Emma said, relieved.

"They'll need help at the airlock. Here, hold the cat." Sanni laid the cat along Emma's thigh and slipped the cup into her hand. "Dip your finger in and feed him drops of water. You'll have to support his head." She hurried off to the adjacent module as the audio feed continued.

"Claude, Claude. You okay?" That was Liz again.

"I can't feel my hand," he answered.

Emma slowly turned in her chair until she could see the screen. White flakes of snow swirled in the dust cloud, blurring the image, but she made out the jumpship cabin tilted at a crazy angle. Limbs from a robot swayed in the cloud and figures in surface suits fumbled around the open docking door.

"Luis?" Ruby's voice had a frantic edge to it. "Luis?" There was a pause and then a wail.

"We've got to get him inside, get the helmet off," Yin said. "Ruby, Ruby. Come on. It's too late. Unstrap the other one."

There were more jumbled voices and Emma watched as the shadowy figures slid a limp body through the jumpship cabin door. Then another one.

Tears overflowed Emma's eyes. She gripped the water cup as tightly as she could.

Jumper Two had come to rest a few dozen paces outside the habitat. Two figures dropped to the ground and crawled while others carried limp bodies. Air compressors kicked on in the adjacent docking module and presently Emma heard voices inside. Claude staggered through the airlock, supported by Yin and Melina. Liz followed with Daan and Sanni. Fog rolled off their suits as they slumped into chairs and a bitter smell, like burnt electronics, filled the module. They'd left life support packs and helmets behind, but hadn't stopped to vacuum off surface dust.

"Careful of Claude's hand," Liz said, panting a bit. "Gently, gently."

Sanni opened the thermal layer and slid it down to Claude's elbows, slowly easing the left glove off his hand.

"I'll handle the compression layer," Liz said. "Someone, get a bowl of water; tepid, not hot."

She cradled Claude's arm and inspected the hand. The skin was very white. Sanni came back with a bowl, and Liz lowered Claude's hand into the water.

"A fuel tank ruptured, and the freezing spray got inside the cabin somehow," she said. "James was in the co-pilot's seat, next to Luis. They hit hard..."

Liz choked a little and shook her head. She cleared her throat. "Is there something warm Claude can drink?"

Ruby stumbled in from the dock, crossed the module, and wrenched open the Spine airlock. Yin followed her.

"James? Luis?" Emma asked.

"They're dead." Daan looked up at the Earth Scan sphere spinning at the ceiling. "Governor, turn the damn Scan off."

"I'm starting to feel something," Claude said after a few minutes.

"My hand's on fire." He grimaced in pain. His hand was pink now, with blue finger tips.

Sanni brought a fresh bowl of water.

"Governor," Danna said. "Are there any messages from MEX we need to answer immediately? Tell them to leave us alone unless they have something useful to add."

"What about Luis and James?" Yang asked, looking towards the airlock.

"We could carry the bodies into the Plaza and pack ice from the pond around them." He went off to find the flatbed trolley they used inside the nederzetting.

"Yin's staying with Ruby for now," Yang said when he returned.

"We need to discuss what to do," Daan said.

"The three of us newcomers won't be much help," Liz said. "We should be resting, lying flat as much as possible for a few days until our blood volumes recover from zero-g. We shouldn't do anything strenuous for twenty days - sols, I mean." She closed her eyes and cradled her head in one hand.

"Use the bunks here in the north habitat," Sanni said. "I'll help Emma." Inside a bunk room, she peeled the suit's compression layer off, and Emma slipped into unconscious as Sanni tossed a blanket over her.

***

Emma lay still in the bunk for as long as she could after waking, but her bladder demanded attention so she reached towards the red nightlight and found the switch. Her duffle sat on the shelf next to her along with her helmet. A sleeve from her surface suit peeked out from under the bunk. Her cargo pants were still wadded up in the duffle where she'd shoved them before leaving the transport ship, a hundred years ago.

A hundred *jaars* ago, she reminded herself as she dressed. She pulled on the surface suit boots to keep her feet warm.

Emma smiled weakly at Daan in the habitat and, moving slowly, climbed the ladder to the upper life support deck and the toilet. When she returned to the lower level, Daan gave her a cup of hot water and a plate of macaroni-like tubes from the food printer. She chewed on a rubbery, tasteless piece.

"Sorry, we're out of tea," he said. "We're low on macronutrients, too. We better recover the cylinders in your cargo. These are nearly empty."

Alarm shot through Emma. She hadn't realized they might lose some of the cargo. It was vital to Kamp, vital to staying alive.

Liz and Claude joined her as she sipped her second cup of hot water. In addition to the effects of gravity, they were also battered from the crash, and Claude's hand was bandaged. Liz found her surgical kit lying in the galley and fished out a bottle of pain meds.

Emma plugged in her pad, opened her message center, and sorted by senders.

"Filip's asking for the habitat video feed to be turned on," she said. "He asked politely; says everyone's worried about us. Is it okay, Daan, for a few minutes?" They took turns talking to the imager, and then shut it down again.

Emma responded to a message from her mother, and found a short message from her father asking if the rovers were damaged in the crash.

There was nothing from Malcolm, which was fine, Emma thought, but puzzling. A crash should have brought all the controllers back from their weekend off. She opened the MEX log and saw him listed on medical leave, but had no time to ponder why.

"We're planning to have a memorial for Luis and James as soon as you feel up to it," Daan said. "Then the bots will take the bodies out to bury next to Ingra. It'll be easier to push them out the south airlock. We'll watch through the bots' imagers."

Even Ruby agreed that video feeds of the memorial should be streamed live. The settlers assembled in the north habitat and each said a few words, then they walked through the Spine to the Plaza, where Luis and James lay on the flatbed under a pile of crushed ice.

It must look eerie over the live streaming, Emma thought, with us standing under dim lights exhaling an ice fog with each breath. Yin and Yang pushed the flatbed, and they all followed through the south habitat to the docking module. The bots were too large to enter an airlock, so Yin positioned the flatbed while Yang suited up to operate the air pumps. When Yin was safely inside, he opened the outer door and a bot's jointed arms reached in.

The robot was like a giant beetle with a smooth oval body, and many-jointed arms with exchangeable tool tips. There were two beetle-bots, bright blue like all the surface equipment - the hands and eyes of the construction squad and general purpose units for the colony.

The bot slid Luis and James from the airlock onto a tool skid and dragged the bodies away. Stone building blocks were staged beyond the maintenance bay at the edge of the shallow trenches where they dug regolith sand. The bot stacked blocks over each body, next to the pile that marked Ingra's grave. The settlers sat in the south habitat, watching the video feed.

After Governor shut off the feeds to Earth, Emma turned to Daan.

"I should get the fish into their pond..." she said.

"Fish." Ruby snorted. "Luis is dead and you're worried about fish." Yin tried to put an arm around her but she shrugged him off.

"Emma's being practical," he said. "Our food supplies are almost gone and we don't know what shape the cargo is in."

Liz started to get up with a groan.

"Stay put, Liz," Daan said. "Come on, Yang. Let's help Emma."

***

Yang and Daan brought the canister down from the habitat's upper deck where Daan had plumbed it into the water recycling system overnight and laid it on the same flatbed they'd used for the bodies. Emma tugged packages labeled for the fish pond from a nearby pile until Yang sat her down in a chair and draped a blanket over her shoulders.

"Just point," he said.

They maneuvered the flatbed across the frigid Spine to the fish module airlock. There, high velocity air ducts skirted the walls, but hung unattached at the bracket where the compressor should go.

"I haven't made any connections to the Spine recycling systems yet," Daan said, noticing the direction of Emma's gaze. "It's too cold out there, so except for power, this module is isolated."

"And except for Governor." Emma examined a shiny white shell, a smooth lozenge as long as her forearm with rounded ends and three small LEDs. The solid green light was illuminated. She touched a black metal bar set all around with short fins - the heat sink protruding through the sealed unit's surface.

"Yeah, I pulled a couple servers from our modules to install here, and inside, too."

When Daan opened the inner door, Emma's spirits rose, and she dropped the blanket clutched to her chest. They stood in the empty fuel module from S-2, repurposed for fish - bright, warm, and humid, with a pond of stone blocks in the center. An aerator burbled in the warm water.

Daan tapped the pond's lip. "I sintered the blocks together with a hand welder, so it's water tight, and I used spare parts from life support. You'll have to keep a close eye on the pH levels in the water since there's no recycling hooked up."

"It's wonderful," Emma said, checking the thermocouple readout mounted on the pond's side. "We need to hang the

81

canister over the side, submerged in the water..." She bent over to help lift the canister and wobbled a little.

"You're still knackered," Yang said. "We'll do that." He positioned the canister.

Emma opened a small port to let pond water gradually mix in. "I'll release them tomorrow, after they've adjusted to the new water. Then I can regenerate the canister filter. This pond should be fine until they start reproducing. By then I hope we'll have the cargo unloaded..." Her voice trailed off. Thinking about the damaged knarr made her think of James.

"I can handle this," Emma said, reaching resolutely for a sack. With her jerk, it sailed up to head level.

Daan chuckled. "Your body doesn't know yet how heavy things are compared to their size. That looks bulky. What's in there?"

"Limnological solids," she said, pulling out a fist-sized lump. "A dehydrated mix of pond life - algae, water bugs, nitrogen-processing bacteria, stuff like that. Liz could tell you all the species names." She unfolded a screened cage with a one-handed flip, hung it in the water, and dropped in the friable lump.

"The cage gives the pond life protection until it's established," Emma said. "After nothing but compressed pellets, the fish will be wild for fresh food and they'd eat it all.

"Liz has bags of soil starts, too. Microbes, bugs, and worm casings. She calls them her subterranean livestock."

Daan watched the lump swell like a sponge. "I've piled all the organic wastes we've accumulated in the greenhouse."

"Great. Then the bugs can work their magic. We'll siphon fish waste from the bottom of the pond and use it to water the beds, share our vegetables with the mealworms, and feed some of them to the fish, which will start breeding. The sand filters the water and what drains to the sump, we dump back with the fish. As neat as your life support systems."

"Then you'll appreciate this," Daan said, enjoying his success. "Mealworms can go on the module's upper deck..." He pointed to the metal ceiling. "But let me show you the greenhouse next."

Through the next airlock, they stepped into a long bay. It, too, was bright and warm and reminded Emma of a Quonset-style greenhouse, but instead of glass it was built of tan stone with carroty orange streaks. The massive arched walls were fabricated from sand, sintered into a sort of stone foam, with closed pores for insulation and three meters thick for radiation shielding. She touched a seam where the surfaces crushed together, creating a tight seal.

"Beautifully consistent." She smiled at Yang.

He pointed down a narrow aisle. "Tharsis sand turns out to be very well sorted. And check out the garden beds. We washed the sand in the maintenance bay, so no perchlorates or other nasties. Just sterile rock dust."

"This is perfect," Emma said. The bay was filled with raised beds built from smaller blocks of the same artificial stone. Knee-high, the beds were separated by aisles, with small ponds scattered among them.

"Here's the sludge I promised you." Daan pointed to crumbling grayish heaps. "Irradiated and sterilized. So, there ya go. Plant us a garden. When's supper?"

His blue eyes danced above a boyish smile.

Emma laughed. "Spinach before you know it. And Liz says the number one problem with aquaponics is overproduction, so I hope you like fish." Her smile faded as she thought about the near-empty nutrient cylinders in the galley. They needed the gardening to go well. "Liz's tools were packed right behind the macronutrient cylinders. I hope we can recover the knarr's cargo."

"MEX is working out a revised access procedure," Daan said.

"The module has a split up the side, so they better hurry," Yang said. "A small dust storm won't cause much trouble, but if we get a big haboob, it'll pack sand into every crevice."

"Come, my lady." Daan took Emma's hand and laid it on his outstretched forearm. "Let's go back to the fish module and I'll show you the mealworm's penthouse."

He waved his other hand theatrically above his head. "But soft! What light through yonder hatchway breaks?"

Emma began a giggle, but half choked.

"Go ahead and laugh, love," Yang said. "It's better than crying."

Emma rubbed her face and smiled gamely.

Chapter Fifteen: Cargo

EMMA FREQUENTLY checked on the fish. She held her breath every time she peeked into the pond, fearing something might have happened to the half-dozen tilapia that would breed a major food supply - if she kept them alive until Liz was fully recovered from the crash and took over.

But all six were still there. Unlike the settlers, they had left the transport for a much larger world and darted around happily chasing food pellets. Sometimes Emma scooped a little duckweed out of its floating cage for them or dropped in some mealworms. They loved that, which was good because there was only one bag of pellets. Before they had fish to eat, she had to grow food for fishes.

Daan often joined her. They were laughing as they stepped into the north habitat for supper one evening, but hushed when they saw Melina and Liz seated at the table, meditating.

"Sorry," Emma said when Melina opened her eyes.

"That's okay," Melina said with a sigh. "I can't seem to get past this headache tonight."

"Do you want something for it?" Liz asked, ending her efforts too.

"No. I should have warmed up more before I started. I get so cold working in the Spine."

"I'll make supper. That'll warm you up." Liz held the edge of the table to help her stand slowly.

"No, no. You sit still," Melina said. "I'll start the food printer. That way, I get to choose the shape." She attempted a smile.

"And I'll heat water," Daan said. "Where is everyone?"

"They'll be here for supper," Liz said. "Claude wanted to take a walk so he went to the south habitat to find them."

Melina started the food printer extruding macronutrients in little shapes like buckyball cages with alternating protein and carbohydrate threads. She said the funny shape made printed food chewy, and texture was the only way to vary the meals. "This printer used to work a lot faster. It needs a new head. We've used parts from both habitat galleys to keep this one going. I wish you'd brought the printer from your transport."

"MEX planned for the S-3 habitat to be dropped on Phobos fully intact," Emma said. "I suppose we'll be happy we have a base there one of these sols. If our cargo's badly damaged, Ruby could fly up and retrieve the nutrient cylinders we left, and the food printer."

Melina harrumphed. "Colony Mars plans. They planned the food supply, too. I gag on half the shapes programmed in this thing." She fiddled with the settings. "I'm surprised Ingra hallucinated about trees. I might try a dash across the surface myself if I saw a decent meal waiting."

"Don't joke about that." Daan scowled at the cup in his hands.

Claude followed Sanni through the airlock. She carried the cat sprawled across one forearm and a yellow duffle in the other hand. She fished out a cushion to lay on the table and a gel pack.

Liz cooed at the cat as she helped shift him to the cushion so Sanni could heat the gel pack in the galley.

"Does he have to be on the table?" Claude asked.

"I'll move him before supper."

"How's the hand feel?" Liz asked.

"Kinda dull right now." He held up his bandaged hand. "But I feel dull all over. The meds, I guess. I can't even work up a good sense of outrage over eating with a cat on the table." He stroked the cat with his good hand.

"He'll get used to gravity soon." Sanni nestled the warm pack against his side and the cat began to purr.

"I didn't have to hold him up when he used the litter box this sol."

The door opened and Ruby hopped in. She announced that Jumper One was back online.

"Did you fix it, or did MEX?" Daan asked.

Ruby shook her head. "I was sitting in the pilot's seat and the displays activated. I ran a pre-flight diagnostic and everything's operational. It just came on."

"Are you spending a lot of time in the jumpship?" Liz asked. "It doesn't have as much radiation shielding as the nederzetting's modules and bays."

Ruby waved a hand impatiently. "My medichip juices up my immune system, doesn't it?"

Liz began to point out that Colony Mars doctors assumed they'd spend most of their time under heavy shielding, but Ruby interrupted.

"MEX is trying to use diagnostics to figure out what went wrong," she said. "They've got the beetle-bots out there imaging Luis's smashed jumpship; like that'll tell them anything. I'm working forward, starting with the last time we used the ships. I'll run a real-time simulation of each system upgrade we received. It can't be a coincidence that both ships shut down at the same time. I'm gonna find out what killed Luis."

Emma hung her head for a moment. And James, she thought. Of twelve settlers sent to Mars, three were dead.

"Come have some supper," Melina said. She set a bowl of buckyballs on the table and scooped some onto Emma's plate.

Emma hooked one with a fork and popped it in her mouth. It didn't taste like much, but did feel springy in her mouth.

She thought of a favorite cafe in Noordwijk. She'd sit in the sea breeze sipping coffee heavily cut with warm cream, nibbling on a cookie or little buckwheat cakes dusted with sugar. Dammit.

Ruby looked over Melina's shoulder at the food printer and frowned. "It takes forever to print those goofy shapes of yours. The first batch will be cold before you're done."

"So print something else if you don't like them." Melina said it with a sigh.

Ruby backed off with her hands raised. "Just saying is all. Is there any hot water?"

It took MEX four sols to decide there wasn't enough information to develop a new procedure to retrieve cargo from the damaged knarr module.

"We'll have to wing it," Yang said. Yin and Yang were experienced with surface work, so they'd take the lead outside.

"The S-3 knarr is different from previous missions," Emma searched for a diagram on her pad. "There's a large door opposite the standard airlock. It's designed to drive the rovers through. If we could get that open, we'd have good access."

"We'll have the beetle-bots cut the airlock away first," Yin said. "And drag it to the maintenance bay."

"There's no way we'll let an airlock go to waste," Yang said.

"The construction squad's loader-bot has a wide bucket attachment. It can roll the module and hold it steady."

"Then the beetle-bots can cut your garage door out of the knarr hull."

"We'll start in the morning." They nodded to each other. "And we'll want more open space in here."

Yin and Yang unbolted the flexion machine from the habitat floor.

"We're going to need room for boxes more than for exercise equipment," Yang said when Liz protested.

"Besides, no one uses it. We're never going back to Earth, so we don't need Earth-strong bones and muscles."

Emma followed them as they dragged the machine to the Plaza, but stopped, shivering, at the end of the Spine.

While Yin and Yang trooped back to the habitat, Emma lagged behind in the Spine's wide aisle. She wanted to test her Martian muscles. Walking felt normal enough, as normal as anything could after months in space. She could move faster with a bouncy step. Not as impressive as the videos she'd watched of people on the Moon, but Mars' gravity was more than double the Moon's.

Still, that was thirty-eight percent of Earth's. Emma thought she'd feel more like she could fly. Moonwalkers ran with long, slow-motion strides. Emma tried, but the hang-time between footfalls was just long enough, and just short enough, to confuse her brain. She felt like she'd missed a step going downstairs and bumped into a water tank.

I haven't had enough time to adjust since we landed, she thought. Maybe it will make sense outside on the surface, where I'll have more room to maneuver.

***

Yin and Yang made slow progress. At first, the beetle-bots could reach inside and lift items out. Then Yin and Yang suited up and took turns stepping inside the tilted module, dragging out boxes for the bots to carry to the north airlock.

The settlers gathered for supper after one particularly long day. Emma felt stronger and had enjoyed watching the external camera feeds, but everyone else seemed irritable.

"Can you tell yet if the macronutrient cylinders are intact?" Sanni asked at the end of one sol. "Working in the cold and dark is bad enough. I don't look forward to starving."

"I hope we can avoid that," Liz said with a worried look. The cylinders in the habitat were almost empty.

"I'd love something that isn't extruded through that food printer. Something fresh. Can we eat a few of the fish?"

Liz shook her head. "Those are the breeders. We can't risk eating any of them until the next generation is safely hatched. We'll have mealworms and potatoes before fish."

"You've got the cases of seeds," Melina said. "Why haven't you planted anything yet?"

"I need to dig the organic sludge into the sand or nothing will grow. Maybe the guys can look for my tools in the knarr?"

The macronutrient cylinders had to be removed first, dozens of them - twenty per settler, each taller than Emma and too wide to get her hands around - occupying over half of the knarr's lower level. They'd be awkward to move, even in Mars' low gravity. Not only did each one contain textured nutrients, but the cylinders themselves were heavy-walled to withstand pressurization into the food printer.

But when Yin and Yang reached the cylinders, they didn't bring any inside.

"Why not?" Melina asked.

"They're all in rough shape," Yin said. "It's pretty obvious they won't connect to the printer."

Yang continued his friend's report. "Valves broken off, dented and split. They're safe enough, frozen, outside, but I don't know how we're going to print meals."

"I'm glad Colony Mars didn't pack it all as powder," Liz said. "They weren't expecting a crash, but if it's frozen it can't blow away."

"It'll be freeze-dried soon enough," Yang said.

Melina looked strickened.

"Remember the backup plan," Emma said. "The beetle-bots can cut a cylinder into sections - the nutrients are frozen solid. Bring in a section at a time so it won't spoil. We can't print fancy shapes, but we can scoop out a meal. Just be careful of metal chips from the cutters."

"Better than starving," Sanni said with a grim smile.

"I'm sick of this stuff," Melina said. "Why did Colony Mars plan gardens of sand? Hydroponics would grow more, faster, in the same space, wouldn't they?"

"But we'd need more pumps and filters, more tubes and fittings, and more spare parts for everything. We'd be chasing our tails trying to keep up with the cargo requirements on each mission," Emma said.

"We're here for the long haul," Liz said. "The gardens may take longer to establish, but by the time the cylinders are empty, we'll be producing enough fresh food to live on."

"I really hate the nutrient stuff."

"You're forgetting something." Yin said. "There are holiday supplies still to unpack."

"We're halfway across the knarr. We should find them soon," Yang said, brightening. "And find something worth eating."

The next sol they brought in boxes of clothes, blankets, filters, gasket sheets for making seals - and the holiday boxes.

"Hurray, shrimp cocktail for supper." Ruby held up a handful of freeze-dried bags.

"Berries." Sanni happily tipped out another box of vacuum-sealed packets.

That night was an impromptu party with no printed pseudo-pastas of any shape.

It was a little scary to think of freeze-dried shrimp being so important to anyone, Emma thought. How long would it be before she felt the same way?

Chapter Sixteen: Construction

EMMA WATCHED as much of the unloading operation as she could through the docking airlock's tiny window. Yin and Yang worked smoothly with the bots, like a well-practiced team.

"You're great roboticists." Emma said one evening as she lifted boxes onto the flatbed. She was recovering from the long journey in zero-g and at times felt normal.

"We're hand-in-glove with them," Yang said. "We've been running the bots for a couple jaars, now, love."

The robotic construction squad had landed two jaars before any settlers left Earth. The bots built the maintenance bay on their own as the final proof of construction techniques on Mars, which included baking water out of the regolith. That supplied water for the nederzetting and, through the fabricator's electrolysis units, hydrogen and oxygen to fuel the jumpship - not an especially high specific thrust fuel, but one the settlers could manufacture from the deep dunes of Tharsis Plain.

Once Yin and Yang arrived on the Pioneer mission, construction accelerated. Emma read all their reports. They jumped on primary and secondary faults, cleaned and lubricated joints, and watched for heat buildup in the motors or degradation in range of motion. The construction squad's productivity had sky-rocketed.

"Quick response is the key," Yang said when Emma asked him about their strategy.

"We're out with the squad every sol," Yin said.

But their approach worried Liz. "That's more exposure than you should be getting," she said. "Radiation level out there is eighty times Earth's average. Our medical projections are based on an hour a sol on average."

Yin didn't argue. "Yes, we do miss Earth's magnetic field."

Yang agreed. "And atmosphere, and not just for breathing."

"I'm just talking about routine cosmic and solar radiation," Liz said. "If there were a high energy event - that would be worse."

"We try to reduce exposure," Yin said. "We spend a lot of the time in the Maintenance Bay, where we're close to the bots but shielded."

"That's not exactly how they briefed us in training," Emma said. "The bots are supposed to be autonomous."

"The squad is smart alright, but we're smarter." Yang grinned. "Supervised autonomy is the key to productivity. Another trick is using the jumpers to move stones."

Liz scrunched her eyebrows together.

"I can ask Governor to calculate your doses, but I bet you're exceeding. Your risk of cancer will go sky-high."

"Not to worry, love." Yin alternated the argument with his friend. "When the hospital equipment arrives, you'll be able to treat cancers, no problem. No one dies of cancer anymore."

"We didn't come to Mars for our health," Emma said, giving Liz a pat on the arm. "I've got to get out there with you guys. I'm recovered - I'm ready to go outside."

"That's good because we're gonna need you."

"Once the lower knarr level's been emptied, you have to help us figure out how to unload your rovers."

"We'll start in two or three sols, tops."

"In the meantime, here's that box of garden tools Liz was on about."

Liz started gardening immediately and Emma joined in. It was hard work driving a spading fork into the regolith sand, and Emma was happy to have Daan's help digging the organic sludge into the sand. He spent afternoons in the greenhouse.

"These stiff shoes were annoying in space," Emma said, pushing the fork into the sand with her foot "Now I'm glad the soles are so thick." She stopped to wipe her face and let a spell of dizziness pass. "This zero-g funk hits me every now and then."

"Partly, it's the thin air getting to you," Daan said. "Manufacturing air turns out to be a slow process. We're having trouble harvesting nitrogen from the Martian atmosphere. The freezer unit doesn't separate CO_2 as well as expected, so we have to rerun batches. A third of this is argon." Daan waved a hand through the air. "Which is fine, of course. We just need more of it."

Emma took a deep breath.

"The nederzetting is like a high mountain top now," Daan said. "I climbed mountains on Earth, so I know about acclimating." He stopped to lean on his fork.

"Climbing mountains? Sounds like nice work if you can get it."

"I used to write travelogues for a living, so I'd arrange to be at the base of a mountain whenever I had enough money for an expedition. I've climbed in the Himalayas, Alps, the High Atlas..."

Something in Daan's voice changed and he stared intently down at his spading fork. "My sister died on Mount Rainier. An avalanche. There was a crack and a snap, and a wall of ice roared down."

"That's horrible." Emma looked at Daan but he kept his eyes down.

"It changed my life. That's when I realized, I was taking a lot of risks to do things others had already done, probably better than me. If I'm going to risk my life, I want to see the Sun rise over a new horizon, in a completely new sky." He jammed the spading fork into the sand.

"Mars sure qualifies," Emma said.

"We've got to get the nederzetting established first. But I hope, someday, to see the Sun set from the top of Olympus Mons. The tallest mountain in the solar system - think what that will feel like."

"That sounds doable now. Ruby could take you in the jumpship."

"Maybe, at first, for reconnaissance. I've got to figure out what would feel like real climbing. Your knarr brought inflatable habitats for us to evaluate. Those could make good camps along a climbing route."

"You need to try my walkabouts. I can tell you all about them." Emma knew some experts inside Colony Mars thought walking on the surface was a foolish, romantic notion. But her father said Mars could never be home until settlers walked across their world.

"The suits are mechanically assisted, aren't they? I'll have to try one to get a feel."

"They're like rovers you wear instead of drive..." Emma's explanation was interrupted by the bay's airlock door opening. Liz stepped over the threshold carefully, balancing herself with one hand on the door frame. "I found the soil analysis kit," she said, holding it up.

"You ladies sit and rest. I'll do that."

Liz sat down slowly, stretching her arms out for balance. She handed him a vial from the kit. Daan dropped in some sand, hopped through the airlock to the fish module, and returned shaking the vial of sand and water.

"That's long enough." Liz reached for the vial and dipped in a test strip.

"Somewhat basic, as we expect, though I should really distill some water for a proper test. I'll check for nutrients later, but I bet the magnesium, potassium, and chloride levels will be what we expect, too. A decent beginning for garden soil. We can transplant the herbs I brought as soon as you've turned over the beds."

They had dwarf banana trees, too. During the long journey from Earth, the plants were growing out of their pots. Liz said they could harvest some herbs as soon as they were planted.

"Let's put all the bananas in one bed," Liz said. "It's not quite as warm or humid in here as bananas prefer, but they'll be okay. I wish we had more light." She looked up at the strings of lights running down the bay.

Daan's chin jutted out. "I put every light we could spare in here."

"Of course. Potatoes need cooler temperatures, anyway, and those'll be our mainstay. It's a good greenhouse, Daan."

"Liz wasn't being critical of you," Emma said after Liz left.

"First the water I use isn't good enough and now there's not enough light. She should appreciate what I've done." Daan looked from the closed door to Emma. His antagonism evaporated and he grinned.

"I'm glad you're here. You understand." He gave her a hug.

Emma relaxed, happy his sour mood passed so quickly. She hugged him back. "Why don't you show me everything you've accomplished in the Spine?"

***

Daan slipped into tour guide mode for Emma. "S-2 brought the life support equipment to recycle air, water, and waste in the bays. Installation was the primary goal of our mission. My Master's thesis was on Elizabethan sonnets, so the only life support equipment I used before joining Colony Mars was for high-altitude climbing."

He showed Emma a plenum enclosure and various tanks, pumps, and compressors; filter beds, vacuum distillation units, and a high-temperature catalytic reactor for waste water; and air revitalizers with regenerable carbon dioxide absorption. All the units were supposed to be sealed, but Emma caught a whiff of the rank smell of sewage here and there. Nothing is perfect, she thought.

"We take readings manually," Daan said as he toured Emma through the systems. "Governor records the data for us, but we tweak the valves and adjust the pressures by hand. It takes a lot of time, but think of all the solenoids and sensors we'd need if Governor ran the system."

"Settler Three brought tons of components for the bays," Emma said. Though Emma's rovers and walkabouts gave S-3 its name of the Explorers, the mundane parts in the knarr were more important - macronutrient cylinders and the tubes, wires, lights, and heaters that would turn cold dark bays into living space.

"I hope they survived the crash," Daan said. "It's a long wait for the next launch from Earth. I pulled lights and heaters from the Plaza for the fish module and greenhouse bay, so I'm going to help get the garden going - make sure my efforts weren't in vain."

The back of Emma's neck tingled. She glanced down, suddenly feeling a bit shy.

Chapter Seventeen: Sun Dogs

YIN AND YANG worked their way deeper into the knarr module and boxes piled up quickly in the docking module. Mostly they contained parts for the Spine, but Melina checked the manifest and dug out a replacement head for the food printer. The last drops of nutrients in the old cylinders would come out in exotic shapes.

"We'd like you, Ruby, to move Luis' ship to the maintenance bay." Yin said over a late supper.

"Grapple onto it with Jumper One anyway you can and fly it over," Yang added.

Yin continued. "No rush. Whenever you're comfortable flying the jumper."

"There's nothing wrong with my ship," Ruby said. "I've isolated the controls from Governor and there'll be no more MEX uploads. No one but me's giving commands."

Yin turned to Emma. "We want you to come with us tomorrow."

"Take a look at these images," Yang laid his pad on the table in front of her. "The knarr is packed in three layers. You're looking at the empty bottom, about three meters high."

"Did you examine the internal frame?" Emma frowned as she scrolled through the images. The bottom third had been loaded with habitat supplies. The rovers were tied down to a middle frame which was supposed to lower on four ratcheted pillars to the garage door on the first level. But one pillar was bent and torn loose from the floor.

Emma pointed to containers of lighting, heaters, rolls of tubing, and sheets to form ducting - supplies they needed to make the bays livable. "We should remove everything that's stowed around the rovers first."

The next morning Emma joined Yin and Yang in the airlock. She took a compression layer off its hanger and stood uncertainly.

"The suit's impossible to get over a uniform," Yang said. He turned pointedly away and pulled off his striped shirt. Yin also stripped to his underwear.

Emma blushed. Of course she had trained to don a surface suit with James and Claude, as well as Liz. She kicked off her shoes and dropped her khakis. She only had the compression layer up to her waist when Yin and Yang were shouldering their life support packs. They waited patiently as Emma squirmed into the suit.

"Sorry to be slow," she said.

"No worries, love. We've done this every sol for jaars."

The crashed knarr lay at the edge of the docking module on the jumpship side. They went out the opposite surface airlock. Emma turned to face the Sun and squinted against the yellow blob in a saffron sky. Below a few streaks of thin cloud, surrounded by tawny halos of dry ice crystals, were four bright spots of light, commas in the sky.

"Sun dogs," Emma said over the helmet channel. "Governor, be sure you record that image."

The horizon spread out in a hump - the gently sloped flanks of the Peacock shield volcano. Sand extended smoothly in all directions, washed out by the glare. It was like floating in space, if space was beige. Tharsis Plain was beautiful.

She felt a tap on her shoulder.

"You awake in there?" Governor had turned on her suit-to-suit comm channel, and one of the Brits spoke. In surface suits, they looked identical.

"Yes, yes. Let's go." Governor had turned on her suit-to-suit comm channel. She followed Yin and Yang around the module, trying a bouncy step like they used. Her feet skidded a little backwards in the sand with each hop.

Through the gaping garage door, the inside of the knarr was dark. Emma flipped on her helmet light. The empty lower level was roofed with beams, panels, and the bottom of the

99

rovers. Rover One, on the module's crushed side, was partly off its tie downs, tilted downwards towards the knarr hull. She examined the broken pillar. There was no way to lower the second level floor.

"Everything is bracketed from above," Yin said. "I don't see how to start unloading."

"I think I can get through there," Emma said, pointing at a space between some of the bracing above. Yin and Yang lifted her, but her suit's backpack caught on the beam.

"I think the hose will reach." Emma unbuckled the strap across her chest and loosened the life support pack on her shoulders. "Hold the pack while I climb, then pass it up to me."

Yang held the pack up high. "Watch that airline."

"Damn. I can't get all the way up. Bring me down." Yin lowered her, and Emma came down pulling a sack with one hand. "I think we can do this. I'll pull down stuff until there's a big enough hole for me to climb up."

"I like you, Emma. You know how to get things done." Emma couldn't tell if Yin or Yang had spoken, but she grinned.

The morning went quickly as Emma dropped down boxes and bags of cargo. She carved out a space high enough to stand in, shouldered her backpack, and opened a narrow aisle to the tilted rover.

"Tell Claude I can see his drill rig drums bracketed to the ceiling above me," she said at one point. "Not a scratch that I can see."

"I'm listening." Claude's voice came across her helmet link. "Thanks for checking."

"Rover One's track chain's still bolted to the storage platform, but the rollers slid out. We should be able to pull the tracks back into place once it's outside. But I can't see one of the tensioners." She pushed on a box and parts tumbled out of a split in its side. "The rover's crushed a whole bunch of boxes against the hull. I'm gonna pull some of this loose."

She passed strip heaters down through a gap in the framing and tugged at some bags that had dropped between the rover's tracks. A few small bags wiggled free, then a few more.

"Careful, love."

A shudder ran through the rover and Emma let out a little shriek.

"Emma. What happened? Are you alright?" Claude and Yin both called to her.

"I'm okay. The rover slid a little more. But..." She grunted. "Aw, shit."

"Talk to us, Emma," Yin said.

"My backpack is stuck. I can't see what's wrong." She braced her feet against a crosstie in the floor and pushed. Another shudder ran through the rover.

"Stop whatever you're doing," Yang said.

"Now what?"

"Is anything pushing on your body?"

"No, I'm okay." She was jammed into the gap between boxes and couldn't turn, but waved her arms and one leg. Yin and Yang could see her through the framework.

"If I could just pull the pack out..."

"Don't move," Yin said. "Don't risk anything falling on you."

"I'll get another backpack from the airlock," Yang said. "You can slip out of that one and leave it right there."

"We'll need some tools, too," Yin said.

"Yeah, we'll disassemble the ties where Emma climbed up and both get up there."

"What do you need?" Claude asked over the suit channel. "I'll stage it for you in the airlock."

"Emma. Can we leave you alone while we get tools?" Yin asked.

"Yeah, go ahead." Emma had been scared but now she just felt stupid. "No rush."

But as soon as she said it, Emma wished they would hurry. It had been a long morning and she had to pee. They planned to go back inside for lunch and she hadn't put the urine collection pad inside her suit. It wasn't very comfortable, and she didn't expect to need it. Now...

Stop thinking about it, she thought fiercely. She watched a clock in her heads-up display and resisted the urge to call Yin and Yang, to ask what was taking so long. She fidgeted.

"Emma." It was Claude. "They're cycling down the airlock now. How're you doing?"

"Oh..." Emma had clamped her jaws tight. "I'm okay."

"You sure? You sound funny."

"I'm sure. I better watch for Yin and Yang."

Finally helmet lights showed through the framework below her.

"We'll do a kludge job down here and have you out in a minute."

Emma fidgeted some more as Yin and Yang talked back and forth.

They had to find the right size wrenches and angle the ties to work them out of the way.

It was too late. The suit's compression layer was tight against her legs. Emma felt warmth spread across her butt. She groaned softly.

"Emma. Still alright?" Claude was monitoring the suit channel.

"Just fine." She did feel better.

It was another half hour before Yin stood in front of her and loosened her shoulder straps.

"There's plenty of air in your helmet," Yin said. "I'll disconnect your power and air hose. You drop down to your knees and crawl out of there. Nice and slow. Yang has your replacement pack."

The click reverberated through Emma's helmet when Yin detached her hose. The air, suddenly stagnate, immediately felt hot and humid. She took in a long breath, which cooled her face, but left her clammy when she exhaled. Resisting the urge to gasp or whimper, she crouched and lifted her arms to slide from the pack straps.

"That was a tight squeeze. Good thing you're no giddy kipper." Yang sounded pleased as he passed the hose over her shoulder and Yin clicked it into her shoulder ring.

"I'll meet you in the airlock," Liz said over the suit channel.

"I'm coming, too." That was Ruby.

Oh, god. Not Ruby too, Emma thought.

Chapter Eighteen: Rovers

EMMA PUZZLED over how to extricate her rovers and shared a plan with Yin and Yang. "You said Ruby can lift the crashed jumpship and fly it to Maintenance, right?"

"Yeah. Piece of cake."

"If we could cut off the top of the module," she said, "could she lift out the heavy cargo from the top layer - the mules and the walkabout suits?"

"I see what you're saying. Then the bots could cut away the upper frame to reach the rovers."

"And Ruby can lift them out. Brilliant."

"Can I go outside with you again?" Emma asked.

"Better let us handle things for a while." Yin noticed her disappointment. "Even we won't go close while the bots are cutting off the knarr's top."

"Or while Ruby's thrashing around with her grapplers," Yang added. . "But she's working on the jumper's crash, so leave her alone right now."

At their next group meal, Ruby explained her upload simulations. She'd found what she was looking for. "The jumpers were programmed to shut down," she said grimly when they gathered for supper in the north habitat. "A timer was embedded in their operating system. That's why Jumper One came back online, too. The timer ran out."

"I don't understand," Claude said. "What was it supposed to be timing?"

"Nothing. And it's not a bug in the last upgrade from MEX, either. The log says the timer was inserted from here. From Kamp Kans."

"Who inserted it?" Claude asked.

Ruby shook her head. "The identification field is blank."

"What? No transponder ID? Governor must have a record if anyone accessed the ships."

"You're welcome to look for yourself." Ruby glared at Claude.

"Logs can be faked, you know," he said. "Has MEX confirmed your simulations?"

"MEX." Ruby snorted. "They couldn't find a road if it had red flags on it. I don't need them to tell me I'm right."

Claude glared back at her.

Emma suddenly realized that she was sitting with Liz and Claude, and Ruby had plopped down next to Yin on one of the boxes dragged in for extra seating. Melina, with the cat squirming on her lap, sat with Sanni and Daan. They wore the same striped uniform, but each mission crew was sitting separately. That should change.

"We found the tea, Ruby," Emma said, walking to the tiny galley. "Let me make you some."

"Oh, I'd love a cuppa." Her expression cleared.

Emma dropped a pellet into a cup of hot water and watched the leaves unfurl. Colony Mars sent them real tea, thank goodness, but only powdered coffee and not much of that. Tea contains theanine as well as caffeine - that was the experts' reasoning. The combination would produce a mellow alertness. Emma handed Ruby the cup, but doubted this discussion would mellow out.

"If you're sure the timer program came from Kamp..." Claude raised an eyebrow at Ruby. "Then we've got another problem, don't we?"

"Yeah, if the log's right, it means one of us sabotaged the jumpships." Ruby locked gazes with Claude.

"Well, *we* were still in space, so none of us did it," he said. "Liz, you're a medic. Can you assess Luis' medical files, see if he was depressed or..."

"He wouldn't need a timer, now, would he, if he wanted to crash his own ship?" Yang asked. "He could dive straight into the surface if he went nutter."

"Luis did *not* want to kill himself," Ruby said sharply. "And he certainly didn't want to kill *me*."

"Maybe it was a mistake," Emma said, carrying a cup to Ruby. "Maybe the timer was intended for something else, something in life support maybe."

"Wait a minute," Daan said. "Are you accusing us?" He flushed with anger and Melina's back snapped straight. A ridge of hair stood up along the cat's spine.

"Stop this," Liz said. "It doesn't make sense for any of us to damage a jumpship, much less kill anyone."

"Maybe someone wanted to keep us out," Claude said darkly.

"Look, if Governor didn't record who uploaded the timer, we don't have enough information to draw any conclusions," Liz said.

"In the meantime, let's have Governor keep the jumper systems isolated," Yin said. "Say two of us have to authorize any uploads from MEX or from Kamp."

Claude looked at him suspiciously.

"Okay, one person from each settler mission - so three of us have to authorize any uploads."

"Daan, I didn't mean..." Emma said.

"Forget it," he said, getting up abruptly. "I've got some boxes to unpack."

She felt unexpectedly lonesome as he left. Dammit. So much for improving relationships.

***

Emma was happy when Liz followed her to the garden. Her bruises had faded and she was ready for some exercise. The cat dashed across the icy Spine and squirmed into the airlock as soon as Emma opened the door a crack.

"I can use the help. Daan hasn't stopped by lately," Emma said. "The worms need more space. Let's take care of that."

Emma shoved several slick-sided tubs through the module hatch to the upper level and tossed up sacks of bedding.

"It's hot up here," Liz said happily. "Just what we need for a good yield."

"Like a summer day." Emma laughed. "How do I do this?"

"Spread the bedding out; mealworms only need a light layer of wheat bran, and it has to last until we have garden plants to shred. A batch of grown beetles will be ready to lay eggs in three months. When those hatch, we can eat our first harvest."

"You make them sound like chickens."

"Mer-row." The cat was batting wildly at a clump of wheat bran on the floor.

"Did he climb up here?" Liz picked him up. He squirmed, reaching paws down towards his clump of bran. "He likes the worms, which is a good thing since they'll be his primary food source. Watch."

She picked up a couple worms and dropped them on the floor. The cat focused wide eyes on their wriggling and slashed his tail back and forth. Liz let him leap out of her arms. He landed on the worms, chewing and purring.

"See," Liz said. "We're both ready to assume our duties - me growing and him eating."

They examined the gardens' progress. Potatoes had sprouted, along with beans and squash. Duck weed floated on the pond surfaces and bugs rowed their way through the water.

Emma squatted by a patch of green threads pushing up through the sand. "A square of vegetables here, started with our precious supply of fertilizer, then a square of nitrogen-fixing alfalfa there. I've been sending a growth report to MEX every morning. They say we're right on target."

"I think I'll recommend everyone spend some time in here," Liz said. "The light and warmth, and greenery once the garden is growing - it'll do everyone good."

"That makes me think of Claude. You changed his bandages today?"

"He's not ready to go to work," Liz frowned. "I'll let him tell everyone after supper."

It was bad news.

"I'm going to lose three finger tips," Claude said. "They're not healing. Liz will lop them off tomorrow."

"Once the dead tissue's gone, you'll heal quickly," Liz assured him.

"I'll finally be able to get some work done." Claude turned to Daan. "I know I owe you time on the utilities."

"That reminds me," Daan said. "We have a surprise in the Plaza. Grab a blanket. It's cold out there." He led them out the habitat module, hopped to an electrical panel, and threw a switch. Light reflected off streaked beige stone throughout the arched interior.

"Ta da! We used all the undamaged lights we could find."

"I hadn't realized how big the Plaza is," Emma said, admiring the arched walls and barrel ceiling fabricated from Tharsis Plain sand.

"This is less than half the lights planned," Sanni said. "But it's like spring after a long winter."

The Plaza was the widest and longest bay, designed to be the nederzetting's town square. There was a narrow pond running most of its length, still heaped with crushed ice. At one end against the wall, worktables and shelves of fabricated stone were the beginning of a community kitchen, and tables and short benches of rock were arranged nearby like a cafe.

"Once it's warm and bright," Liz said, "I'll ask Yin and Yang to fabricate pots large enough for banana trees. Some greenery will soften the rusty color of the stone."

"So now you don't like our stone," Ruby said.

Liz started to protest, but Ruby waved a hand. "Forget it. I have more important worries. We left the power receiver from S-3 in orbit. If we want to get it landed before the seasonal storms, I need to fetch it soon. We'll want the power for Daan's new lights and everything else from the knarr. Yin, Yang - help me refuel the jumper tomorrow and I'll bring it down."

Ruby looked around at the others' surprised faces. "MEX has cleared the jumper and, more to the point, I've cleared it. There's nothing dodgy in the AI programming now. I can't cower down here like a rabbit in a hole. Once we hook up another power receiver, we can pump some heat into this bay."

Chapter Nineteen: Pressies

JUMPSHIP ONE was at the south docking module, so after breakfast Emma and the others walked down the Spine and Plaza, and through the south habitat. Melina carried the cat and set him on the stationary bike to claw at a thread hanging from the seat.

Liz frowned at the empty bolt holes in the floor where the exercise equipment belonged. "You removed the flexion machine here, too."

"Give it a rest, Liz," Daan said. "I'm tired enough without an extra hour of resistance training."

Ruby was already onboard, running checklists, when Yin told Governor to open the live stream to MEX. "Yang and I will suit up and walk to the maintenance bay. We'll monitor the bots refueling the jumper's hydrogen and oxygen tanks from there."

With full fuel tanks, Ruby rose out of the atmosphere on translucent blue flames. No one made a move away from the screen. It would be hard to do anything else while Ruby was in orbit.

"Shall we make tea?" Liz stood by the galley uncertainly. Yin, Yang, and Ruby bunked in the south habitat and she was seldom in their galley. "I don't want to intrude."

Sanni hopped over to help. "This galley is laid out exactly like the north habitat." She handed cups to Liz.

Yin and Yang were back inside by the time Ruby reached the power receiver's orbit.

"Everything looks good for retrieval," Ruby said.

She above the receiver, so the mesh dish of its antenna was pointed straight at the ship's imagers, a lacey white rectangle floating over a terracotta planet mottled with gray.

"The atmosphere's very clear right now." Yang sipped his tea. "It's a good sol to bring the receiver down." They quietly watched the approach.

"I hate to do this..." Ruby sounded sour. "But manual operation isn't delicate enough for the grab."

Ruby turned the grappler operation over to Governor. The AI coordinated telemetry from the ship and the receiver, closing the grappler tips gently on the receiver's capture lugs.

"See, I told you the ship is fine," Ruby said. But she ran an extra diagnostic before reentry.

They watched the screen, focused on the receiver dangling below the jumpship. Emma recognized the Tharsis Plain pass below with its distinctive pattern of huge shield volcanoes.

"I'll land on the next pass," Ruby said.

Governor switched to the nederzetting's outside imagers.

The receiver touched down gently on a stone pad sixty meters east of the Plaza, engulfed in the dust raised by intermittent engine firings.

"Brilliant," Yin said.

"We have time to hook it up before supper," Yang said as they headed to the docking module.

"You've got to drag cables awfully far," Emma said.

"Next jaar we'll build a medical bay connected to the Plaza, and we'll hook the receiver to it directly then," Yang said.

"To provide redundant power for the hospital and labs," Yin added.

Oh, yes. Emma flushed. She had studied the construction plans and should have remembered.

***

In celebration, Liz and Sanni volunteered to prepare the meal they'd missed when Jumpship Two crashed. They headed to the north habitat to get started while Ruby was docking. In honor of a special event, Governor left the imagers on in both habitats streaming Ruby's welcome home live. They waited for Yin and Yang to return and repeated the welcome.

111

Yin waved goodbye to Earth. "I've signed off for the sol."

"Cracker good," Ruby said. "Are these chives?" She sniffed at a bowl of beige carbohydrate mush dotted with bits of green.

"Yes," Liz said. "I harvested some thyme, too."

"I'm looking forward to supper for a change," Claude said, sitting down next to Emma. He waggled his bandaged hand. "I may have lost some fingertips, but it doesn't hurt to hold a spoon anymore."

"I bet your wife was upset about your hand," Emma said.

"I didn't tell her, and she promised not to watch the Colony Mars feeds."

Emma was sorry she'd brought up Claude's wife. His face fell as he answered.

"We agreed not to contact each other so she can move on with her life."

Emma gave his arm a squeeze and glanced around the table. Melina was picking at her mush, searching for bits of metal with a single tine of her fork. Sanni stirred her nutrients into a pinwheel swirl. Daan dropped his daily micronutrient blob on top of a single pile, like snow on a mountain. No one was paying attention to them.

"Look, even the cat wants to nibble something green," Melina said. The cat was clinging to her lap and chewing on a sprig of thyme she dangled. "Ow. Watch those claws."

"Governor, send the new receiver's coordinates to the power station," Yang said as he carried tea cups to the table. "And initiate system diagnostics. If everything pans out, we can run utilities to the new gardening bay - install lights and start warm air circulating."

"Good. I get the willies every time I walk past that yawning dark arch," Melina said.

"Dark and cold," Ruby added with a grumble.

Yin and Yang built another new bay stretching out from the Spine, but the connecting archways remained blocked up.

The fabricator continuously harvested nitrogen and argon from Mars' thin atmosphere, and the beetle-bots dragged the tanks to an airlock where they released the gas into the module.

As soon as the nederzetting accumulated sufficient internal pressure, Yang cut through. But a bay wasn't useful without utilities.

"I have more seeds I can plant, once another bay warms up," Liz said.

"What do you want first, heaters or lights?" Daan asked politely. He wasn't brusque with anyone but Emma. "Most of the heaters had their connectors sheared off in the crash, but I think we can repair them. Installing lights will be harder. A lot of the heat sinks for the lamps are cracked. The diodes were packed separately, but we have to assemble the fixtures before I'll know how many lights we can get working."

"Heaters first, then," Liz said. "You can work on the lights while the ice in the new ponds melts."

"That's another thing," Daan said. "Once ice melts in the Plaza pond I can start the water recycling system in the Spine. And ramp up the air compressors. Melina, Sanni, and I won't be able to keep up with maintenance and install new systems."

He gave Claude and Emma a crooked frown. "We could use your help, like Colony Mars planned."

"I can insert diodes into fixtures one-handed. And the bandages come off soon." Claude held up his hand.

"And I can handle maintenance for the habitat systems." Emma said. "Or installations. Whatever you want."

"Aren't you worried about working with saboteurs?" From Daan's tone, he wasn't joking.

"Daan - what I said about the timer in the jumpers... I never meant any of you'd caused the crash." Emma didn't know why Daan wouldn't accept her apology. He was a pigheaded...

"The bays will warm up faster than you think, mate," Yin said, interrupting her thoughts before Daan could reply. "Those stone blocks are excellent insulation."

"The wind's been sorting the Tharsis sands for eons, so the grains we feed to the fabricator are within a narrow particle size distribution," Yang added.

"It's slow going, but easy to laser-sinter together into whatever shape we need."

"Three meters thick for the above-grade arch and five meters thick for the floor."

"The bay's a tunnel built on the surface instead of dug into the ground."

"And Mars is burying the bays for us in sand dunes. Little by little, every storm season our shielding gets better."

"I'll be happy when I can sit on your rock benches without freezing my butt off," Ruby said. The words were grumpy, but she smiled as she scooped out buckyballs flecked with chives.

"After supper, let's do a group meditation. We deserve some relaxation time." Liz smiled, hoping, no doubt, to get them working together again.

Emma sighed. Maybe Daan would get over the unintended insult.

Chapter Twenty: Haboob

I T WAS SEVERAL sols before Yin and Yang cut the top off the crashed knarr. First the beetle-bots had to drag stone blocks over to brace the module, and then the loader was free to scoop up sand. Once a wide sand ramp was packed against the module, the bots fitted blades to their limbs and opened the knarr like a can of soup.

Daan turned the north habitat table into a work bench and everyone joined in, replacing broken diodes in lighting fixtures. Each new diode snapped into place with a muffled pop. It was tedious work, but not difficult.

It felt good to work together. Tensions eased while they chatted. Melina kept watch on the cat as his eyes darted back and forth, following their moving hands. He occasionally tried to swipe a diode.

"I never thought sweet tea would be such a treat," Daan said, holding up his cup to the imager when he stopped for a break. The Earth Scan sphere spun a warm, contented yellow at the habitat ceiling. Filip had cajoled them into streaming feeds to Earth for an infotainment special.

Everyone's mood lightened. Ruby's successful flight and sugar for the tea. Maybe all they needed was some good luck.

***

An MEX transmission arrived as they cleared the table for supper. Governor read the heading aloud: "We have an issue to discuss."

"Oh, hell," Ruby said, and opened the transmission on the habitat screen.

Instead of Filip Krast, the lead controller who usually messaged them, the Settler Four mission manager was seated at a desk. He cleared his throat and spoke directly into the imager. "We've been running some scenarios, and we're worried about the lack of redundancy for landing S-4 on Mars. If there was a problem with the one remaining jumpship, S-4 could be stranded."

Ruby swore. The cat's eyes snapped open wide and he scurried into a bunk room.

The manager continued. "Now, I know you're going to say they have months of extra supplies and we'd fix any problem by then... and the consensus here agrees. We're going full-bore ahead with the schedule. This message is intended to keep you informed. MEX will revisit the issue before authorizing a launch."

"Well, damn," Claude said when the transmission ended. "Why bring it up if they're going full-bore ahead? Would they really cancel the launch?"

Sanni gazed down at the floor stoically, but Melina's eyes widened.

"They can't do that to us," she said. "S-4 is bringing medical supplies."

"How badly damaged is Jumper Two?" Emma asked.

"Piss awful," Ruby said.

"We could probably beat the frame out straight enough to use," Yang said. "But two of the engines are pretty much smashed."

"We don't have high-precision fabricators to build new parts," Yin said.

"We've got other engines, don't we?" Emma had an idea. "Salvaged from the transport ships?"

"Well, yeah." Yang rubbed his chin thoughtfully. "We've got all nine of the thruster engines that brought the transport ships to Mars stored in the maintenance bay."

"It's still no good," Ruby said. "The jumper's cabin split wide open in the crash."

"What about the hull from the knarr?" Emma asked. "Can't we cut strips to weld over the split?"

"Maybe. I'd hate to send someone into space jerry-rigged like that."

"We can use remote control." Emma waved a hand enthusiastically. "The rovers have telepresent capability - you can operate the manual controls from your pad. I could pull a unit out and tie it into the jumpship."

"That's an idea," Ruby said, a smile spreading across her wide face. "How long before I can lift the rovers out of the wreck?"

"Before planning surface projects, please check the weather alerts." Governor activated the display. The AI didn't often speak spontaneously, but it was always listening, and opened an image. A storm had popped up in the southern hemisphere, emerging from the deep Hellas Basin, lofted upwards from the sun-warmed crater floor by winds rushing along a canyon break in the wall.

"Blimmin' heck. We're cursed." But when Ruby set her mind to something, she was hard to stop. "Governor, tell MEX to make themselves useful and run their weather models to check the forecast."

That was a poke at MEX. Despite a large weather team, they didn't understand how an updraft from Hellas could envelope the whole planet within a few sols.

"I'll send the bots for some ceramic-wool blankets from Maintenance," Yang said.

"Brilliant idea you had." Yin smiled. "Printing those blankets with the fabricator."

"They can wrap the knarr to keep out most of the dust. Then I'll bundle them off to Maintenance until the storm clears."

"The forecast doesn't look so bad, and the storm season's only just started. It shouldn't shut us down for more than a fortnight."

"That gives us time off for a solstice party."

"Do you always celebrate the first storm of the season?" Emma laughed. A plan to fix the jumper lifted her spirits. "Or

117

are you just looking for an excuse to open the party boxes again?"

***

For two weeks they worked repairing lights and heaters from the crashed knarr. When the storm cleared Yang and Yin hauled in more boxes of components, moving everything away from the walkabout suits in their plastic crates.

As Ruby's jumpship hovered, sparkling ice crystals from the engine exhaust mixed with blown dust. She lifted a walkabout crate from the knarr, set it on the ground, and grappled the second one. Next she lifted a mule, a miniature walking habitat designed for a single settler to camp on the Martian surface. Hovering used a lot of fuel and she had to retreat to the maintenance bay to refill her tanks. As soon as the jumpship left, dust obscured the knarr and drifted into the open top.

"This will take longer than I expected," Yin said when they came back inside.

"Ruby can only make a few lifts a day," Yang said. "The jumpship stirs up so much dust it ruins visibility."

"We'll need to electrolyze more hydrogen and oxygen to fuel the jumper before we try again."

Over the course of a week, they removed the top cargo layer. Emma took every chance she could to hop into the docking module and look out the airlock porthole, craning her neck to see the top of the knarr.

"Tomorrow we disassemble the frame and expose the rovers," Yang said over scoops of protein and carbohydrate mush one evening.

"We brought you something special, Emma," Yin said. "Take a look in the dock."

Emma hurried to the module before the evening meditation began. Two sleek plastic capsules, waist high and two meters long, occupied half of the floor.

"My walkabouts." Emma turned to Yin, who'd followed her.

"We thought it would be easier to unpack them here instead of Maintenance."

"How'd you get them inside?" Emma laid both hands on the closest capsule, making sure it was really there.

"The beetle-bots slid them into the airlock one at a time, and we used hand jacks inside."

"Thanks, Yin." She hugged him. He grinned and patted her back.

"Just don't get me in trouble with Ruby. She wants you to concentrate on fixing Jumper One before anything else."

"No problem. I know the priorities."

Self-disciplined, Emma thought. That's me.

Another few sols and the boxes from the middle layer were unloaded. Yang's blanket hadn't been a perfect cover. Even after vacuuming with the airlock system, the burnt-metal smell of Martian sand followed the cargo inside. They all coughed and sneezed as they carried boxes to the Plaza and stacked them by an air return filter. Daan and Sanni had to change the filter twice before the smell faded.

Fortunately, dust fell through the middle layer for the most part, down to the bottom of the knarr. Yang was able to brace Rover Two and remove the storage brackets without further trouble.

Emma got a message over her pad to meet Yin at the north surface airlock, the one closest to the wreck. She unplugged the pad from the wall, excused herself from dragging rolls of wire to the Plaza, and hopped to the docking module.

Yin and Yang were standing at the open door to the surface-level airlock, already in their suits, grinning.

"We've got a rover upright," Yin said. "There's time to test it out."

"Let's unpack it and test the controls," Yang said.

"Come on and suit up. We won't peek."

119

Emma hung her shirt and khakis in the airlock and began working her way into a compression layer. She was pulling on the thermal layer when Ruby arrived in a surface suit.

"I keep my suit in the south habitat's dock," she said by way of explanation as she watched Emma stomp into boots. "I'm coming along to help."

Emma felt a tingle of excitement when Yin sealed the inner airlock door. She was about to activate a rover on Mars, something she'd planned with her father for a long time.

"I'll stream the exterior imagers to MEX, shall I?" Emma said. "My Dad will be watching for news about the rovers."

"Okay, helmets on everyone," Yang said. "Check your air systems and power levels."

Emma sealed her helmet with a twist-click. Its plastic smell faded as air began to circulate.

"Communications okay?" Yin's voice sounded in Emma's helmet.

"I..." Emma stopped, cleared her throat, and tried again. "I hear you loud and clear." She tried not to fidget while the airlock pumped down.

Yang opened the outer door and Emma stepped onto Mars once more. She was determined to get a better look around this time.

She stomped a foot, kicking up fine burnt orange dust that hovered around her blue boot and clung to her leg. She tipped her head to look straight up. There were no dry ice clouds. The Sun had the featureless terracotta sky to itself.

We really need more words for shades of orange, Emma thought.

Behind her were the modules and to her right sand dunes piled against the Spine blocked her view. Emma turned left.

Peacock Mons crouched half hidden below the curve of the planet, but its peak was visible, the highest point of a broad, gently sloping lump of a mountain with a collar of shadow at top. Emma felt tears well up in her eyes. It was beautiful, even with most of its features softened by dust in the thin, cold atmosphere.

"Guys, forget the rover for a minute," Ruby said. "Let's take a tiki tour and show Emma around."

Yin, or maybe it was Yang, shouted agreement. The two of them charged off across the sand, racing each other with loping kangaroo-hops.

"You better go slow. Don't lean forward too far," Ruby said to Emma. "Practice inside doesn't get you ready for how slippery the sand is on these foundation stones."

Yin and Yang had produced all the nederzetting bays by digging wide trenches many meters deep and pushing fabricated floor stones back into the holes. Because the stone was like a solid foam, with many closed pores sintered for insulation against the Martian cold, there was excess sand from the dig to fabricate into blocks for the barrel-arched walls and ceiling of each bay. Even so, there was left-over sand. Emma could now align the diagrams and images from reports she'd read with dunes nearby.

The floor extended far beyond the bays, to avoid excavating near any bay walls. She scuffed her feet along until she found the edge of the stone apron - future bay floors - that extended for ten meters beyond the current bays.

"Stop acting like an inspector," Ruby said. "Let's have some fun."

Emma followed Ruby, gaining speed as she hopped south along the Spine. Mars' gravity was less than Earth's, but she'd lost muscle and bone density, so she didn't feel like a superhero. She skidded and fell to one knee. More carefully she walked around the buried south modules, bouncing from foot to foot past their airlocks and power receiver.

She didn't realize how steeply the ground sloped upwards where a drift covered a new bay. Her feet slid out beneath her and she fell forward onto hands and knees. Emma held her breath as she checked the heads-up display. Pressure held constant in her helmet. She let her breath out all at once, fogging her view.

Ruby helped her up and brushed sand off Emma's suit, looking for any damage.

"Good on ya," she said, laughing. "Next time, keep an eye out four or five hops ahead."

"Go arse over tit?" Yin and Yang hopped up next to them, breathing hard, their grins showing between each helmet-fogging pant.

"Don't worry," one of them said. "We've fallen loads of times. The suits are tough. Little hops, I think, for the rest of the tour."

"Where's Olympus Mons?" Emma asked as they rounded the drifted hump of the bay.

The Sun was fairly low, a bright blur in the sky above a thin white cloud where Emma estimated the volcano should be. The mountain, if its top was even visible from twelve hundred kilometers away, blended into the fuzzy orange sky. "I thought you said there weren't any dust storms nearby."

"No storms," a Brit said.

"But there's always dust," the other Brit said.

"Even a regional storm on the other side of the planet kicks up dust worldwide."

"The curse of Mars."

They continued along the Spine, Yin and Yang pointing out where they planned to add more bays, and swung out around the greenhouse.

At first, Emma didn't recognize the crashed knarr module. It was partly covered in Yin's ceramic blanket and drifted sand. Rover One tilted awkwardly, one set of track chains half off.

I'll worry about that later, Emma thought. She turned to Rover Two, which sat upright on its tracks, swaddled in packaging.

"I'll show you how the roof canopy comes off the rover's power receiver," Emma said.

Emma kept up a monologue about the rover's features as they removed the cushioned sheets. Finally, she hopped backwards to admire the machine. The front cab had large windows and hung over a pair of treads that propelled the boxy body. It was sky blue, Earth sky blue, with Colony Mars' logo on the side.

"That blue coating is glassified; fused to its skin," Emma said. "Should last forever."

"It's a beaut, alright," Ruby said. "But will it run?"

Emma opened a channel to Governor. "Send the activation code. Engage the AI interface. There's a start-up diagnostic that will run. It takes a minute."

Governor announced the interface was established. "I have merged with the rover's AI."

"Go dock at the north surface airlock," Emma said.

A slight shiver ran through the rover. Then it extended two outriggers and, pushing against the sand, pivoted itself sideways, retracted the outriggers, and trundled off towards the docking module.

"Well done," Yin said. "Is that the remote control you were telling us about?"

"No. The rover can execute some basic programs, just like the jumpship can. Governor feeds it parameters, and it can dock. Watch this."

Emma hopped ahead of the rover and stopped in its path. The rover stopped, too.

"It won't run into anything. It's waiting for instructions," Emma said. "Or to continue with its program." She jumped away and the rover resumed its course.

They followed it to the airlock and watched the door's static charge drive dust away. The rover extended its short docking tunnel and sealed against the airlock.

"All set," Emma announced. "The rover was shipped with a full atmosphere, so as soon as the airlock cycles we can open it and unpack the cargo. It's packed with fragile items and gifts from families."

"Didn't you sneak a peek at the gift manifest before you left Earth?" Yin asked.

"Nope. It's a big surprise."

"Don't tear the packaging," Yang said. "Save everything,"

"We need to hop down to the south airlock to let ourselves in."

"Yeah. Let's get inside and open our rover pressie."

Excitement was contagious, so Emma bounced on her toes as she waited for the airlock to equalize. But she didn't know if there was anything special for her inside.

Chapter Twenty-One: Haiku

SINCE THE ROVER occupied the north airlock, they hopped to the south dock. Yin and Yang both changed into striped shirts and khakis. Emma wore her suit to walk to the north habitat. The faint burnt smell of Martian dust clung to her despite the vacuum cleaner in the dock, but she'd left her clothes in the north airlock and didn't fancy traipsing through the bays in her underwear. Besides, MEX requested a live stream when they opened the rover, so the habitat imagers were probably already on.

Emma doffed the suit in her tiny bunkroom, which would now smell of the Martian surface for sols, she thought ruefully. She pulled on a striped shirt and cargo shorts. The habitat was full of chatter and bits of packing material when she pushed open the privacy flap and stepped out.

The rover was stuffed with cargo. There were imaging components, servers for Governor, and fragile spare parts, but the first items they reached were in the rover's airlock. They found more packages of specialty foods like chocolate, dried fruit, cheese, hard candies, and powdered drink mixes, even beer and wine packed in flexible tubes to withstand freezing during the journey through space. Best of all were the personal gifts.

Colony Mars invited family members to send gifts for the settlers in each transport and most were surprises. Even Ruby didn't complain about the live stream, since her family would be watching along with Colony Mars' premium subscribers.

"Here, Emma. Something for you." Liz passed a box. Emma didn't think anyone had packed a gift for her. There were two thick palm-sized disks and a holographic projector - including *batteries* - from her mother, with a note saying she'd loaded them with favorite sculpture files. And a ratty old stuffed dog with one eye missing.

I didn't know Mom had kept this, she thought, hugging the toy under one arm.

She pulled out wads of bright fabric that had been stuffed in the box as cushioning and laughed out loud. Silk undies!

Jammed along the box sides were a few of Colony Mars' super-light, super-strong plastic bags filled with desiccated toothpaste, and a half-dozen replacement heads for her toothbrush.

The tooth powder padded a tin with cheese and salami - since she was a little girl, Mom always got tins like this for Christmas. She'd had to think ahead and send all this to the spaceport last June to load in the knarr. Mom wasn't totally scatterbrained after all.

Tears filled her eyes and Emma ducked into her bunk. She carefully laid out each item. There were so many little things she'd never have again.

She ran her fingertips across the bottom of the empty box. There was nothing from her father, not that she'd expected anything.

Laughter rang outside so, after wiping her face, Emma pushed through the privacy flap, zipping it closed behind her.

"I'll share my can of vegemite," Ruby said, waving it for everyone to see.

"I got something special." Liz caught Emma's elbow and smiled secretively. "I'll show you next time we're in the greenhouse bay."

"Ho, ho." Claude held up a double-headed hammer. "A rock pick. This is the best technology for prospecting and I don't need fingertips to make it work." He gripped the hammer's handle with a smile and rummaged through his box. There was a sweatshirt from his university and a handful of curled and faded clippings - cartoons that probably once decorated a lab door.

Claude pulled out a clear plastic tube and looked puzzled for a moment. There was a plant inside, its oval leaves dried to grayish green and tiny flowers still blue. Claude shook the tube and small seed pods rattled.

Claude looked up and caught Emma's eye.

"What did you get?" he asked.

She showed him her childhood toy dog, but his laugh sounded hollow.

"I have flower seeds," he said, holding up the tube before Emma asked. "I'll have to talk to Liz about getting a little space in a greenhouse to plant them. They're called forget-me-nots."

Claude cleared his throat. "I think I should stow these." He stepped into his bunk, closing the flap behind him.

Daan shouted over the chatter. "Let's have one hell of a party."

Despite the celebration, Emma couldn't relax. She slipped into her bunk and zipped the privacy flap. Her mother's gifts lay on the bunk.

Emma slid the disk into the holographic player and tapped through the metadata without reading. The image was a sculpture, a sort of upside-down tear drop balanced on a ball. She was about to advance to the next image when she noticed an audio icon and touched it.

"Mars is the stepping stone for humanity's voyage into the universe." Her mother's voice - her mother had recorded captions.

She giggled as she recognized the quotation. It was some inspirational drivel from Colony Mars, maybe from a tee-shirt.

Next came an image of two naked men warped like a 3-D funhouse mirror. They were running, one reaching forward to the other, who reached back. "Mars is the challenge of our age. If the baton falls from one hand, pick it up."

All the images were inspirational, the originals cast in glass or steel or bronze. "Passion for exploring the universe," "attraction for the unknown," "childhood dream."

"Inspire people everywhere - catalyze growth, prosperity, knowledge, and unite the people of the world."

Yeah, right. Whoever said that meant the world of Earth, expecting to gain the benefits without risking their own sorry necks.

"When the sun expands, Mars will be our spaceport to the solar system."

Emma snorted. The sun won't expand for a billion years. What makes anyone think Homo sapiens will still exist? It wouldn't even take an apocalypse - just evolution into progeny so far removed we couldn't recognize them.

"An honor to stand on the edge of destiny."

Wait a minute. That was from one of her father's speeches. She remembered a catch in her throat and tears in her eyes as she'd listened to him. The line sounded silly out of context - pompous and effortless for someone who never intended to step over that edge.

She flipped off the hologram player and, avoiding anyone's eye as she stepped out of the bunk, slipped to the docking module. Yin and Yang were there.

"I thought I'd unload a few things..." She noticed a line of boxes half-circling the module.

"We thought the same thing," Yang said, sliding another box along the floor.

"We like to get an early start each morning, so we're gonna empty the rover."

Emma grinned. "Pass me a box."

***

Before the next sunrise, Emma suited up with Yin, Yang, and Ruby at the airlock. Since the rover was pressurized, they opened the door straight away and stepped in.

The rover's onboard airlock ran behind the passenger seats. Directly opposite the inner door were two narrow hatches that would mate with the walkabout suits. The passenger cabin was to the right.

Emma turned left. "I brought bottles of water." She dropped them on a narrow counter. "But the only other thing we have is air. The sanitary facility isn't charged yet."

"No worries," Yang said. "The maintenance bay has everything we need."

Ruby's tour of the rover didn't take long. From the inner door Emma pointed out the tiny galley and hatch to a life support closet at the rover's rear.

Emma slid into the driver's seat, checking cabin records for pressure and temperature. "I'll do a quick-start on life support. The rover held air pressure fine in the knarr, but this is its maiden voyage. Better put on helmets."

"So nice," Yin said as the rover undocked. "Driving to work instead of walking."

"No traffic either," Yang said.

Emma drove across smooth sand, pinkish-gray in morning light, towards the maintenance bay a kilometer away. They passed the bright blue loader. It was no longer needed to unload the knarr and had returned to scraping up sand.

Emma stopped the rover to watch a bucket of sand dump into the fabricator's hopper. A screw feeder was currently angled up to the top of several metal arcs, bypassing the molecular separators inside the main body and too high for Emma to see properly through the window.

The fabricator was their factory. Inside were furnaces for baking water out of pores in the sand and electrolysis units for converting it into oxygen and hydrogen.

"Water and oxygen have been easy to collect," Yin said.

"It's the molecular separators that give us trouble," Yang said

"Our capacity for freezing out CO_2 to purify the nitrogen is low."

It was hard to think of the big box as a robot, but it had a lot of onboard intelligence that communicated with Governor. That was merged with Governor, really. All one AI.

"The fabricator head has a small feed bucket. The whole assembly rides on an XYZ frame," Yang said. "The head delivers sand to the proper coordinates and a laser sinters the particles into place at the specified density."

They watched the head for a while but it barely moved along the block of stone, forming one of the tabs or grooves that locked stones together as a bay was assembled.

"Governor can run everything robotically," Yin said. "Like your rover, the squad can perform basic operations on its own, but when we take over, things go faster."

"We're an entire bay ahead of MEX's construction schedule," Yang said. "Manufacturing air is the long pole in the tent now."

"Can't really complain, I guess. Something had to be the long pole in the tent," Yin said

"Some of the experts at Colony Mars are saying 'I told you so.'"

There had been heated debates over where to locate the colony. The Tharsis Plain was three thousand meters above Mars' average elevation. That was high enough for the atmosphere to be noticeably thinner and the regolith held less water. But the sand was perfect for construction.

"Fabrication works better than anyone expected," Yin said. "The Tharsis dunes are perfectly uniform for the full five meters we dig out to install a bay floor. We can shovel the sand straight into the fabricator, which saves a lot of time."

"I've read all your reports," Emma said. "But there's one step you slowed down..."

"Yes, when we sinter the blocks together - like welding to seal the surface of the stone - heat builds up in the seam. If it gets too much hotter than the rest of the block, the stone cracks."

"We lost a few arches before we realized what was happening."

"Yang modified the bevel where the blocks meet and we get a better seal now, too."

Emma watched the loader's backhoe attachment extend and dig onto the sand. "How are the solid lubricants holding up..."

They eagerly discussed the minutia of construction. Emma felt like her brain was fully engaged for the first time in weeks.

"We'll do proper mining once all the basic bays are complete and there's time to prospect for something more interesting than sand," Yin said.

"Claude's brought some brilliant equipment for prospecting," Yang added.

"These humongous volcanoes must have burped up some useful minerals."

The maintenance bay was easy to spot in the early morning. Its shadowed face was gray against the brightening orange sand - a sharp-edged shape skirted by sand drifts. The precise location for Kamp had been decided when the module carrying the fabricator touched down. The other modules had landed with a kilometer - excellent accuracy after a journey of five hundred million kilometers. Loaders and beetle-bots had hauled their module's equipment to the fabricator and began construction. The maintenance bay had been their first bay, and the Pioneer jumpship later retrieved the outlying modules.

Now those modules stood in a row at one end of the maintenance bay, stripped and empty, waiting to be cut up and recycled as needed.

The beetle-bots kept a parking pad clear. Emma activated the rover's docking program and sat back.

"Welcome to Maintenance, our home away from home." Yin led the way through the airlock.

"We spend twelve hours a sol here or in the loader's cab," Yang said.

"Don't take off your suits," Yin said. "We'll go out on the warehouse floor in a minute and it's not pressurized. That roll-up door for moving the big robots can't seal airtight."

Yang casually leaned against the wall, then reached up to an imager mounted above his head. For the first time Emma could remember, worry creased his brow. "Let's talk a bit. Imager's off, recordings are off."

"We're always the upbeat pair, always the good news," Yin said. "But we're worried. You understand what we're doing, so we can talk plainly."

The sudden change in mood made Emma a little dizzy and she hugged her helmet to her chest. "Sure."

Yang. "You know we had some problems when we first landed. Sitting inside a module all sol, monitoring the robots. We got twitchy. All of us did."

Yin sat next to her. "Claustrophobic. It was worse than the flight from Earth. We knew that would end, but this." He spread his hands. "This was forever."

"That's when Ingra said we had to build the bays faster, to give us some room to move," Yang said. "And Yin and me, we worked up our improvements with the Colony Mars construction team, and started going outside every sol."

"I thought that was because of some programming upgrades," Emma said.

"Yeah, because we insisted." Yang rubbed a gloved hand along his leg. "When Settler Two arrived, we thought we had it made. The Plaza was done, Melina was a ball of fire, Sanni steady as a rock, Daan kept talking about climbing Olympus Mons, and Luis made Ruby happy."

Yin's grim expression loosened to a smile. "A happy Ruby is good for everyone."

"They brought more lights and more heaters," Yang said. "Yin and me, we opened the Spine as soon as we could."

Yin pulled off a glove to wipe his face. "But it didn't last. You see how Melina is now. Could you even describe her to me? She hardly registers as alive. Sanni hides it better, but she's in trouble too. Daan's prickly as a thorn bush, and Ruby's downright paranoid."

Emma's shoulders relaxed. So it wasn't just her having trouble with the others, and now she had allies. "I've felt it too. With Liz's help, with the psych department in Holland..."

But Yin had a different concern. "With all the drama inside the nederzetting, no one's paying attention to our real problem. Mars."

"Yeah," Yang said. "This planet would kill us in an instant. Some knackered mistake could breach the habitat. Get sloppy with dust control and it's fibrosis of the lungs."

"Or something worse." Yin said. "Too many equipment failures, or Claude can't find minerals to make fertilizers or metals to repair parts, and it's slow-motion death from cold and starvation. More missions can't bring enough food and supplies to make up the difference. Not for long."

Yang flattened his thin lips together before continuing. "Gives me the collywobbles."

Emma's mouth went dry. "Haven't you talked to MEX? What do the experts say?"

"That the psychologists will work it out. That Yin and me are doing great and just keep it up. They don't appreciate the trouble we're having manufacturing atmosphere. They say, no worries 'cause it's within nominal, but that's rubbish."

Yin's dark eyes locked with Emma's. "You understand the robots. You realize what we're working with, what we need to accomplish so we don't die out here. You can help us keep construction going. Ingra said, more bays is top priority. That's what Yang and me are good at, so that's what we're going to do."

Yang set his helmet down. "And it's what makes us happy, so we're one less problem for the psych department."

Yin's smile glowed against his black skin. "Now, back to being good news." He reached for the imager. "Leave your helmet here for a minute, Emma, and we'll show you the control room."

Emma followed them up a vertical ladder, through an oblong hatch that accommodated her suit's backpack. Up top, she entered a narrow room with windows on one side overlooking the bay below. Following Yin and Yang's example, she removed her helmet.

"These are control interfaces for the bots. Life support and a full sanitary unit are through there. Our galley is that way." Yang pointed to the doors in turn.

Emma stepped to the windows, six rows of small panes overlooking the warehouse floor below. A shaft of light from the control room reflected off something metallic.

"It's too dark to see," Emma said. "Is something moving down there?"

"One of the bots, using infrared to maneuver. It doesn't need the lights and we routinely keep the roll-up door closed. Less dust to sweep out that way."

"Yin, this bay was constructed in-situ, here on Tharsis, wasn't it?"

"Sure. The construction squad built it before we arrived."

"Where'd all the glass come from, then?" She rapped a knuckle against one of the small, thick panes.

"It's a slow process, but the fabricator made these windows."

"There's enough of silica in the sand."

"Glassmaking is one of its programs."

"You're thinking we can replace the jumper's windows. But take a look." Yin flipped on the warehouse lights below them.

Emma drew in her breath trying not to gasp out loud. The crashed jumpship lay in the center of the floor, its cabin turned towards her. The ship was tilted at a steep angle since both engines on one side were smashed and folded inwards. The entire frame was twisted.

"Let's go down and take a close look."

They climbed back down the ladder. Ruby waited in a second airlock that opened to the bay floor. They donned their helmets, the airlock pumped down, and they stepped out near the ruined jumpship.

The front of the cabin crumpled inwards against the pilot and co-pilot seats. Only the shattered screens and a few manual controls stood between the seats and the collapsing frame. Emma understood clearly now why James and Luis were dead.

She took a deep, shaky breath and clambered into the cabin to open the ceiling panels. Most of the ship's control systems were mounted in the ceiling. "Well, this is a mess. There's no way Governor can interface with this thing. Let's look at the engines you've scavenged."

Nine thruster engines, salvaged from settler transport ships, stood in a row along the wall. Emma spotted Rover One once she was past the ruined jumpship. She stopped to examine its track rollers, carefully aiming her helmet imager to capture pictures to send to Earth.

"I don't see any significant damage. Can I use the beetle-bots to pull the track chain back into place before we leave?"

"You're the expert," Yang said. "You can do whatever you want."

Emma grinned. To be welcomed by two brilliant roboticists was all she could ask for.

Chapter Twenty-Two: Walkabouts

LIFE IN KAMP settled into a routine. Liz shouldered the greenhouse tasks. Claude joined Daan and the others assembling lighting fixtures, rewiring heaters, and catching up on maintenance for the life support systems.

The weather remained clear in the first months of storm season, so Yin and Yang continued fabricating building stones and harvesting atmosphere. Ruby split her time between moving stone with the jumpship and helping Daan's team.

That left Emma free to redesign jumpship controls. She threw herself into the effort. Designing the interface was a good reason to contact her father. He never mentioned their last call on Earth and they fell into a familiar pattern. They had something to share now and he worked on the problem personally.

She'd been worried he might object to stripping the unit from Rover One, but instead the project excited him. Demonstrating the adaptability of the unit was good for his company. Critics within MEX who had argued for simple buggies had to suspend their grumbling, since jumpships were vital to the colony plans. He hoped to sell Colony Mars another pair of rovers for a later mission.

"This reminds me of when we built your first servo mechanism," he said at the end of one message.

"I kept that servo for years." Emma smiled at the memory. It was one of the few occasions her father had spent time at home.

She bent over her schematics until his next message arrived. That was pretty much the way Emma and her father always communicated and the transmission lag was too long for conversation anyway.

It was a relief, in a way, to avoid direct conversations with Earth, even with her mother. Her mother's messages, which arrived at irregular intervals, were so chirpy and so cheerful. Conversation could have been exasperating.

Design and testing took time. Emma was still immersed when Liz brought her first bowl of beets to supper, then squash sautéed with green onions, and later a few tomatoes. Each new vegetable was a cause for celebration and energized Daan and Melina, who otherwise complained they were tired all the time. Emma noticed headaches herself, but usually shrugged them off. Just eyestrain, maybe.

A major haboob storm soon ended construction. As soon as the weather alert sounded, Yin and Yang told Governor to stash the squad in Maintenance. Governor calculated the best orientation to fit the rovers in with the bots. The fabricator lumbered slowly across the sand on its wide treads as the eastern sky turned into a boiling mass of deep red clouds. The warehouse door rolled closed and the bots shut down.

Liz harvested the first batch of potatoes as compensation.

"No more of that macronutrient sludge," Melina said as she raised a boiled potato on her fork.

"There're a few more servings in your future," Liz said. "I dug these as soon as I as reasonably could. The rest of the crop should stay in the ground for another month."

"We stacked cylinders in one of the airlocks and turned off the heater," Yin said.

Melina sighed. "Don't spoil this moment with talk."

The arrival of the first planet-wide storm was disheartening. Even though the habitats' temperature and lighting levels never varied, the sols seemed darker.

***

Liz stepped through the doorway, the cat in one arm and a bag of squash under the other. A cat didn't mix well with tiny electrical parts so Liz kept him in the greenhouse during work shifts.

She had to drop the cat to close the door.

"Will you get that cat out of here," Claude said. He was staring fixedly at a wire dangling from the fixture he was assembling.

"Damn." The cat leaped at the wire and pulled the fixture to the floor. He streaked away as it landed with a crash.

"Don't yell at him." Melina followed the cat to her bunk. She usually left her privacy flap open at the bottom to lure him in and kept a handful of mealworms along with his toys from the Moon.

"Time to clear the table for supper anyway," Sanni said.

"Good. I'm tired of this." Claude rubbed his eyes with the heels of his hands.

"You'll notice MEX hasn't been bothering us about live feeds," Ruby said, swinging her hand over the little boxes of diodes. "No one wants to watch this piss awful work."

"I've got the latest engine test results from MEX," Emma said to Ruby. "Let's skip meditation tonight. We can work in the south habitat after supper."

After spending an hour with Ruby in the south habitat, Emma walked through the Plaza to her north habitat bunk. It wasn't that late, but she felt tired and had a dull headache. Something caught the corner of her eye. A chill ran down her back. Something was following her. Emma turned and stared at the ice, a decaying glacier of fissures trickling with meltwater thanks to the rising temperature.

"Cat? Kitty-kitty-kitty?" Nothing.

Inside the north habitat, Sanni had the cat on her knee while Melina dangled a string. He batted at it frantically.

"I'm glad the cat's here," Emma said. "I thought he got left out in the Plaza."

"Why's that?" Sanni asked.

"I could've sworn I saw something by the pond. I thought maybe it was the cat. Just a shadow, I guess."

Melina lifted her eyebrows and tilted her head towards Sanni. But Emma was too tired to worry about them. "I'm going to bed."

A couple sols after the haboob cleared, Yang declared the dust settled enough to use a rover. He woke up the construction squad but only moved the fabricator a little way out of Maintenance, ready to retreat if another storm approached. The beetle-bots used shovel tips on their limbs to scoop drifts away from the docking airlock and into the loader bucket. The bots carefully cleaned the outer surface of the airlock and resumed fabricating stone.

Emma immediately told Governor to bring a rover to the docking module. She and Ruby were anxious to mount the transport engines on Jumper One.

They drove Rover Two to Maintenance every sol for a while, wringing out systems and dry-fitting components. The more time they spent together, the better Emma and Ruby collaborated.

At the end of one morning, Emma and Ruby were in the maintenance bay's narrow control room, watching the read-outs as a bot ran cables from the jumpship cabin to the scavenged engines. Emma made notes on an intermittent reading.

"Your system design is going to work," Ruby said. She nodded her approval.

"Robotics is my field."

Ruby looked satisfied as she started the engine diagnostic. "I've always liked working out here. I can really concentrate."

"I'm glad we're working together on this," Emma said. She hesitated before going on. "At our course-correction party, and then later in orbit... I'm afraid you and I got off on the wrong foot somehow."

"Yeah, well..." Ruby continued to monitor the read-outs. "I heard some rumors that put me off."

"Rumors?"

"Donations soared after Ingra died. What if they want to see something... I don't know. Something dramatic. Again."

"*They* who? Who told you that bullshit?"

Ruby shrugged. "It sounds like bullshit to me now, too."

"So you and me - we're good now, aren't we?"

Ruby finally looked up and smiled.

"Yeah, we're good. But I still say we've got to be independent. The Colony Mars outfit won't be there forever. We can't depend on them to call the shots."

"Is that why you're here?" Emma asked "To make sure Mars stays independent?"

Ruby snorted. "I'm here to fly into space. I wasn't going to make it on Earth - a girl from the wop-wops of nowhere. I may only take a jumpship into orbit once a jaar, I may die on one of the hops, but the tradeoff's worth it."

***

In mid-season Governor relayed an alert from the weather satellites - a vast cloud of dust was emerging from the Hellas Basin. The storm was forecast to spread rapidly north and west towards Kamp. They'd be engulfed in a few hours and the storm would continue for weeks.

Yin and Yang sent the beetle-bots scurrying to drag up nitrogen and fuel tanks - the fabricator had been harvesting atmosphere. The bots released the gases into the nederzetting before retreating to the safety of their maintenance bay.

Jumpship work was on hold again.

Two walkabout suits still lay in the north docking module. Emma had resisted the temptation to unpack them, but now she had time.

"Want some help?" Claude asked as they cleaned up after breakfast one morning. "I could use a break from the repair bench. Mounting all these little god-damn-it parts gives me a headache."

"What do you think of exploring in robotic suits?" Emma asked. Claude had never said much about the walkabouts and she'd bumped up against enough skeptics at Colony Mars to be defensive.

140

The idea, her father's romantic idea, was that settlers should venture across the Tharsis Plain on solitary multi-sol expeditions. Like Daniel Boone or Davy Crocket, he'd said. The walkabouts were robots you crawled inside, rovers you wore, pressurized exoshells to enhance human speed and strength. Emma's personal expertise was the tail design. Walking on loose sand required a third leg for stability and the suit needed a counterbalance when traveling at high speeds, so it had a tail.

"I think exploring is essential." Claude said. "Prospecting is what brought me to Mars."

Claude paused with two bowls in his hands, the muscles in his jaw tight. "When I was young I had ambition, and potential. But what did I accomplish? Teaching others to go out and do what I didn't. There's nothing sadder than thinking about what might have been."

He barked a short laugh "Once I get out on the surface... In a month of solid field work I can learn more about Mars than any expert knows today. That's what makes all this..."

He gestured to the pile of lighting fixtures piled against the habitat wall. "Tolerable."

That was how Emma felt. "Yes. I'd love some help."

"If I wait too long, we'll be preparing for Settler Four's arrival," Claude said. "I'll be stuck for another two years... Excuse me, another jaar. I didn't give up so much to spend the rest of my life living like a rat in a culvert."

He held up his truncated hand with two joints missing from the last two fingers, one from the middle finger. "I'm alive. I've got to make that count."

Emma let out a long, slow breath. "There are times I think I made a mistake coming to Mars. I wake up in the middle of the night and wonder what the hell I've done."

Emma felt tears behind her eyes and berated herself. She'd never said that to anyone, not to Governor's psychology program, not even to Liz.

"No one else acts like they gave anything up. I wonder if I belong here."

141

"I gave something up," Claude said. "My career, my home..." He looked down suddenly.

Emma completed the thought to herself - your wife.

What had she left behind? Her father... she could message with him like she always did. Her mother... there was an annual visit where she was dragged around to poetry slams and art exhibits and talked to people she didn't understand.

I could have looked harder for people I did understand, she supposed.

There was terrific work being done in robotics for private homes, farming, and manufacturing. That work hadn't grabbed her. Maybe she'd been too hasty, too narrow-minded. Racing across the surface of Mars wasn't the only way to blaze new trails.

She turned away from Claude and sniffed hard. This was a worthless train of thought, and she refused to be self-indulgent. That's what grit's all about. Discipline and self-control. Stick to the plan. It's why I'll get to stride across the surface of Mars in a robotic suit. Thousands, maybe millions, of Earth-bound people envy me.

"You and me, we're in the same boat," Claude said.

"And Daan."

"Daan's a rat in a culvert." Claude shook his head derisively.

"No. He wants to climb Mount Olympus."

"I don't know what he wants. Neither does he."

Building a safe home was indisputably their priority. Emma knew that, she'd trained for that. They all had. But it was so tedious.

"Yesterday, I carried a roll of wire to the new garden bay..." Claude looked over his shoulder and leaned closer. "It's so dark and cold, I started to shiver. Suddenly I couldn't breathe. I felt like I was choking. I ran and hid between the Spine tanks till my heart stopped pounding in my ears."

Emma blinked at him, stunned. "Could there be an air leak?"

"No." He shook his head. "I checked later."

"Did you tell Liz? Or talk..." She paused. "You could talk to Governor's psych program."

"I told Liz about the heart rate. She couldn't find anything wrong."

Emma frowned with concern.

"Hey, it's nothing. I don't know why I mentioned it."

Claude stepped into his bunk and came out holding his rock pick. "How well can your walkabouts manipulate this?"

Emma smiled, relieved to be back to work. "That's one of the first things I want to find out."

The crash had damaged the lower half of the knarr, but the walkabouts had been stowed in the top layer and were intact. Emma and Claude cut the bands and the capsules fell open like clamshells. Each suit lay on its belly, arms close to its sides and tail folded up. They were bright blue like the rovers.

"Governor. Send the activation codes," Emma said.

With a faint hum, the suits seemed to relax. The rigid arms slumped.

"Are you in contact with the suits' AI? Go ahead and merge."

"So, Governor will be able to operate the suits?" Claude asked.

"For basic programs, yes. Just like the rovers. I'll show you. Governor, when startup diagnostics are complete, stand the walkabouts up."

Emma and Claude stepped back. The walkabouts, side by side, moved in unison like soldiers. They pushed up onto hands and knees. Their wrists telescoped out, tipping their shoulders upwards. Each tail swung out behind, each right hip and knee bent to bring a foot against the floor. They stood. The hands retracted and the tails stiffened, leaving a curl of a half-dozen joints on the floor. They stood like three-legged stools.

"They look so big," Claude said. "And strange."

"Governor can operate the access hatch, or you can open it manually like this." Emma flipped up the cover over a button on the suit's left shoulder and pushed. There was a whir of motors and the life support backpack disengaged with a clunk. It hinged upwards revealing a door in the back of the suit.

She spun a small wheel until another click indicated the latch was free. "You can twist around and get a hand on the inside wheel, but it's easier to have someone help you in and out of the suit."

She pulled the door open and leaned in, checking the heads-up display. "Use these handholds and slide your feet in first. Feel for the stirrups in the lower legs - they adjust automatically. And the control gloves in the arms for operating the claws."

"What happened to the 'keep technology simple' mandate?" Claude asked. "This thing must have more sensors and motors than the whole Spine."

The walkabouts are absurd, Emma thought happily. Absurd and beautiful. She wasn't sure how her father had sold them to Colony Mars, but unexpected robots were definitely the most satisfying to build.

This was why she was here, why her father had encouraged her to come to Mars. With the walkabouts she would shake off her malaise and claim the Martian surface as home.

Chapter Twenty-Three: CO2

"I NEED HELP in the greenhouse," Liz said to Emma one morning while the haboob still trapped them inside.

"Sure. I've left you with all the chores lately... Sorry." She smiled apologetically.

"It's not that. I want your advice on something."

Inside the greenhouse, Liz led the way to a bed of beans.

"These are my Type Two pintos. Like the experts predicted, they won't need to be staked in Mars gravity."

"Yeah," Emma said. "They look fine."

"Not so fine." Liz pulled a tape measure from her pocket and held it against the nearest plant. "Compared to our test gardens on Earth and Lunar Base, these plants are half the size they should be."

Emma had sudden visions of starving. She dropped to her knees in the aisle and looked closely at the plant.

"I'm pretty sure I know what's wrong," Liz said. "The carbon dioxide level in here is too low."

"We've outsmarted ourselves." Emma nodded as she realized the problem. "We sealed the greenhouse to keep in heat and humidity..."

"And sealed out the carbon dioxide we exhale. You, me, and the fish breathing in here don't provide enough for the plants."

"No problem. Yin and Yang can bypass the separators and compress surface atmosphere directly. It's ninety-five percent CO_2, and the traces of other gases won't hurt a thing. Drag their cylinders in here and release all the CO_2 you want."

"Good, I was hoping you'd say that." Liz sat on the edge of the bed. "Isolating the greenhouse also means the Spine's air sensors don't help me track levels in here..."

"Also no problem. Governor, send Yin and Yang a summary of our conversation. Daan, too - tell him we need a portable CO2 sensor. Oh - say - when he has a minute."

They fed the tilapia as they waited for replies, including one fish in a nursery pond.

Emma's shadow fell across the pond and tiny babies dove for safety in momma's mouth. Emma stood still until the fish opened her mouth and released her fry back into the water.

Liz beamed as if she were the mother herself. "I love how tilapias guard their babies."

The fry circle close to their mother. She flicked her tail to stay in place, occasionally showing red-rimmed fins. Soon she wouldn't let the babies back into her mouth and Liz would return her to the breeder pond. Just like babies everywhere, Emma thought, they have to go their own way.

"Hey, ladies," Yin's voice - or maybe it was Yang - spoke from Liz's pad. "We'll bring you a cylinder of good old Martian air as soon as the dust clears."

"Excellent. Thanks." Liz turned to Emma. "Actually, I hate to wait."

"What have we got to burn?" Emma asked. "Maybe packaging from the knarr?"

"Fire? Inside the nederzetting? Isn't that against Colony Mars rules?"

"Against their guidance, sure, but I think we've got a good reason. We can light small piles in the center of a bed. Move the lights away if we need to. I'll talk to Daan when he calls."

"While we wait..." Liz's worried expression cleared. "I told you I got something special the other day. Come see."

Emma spotted stalks of tiny yellow flowers in a lettuce bed - for seed that would guarantee their next crop - but Liz led farther down the bay.

"Here it is." She led Emma to four irregularly spaced sprouts, each with a half-dozen leaves.

"Liz, is that cannabis?" Emma laughed.

"We say 'the purpose of humanity is to nurture life.'" Liz laughed with her. "And this life will nurture us in return."

"You're the farmer. But won't MEX object to stoned settlers?"

"Not when they see the Earth Scan sphere blossom with approval. We need to relax, to unwind, and improve everyone's appetite. Besides, this is a mellow strain."

"Smoke's not good for the lungs."

"Yeah, no smoke. But the spring equinox, Mars New Year's Eve, is a great time for a party. There's a traditional spring drink, a milk tea of cannabis with spices. I'll make that."

"Where's the cat?" Liz looked around. "I like to keep an eye on him."

Squash vines in the next bed rustled. "There he is." Emma dove in.

The bay door opened as they searched. Daan stuck his head in. "Hey there. I've got your sensors." He hefted a surface suit backpack on one shoulder.

"This has a full set of life support sensors. Plug it in like this and Governor can read the levels. You know, you can go up to five thousand parts per million CO_2 if you'll promise to spend less than eight hours a sol in here."

"That won't be necessary," Liz said. "There's a point where more CO_2 won't help. We're nutrient limited in these sands. I'll be happy around four hundred."

A coil of lights hung from Daan's other shoulder. "I'll need another pair of hands to help me hang these."

"Emma can do that. She'll be glad to get out of our next chore," Liz said. "I'm about to sift mealworm bedding."

Liz retrieved the cat and bounce-walked down the aisle, leaving Emma and Daan.

Daan had a dozen strings of lights.

They stood on the rims of the beds. Lights hung from poles pushed into the sand to keep the lumen level on the leaves as high as possible without snagging anyone's head. They stretched the new strings from pole to pole and plugged them in to cords dropped from the ceiling.

"Good job," Daan said with satisfaction when they finished. "Let's take a break."

They sat on the stone edge of a bed. Emma rolled her shoulders, sore from all the reaching.

"Have you noticed how hard it's getting to open the airlock door?" Daan asked.

"Yes. I practically have to pry it open." She'd taken to bracing a foot against the frame to haul on the door, but Daan had been so sour she hadn't complained.

"P V equals N R T." He smiled at her momentary confusion. "A basic equation. As the temperature in here goes up, so does the air pressure. Even a small increase creates enough force to notice, and you lose warm air to the Spine. I'll hook up an air pump so you can equalize pressure before opening the door."

"That'd be great." It would be nice to have the airlock pump, but it was even nicer to talk amiably with Daan.

"I've been working on a poem and I finished it while we worked."

"You told me once that you're a writer."

"On Earth I wrote travelogues for money and poetry for myself. Want to hear it?" He cleared his throat.

"Dust blurs the stars as

"Moons cross paths through rusted skies

"Above orange plains.

Emma gulped. Poetry!

She'd never read any poem unless it was a school assignment.

Daan chuckled. "Don't worry; I won't recite angst-filled soliloquies at you."

It felt good to laugh with him.

Chapter Twenty-four: Exploring

DAAN PLOPPED the cat in front of him and raked his fingers back and forth from neck to tail. Fluffs of amber fur floated away in a ventilation current.

The settlers were sitting at the stone tables in the Plaza enjoying the wide space with its high arched ceiling. The floor was still cold and Emma wore her surface boots. A draft tumbled from the last chunks of ice floating in the pond.

"It's no wonder the cat's so wild," Sanni said. "You play too rough."

"Aw, he loves it," Daan said. As if agreeing, the cat arched his back and purred loudly, then suddenly rolled on his side, hugged Daan's arm, and bit his hand.

"Then why is he biting you?"

"It's a love bite," Daan said, clenching his teeth against the prickle of the cat's claws and teeth. "He's not breaking the skin."

"Here's a bit of fun we can have while we wait out the storm," Yang said, unplugging his pad from an extension cord running across the floor. "The pressure's high enough for us to open one of the new bays."

"Brilliant," Yin said. "There's no point in building them if we don't move in."

Daan left the cat licking his fur flat and they all followed Yang around the pond to an arch in the stone, protruding at the edges but flattened inside. Yang opened a tool box on the floor.

"I've been watching the pressure go up, millibar by millibar as the air warms," he said.

"This bay will be the lab and hospital, where the S-4 equipment will go," Yin said. "We don't want to give MEX any excuse to delay that mission because we're not ready."

Yang slapped his hand on the flat wall, grinning at his audience. "On the other side is the empty module from Settler Three that Ruby brought down. The beetle-bots opened the airlock doors before sealing it against the Plaza and we built the new bay against the airlock on the other side. At least, I hope it's on the other side." He laughed at his own joke.

He took out a hand drill, fitted in a bit half the length of his arm, and plugged into a nearby outlet.

Yin fished a small metal valve with a wide gasket out of the toolbox and spread his feet apart, standing like he was about to jump.

Ruby folded her arms across her chest. "Quit goofing around and put in the valve."

Yang stepped back, lifted the bit to the wall, and began drilling. Rust colored dust fell from the hole as he worked the drill back and forth, clearing out the cuttings. Only a trace of Mars' irritating surface smell tickled Emma's nose. When the bit had nearly disappeared into the wall, he released it from the drill chuck, added a length of rod, and resumed. Soon he had to take a few steps backwards to clear stone dust from the hole.

Then, with a *whoosh,* the bit broke through and Yang jogged backwards to pull it out. Yin sprang forward and shoved the valve into the hole. He turned the handle and the valve whistled as air rushed from the Plaza into the module beyond. With a little tweaking, the whistle died, replaced by a continuing hiss. Everyone applauded. Yin and Yang bowed.

"Once the pressure equalizes," Yin said, "we'll cut the opening clear, and it'll be ready for utilities."

"Right now it's another icy void sucking the heat away," Ruby hugged herself tighter. "Just when the Plaza was warming up."

"I've got to install high velocity air compressors in the module," Daan said. "It would be easier if you built ducts into the floor, like with the other bays."

"The airlock has to seal the bay," Yang said. "So you've got to install gated hoses. Sorry."

"It seems like a lot of work for nothing," Daan said, grumbling. "Bays never leak."

Most of the bays Yin and Yang built attached directly to the Spine, the fabricated stones shaped to dovetail together, their wide surfaces crushing together and sintered from the outside to seal. For some key spaces like Medical, they incorporated a transport ship module for extra protection - a safe room to scramble to.

"Might as well start on the tedious part," Yin said. He tossed Yang a wide chisel from the tool box and hefted a couple hammers.

"But the pressure's not equalized yet," Emma said.

"No worries. It'll take us a week to chip through to the airlock."

Of course, Emma thought. The wall's three meters thick. She looked down, hiding a flush of embarrassment. Strange that she'd forgotten that.

***

Ruby was right about the cold. After Yin and Yang cut the stone out of the bay arch, the whole Plaza was frigid again.

"So let's all pitch in and move the utility supplies into the bay," Yang said when Ruby complained. "It won't take long to get the place hooked up for heat and light."

"What's in here?" Emma asked as she stepped into the medical bay with an armload of wire coils. Her hand light cast deep shadows from waist-high blocks of beige stone.

"Don't touch anything," Yin said quickly. "Not with your bare hands. We built stone benches and shelves into the bay as we fabricated. The stone's still as cold as the Martian surface. Cold enough to burn your skin."

***

Before turning the bots loose after the storms cleared, Yin fabricated a mortar and pestle, and a heavy, thick-walled bowl.

151

He promised the lasers glassified sand thoroughly, so there were no leachable toxins.

"It's spring equinox on Mars, our New Year's Eve," Liz said as she concocted her holiday tea. "It happens to coincide with Thanksgiving back home in Manitoba this year. No matter how you look at it, it's time for a party."

Liz turned on the Earth Scan as well as the live stream and positioned an imager over the galley counter while she steeped cannabis flowers in hot water and mashed in milk powder and sugar. Everyone hovered around. Earth Scan was a small orange sphere. Life on Mars was apparently old news.

"I don't have all the ingredients for proper bhang tea," she said. "I wish I had almonds..."

"It smells fine," Sanni said.

Liz spooned a little into a cup and handed it to her.

"Tastes fine, too." Sanni smiled. "I think this'll soothe my headache."

Liz filled Sanni's cup and passed everyone a drink.

"I'd rather have a beer," Claude sighed. "Or a sausage. I wish you were growing pork tissue."

Liz chuckled." Maybe in some future lab. I doubt anyone would want to share a transport ship with a pig."

"For now it's easier to grow fish and worms than the nutrient media needed for muscle tissue. Besides, I enjoy growing fish and worms, and I honor them. They're living creatures. It's hard to think of cultured tissue the same way."

"Which mission will bring barley and hops?" Claude asked. It was rhetorical; beer wasn't on any mission list.

"Maybe instead of eating the potatoes," Melina said. "We should make vodka."

"I thought you Greeks drank that funny licorice stuff."

"We drink what we can get," she said with a wan smile.

"It's good to hear Claude joking around," Emma said to Liz as they set out plates. "He's been so quiet lately. We've hardly talked about his prospecting trip in weeks."

"You feeling okay?" Liz asked Melina. "You sound tired."

"Just working too hard, I think," she said. "I've been pulling wire in the new bay. It's funny, but I look at the schematic, and I know how the wires should run, but my hands don't want to do the job. It's not like me." She held up a hand and stared at it as if looking for the problem. "Don't say anything to Sanni, okay? She never complains about anything."

"I have something to cheer you up." Emma pulled a plate from the chiller unit. "Fish fillets."

Liz set the bowl of bhang tea on the table and rummaged for a frying pan.

"Let's put some music on," Claude said, plugging in his pad and scrolling through files.

"Something we can dance to," Sanni said with a pirouette.

Sanni was usually so restrained that Emma started to giggle. It was contagious and they all laughed.

"Ah, the smell of frying fish," Melina said.

"Everything will smell like fish for days - sols," Claude said. "Well, it will." He answered Melina's reproachful gaze.

"Remember from training? Fish smell is hard for the air system to remove..."

"Who cares? Real, fresh fish." Melina sighed. "I feel human again."

"Nuke some potatoes, too, will ya, someone?" Daan said. "I haven't been this hungry in months."

Chapter Twenty-Five: Meteor

S HORTLY AFTER the New Jaar's Sol Zero, Yang declared the storms cleared enough for a trip to Maintenance. Emma and Ruby joined him and Yin.

The trenches Emma had seen before were freshly filled in by the storms, featureless dips in the sand.

"We just keep scooping out the same trench over and over, jaar after jaar" Yin said.

"Handy, actually," Yang said.

Emma enjoyed working in Maintenance even though she spent most of the time on the bay floor in a surface suit. She and Ruby finished rewiring Jumper Two for the telepresent controls. Yin and Yang sent the loaders and fabricator out under Governor's control so they could supervise as beetle-bots hoisted equipment on the warehouse floor, which had become the main workshop, too.

With its telepresence units donated to the jumpship, Emma drove the rover back to the nederzetting that night, tired but happy. They all returned early the next sol.

After a week of effort, Emma merged the jumper's refurbished controls with Governor. Ruby took over the incremental shake-down, verified every control function, and exercised each valve in the fuel lines. When the bots first dragged the ship out of Maintenance, Ruby lifted it only high enough off the ground to check the gyros.

Ruby had a series of test flights planned. "I can take it from here."

Yin and Yang went back to fabricating construction blocks, anxious to try some improvements they'd developed over the storm season.

Emma resumed her tasks in the nederzetting, where the mood was solemn. She found Melina sitting at the habitat table one evening, resting her forehead on her crossed arms. The cat was curled against her, purring contentedly. She only stirred when the rest of the settlers came in for supper. Emma moved the cat off the table and he hopped to the bunks, poking at the privacy flaps to find one loose so he could crawl in and resume his nap.

"It's the cold in that new bay," Claude said, looking at Melina with sympathy. "I feel it, too. I'm achy, like the flu's coming on."

"Maybe you should wear your suit's thermal layer," Ruby suggested. "I'm nice and warm all sol in the maintenance bay and I feel fine."

"A suit's too bulky," Melina said irritably, rubbing her forehead. As soon as supper was over, she skipped the evening meditation and went to her bunk.

Liz chewed on a corner of her lip as Melina left. She was worried but Emma no longer had sympathy. Melina endlessly dragging herself around was annoying. She wished she had a reason to go back to Maintenance in the morning. She enjoyed the work there.

***

When Claude opened the module door Emma was watching fish snap and splash as she dropped in mealworms.

"Close the door behind you," she said when he started towards her. "We need to keep the heat in."

He shoved the door closed without looking back and plugged his pad into the first outlet he saw.

"Look at this." He opened a weather satellite image centered on the Tharsis Plain. There was a fuzzy blob of beige east of Kamp.

"That's a funny looking storm," Emma said.

"Ah ha, because it's not a storm. The satellite issued and canceled an alert so fast you probably didn't notice it. This is something else."

"You look happy, so I guess it's a good thing?"

"Meteor strike."

Emma gasped despite Claude's satisfied grin.

"Oh, come on, it's no surprise. Thousands of tons of micrometeors fall on Mars every jaar. Something as long as my forearm hits every sol, just like on Earth."

Emma examined the image. "A cloud this size must be from something bigger."

"A once in a century meteor." Claude waved his free hand in excitement. "I bet it's gouged out a crater fifty meters across. And deep. Deep enough to expose whatever's under all this sand."

He radiated enthusiasm. "I've got to go out there. MEX gave us standard procedures for prospecting and the rovers are ready to roll. It's time the Explorers Mission went exploring."

"You want to try your swarm-bot drill?" Emma asked.

Claude beamed. "Absolutely. Let's put it to a vote." He opened the prospecting procedure on his pad.

"I'm sending the satellite images and drill procedure to everyone. I'll need to run the startup sequence and find some place to drill a test hole before leaving Kamp."

"How about the warehouse floor in Maintenance?" Emma asked. "From there we can load the drill onto a rover."

"I'll ask MEX if they have any problem with that," Claude said.

"I'll be your driver." A tinge of excitement colored her usual fatigue. The prospecting procedure called for a crew of two. They'd need a rover to haul the drill to the crater, and they could test an inflatable habitat, too.

Replies to Claude's request came in quickly.

"Claude's drilling doesn't interfere with my construction," Yin said. "I vote yes."

"I'd like to see the rest of you have as much fun as Yin and I do," Yang said. "So, yes."

"It's good to see you enthused, Claude," Liz said. "Get out into the sunlight; do what you came here to do. *Yes* from me."

"That's a majority," Claude said, yanking out his pad's plug.

A familiar tingle of excitement, missing for too long, ran up Emma's spine.

***

At lunch, Claude talked through his plans.

"Why didn't we get a warning from MEX?" Ruby asked. "Didn't they promise the Near Earth Object network would pick up threats to Mars, too?"

"I've messaged with Filip about that," Claude said. "The network scans for objects in the planetary ecliptic plane. This meteor came from above the plane, nearly straight down onto Mars. It's probably from outside the solar system." Claude smiled. "It's a great piece of luck."

"It's a piece of irony," Sanni said.

Liz nodded. "People want Kamp to be a backup plan for humanity, in case an asteroid hits Earth. Instead we almost got nailed."

"So back to my proposal. So far, five of us said yes. Do the rest of you see potential problems?"

"You'll be all alone out there, exposed on the surface," Melina said. She bit her lip and looked around for support. "I vote no."

"Melina's got a point," Sanni said.

"I go into space alone," Ruby said with a shrug. "I'd be brassed off if you told me I couldn't take that risk. So it's okay with me."

"If I'm going to climb Olympus some sol, someone needs to get out on the surface," Daan said.

"Claude won't be alone," Emma said. "He'll be with me." Emma grinned. Prospecting was one justification for the walkabout suits - they made equipment set-up easier. She tapped out a message to her father, letting him know the walkabouts were about to get their feet on Martian sand.

***

Setting up Claude's drill test required shuffling equipment around. Yang docked Rover Two at the south module while Emma slid into a walkabout and crawled it out the north airlock, listening carefully to the soft whir of motors and hum of the life support pack.

She lowered the suit's tail and shifted her weight from foot to foot, then made little hops.

She'd piloted a prototype suit across an arctic island in Canada as a stand-in for the Martian surface. She'd run this walkabout - this very unit that encased her now - on a treadmill in a virtual reality room, suspended by a harness that carried two thirds of its weight to simulate low gravity. But this was real. This was Mars.

After months of confinement, the expanse of Tharsis Plain was endless, the horizon a brown band between the dull orange sky and terracotta dunes. Her heart pounded in her ears.

She closed her eyes and breathed deeply. It was important to observe the suit's performance calmly.

She leaned forward to raise the tail and took a few short hops.

To hell with calmly.

"Yee ha." Emma kicked off hard with both feet and the walkabout soared, landed with its feet together, knees absorbing the energy and feeding it back into the next hop. The plain rushed by in a blur as she flew along the meandering base of overlapping dunes, like a dry river flowing through barren fields.

The tail balanced automatically, the motors whirred pleasantly.

"I know you're having fun, Emma, love." It was Yang, or maybe Yin, on her suit's comm link. "But come back and close the airlock door. You're letting dust seep in."

158

That jarred her.

I don't make mistakes like that, she thought.

She hopped up the side of a dune, slowed by sand shifting underfoot, and circled back. The nederzetting was a collection of humps and ridges blending into the dunes. She'd traveled farther than she realized.

With the airlock secured, Emma hopped sedately to the southern modules where the rover was docked and backed the suit into position. "Governor, reel me in."

The AI raised the suit's pack, cutting off air circulation, and the helmet fogged with her first breath. It deployed the rover's roof crane, grappled hold of the suit, and lifted it against a walkabout access port. Emma slid out to find Yin, Yang, and Claude waiting for her.

"The walkabout's functioning perfectly." She did a bouncy jog through the nederzetting back to the north habitat to move the second suit.

Rover Two met her at the north dock. Claude's drill rig waited outside, so Emma crept through in the second walkabout and loaded the drums on the rover's rear cargo bed.

"I'm going to hop down to Maintenance," Emma said on the rover channel. "You need the practice, Claude. Get into the other suit and come with me."

They followed as the rover rolled to Maintenance. The sand was smooth and packed, providing a perfect test route for the walkabouts. Emma bounced from foot to foot, watching Claude's cautious progress.

"This is great," she said. "How are you doing, Claude?"

He grunted breathlessly.

"You're working too hard. Relax and ride the suit. Look around, enjoy the view."

Claude only grunted again. He'd never spent more Earthside training time than required in a walkabout and, Emma had to admit, the suits moved differently in Mars gravity.

"Lean forward and kangaroo hop - both feet together. It's easier."

Yin called ahead so the beetle-bots had the bay door open. With the robot squad back at work along the trenches, the center of the bay was clear. Emma and Claude rolled the drum inside and plugged in a power cable. While Yin and Yang rode the rover around to the usual airlock, they opened a view-port in the waist-high drum.

The drill was a robot swarm, thousands of ant-like microbots. The bots would burrow straight down through a fitting in the drum's bottom, passing grains of sand from bot to bot and sintering the walls of the finger-wide borehole as they went. If they encountered rock, there were dozens of drill bits bracketed to the drum's inside. They'd pass a bit down, anchor it to the borehole wall, and twist it slowly into the stone until it dulled. On the surface, a small power receiver would keep them energized, and they could pass an electric charge down, bot to bot, by tapping their butts together. Not very fast and not a very big hole, but the lightweight rig was easily shipped to Mars.

"I worked with microbots in school," Emma watched the bots begin to move as they charged.

"There's a practical limit to how deep they can drill, which is why the bottom of a new crater is perfect," Claude said. "Natural channels cut into the surface are another promising spot, or higher on the volcano, above the plain, where it's fairly free of sand."

"I'm sure the lithology is interesting..." Emma had never been especially interested in rocks. "But we need metals to fabricate spare parts and build new equipment. To grow. Won't ores be deep?"

Claude sighed. "Perhaps. That's a chicken and egg problem. Our construction bots aren't designed to dig very deep. We need metals to build more machines, and we need more machines to dig deep ores. But we may get lucky. On Earth there are ore bodies where copper sits right on the surface. Gold rush miners picked nuggets out of streams, and there should be iron and nickel meteorites. There're a lot of possibilities. We just need enough to get started."

Once the drill was set in place on the bay floor, Emma and Claude hopped out the rollup door, around to the rover to dock the walkabouts, and hurried through to the Maintenance control room. Yin and Yang were monitoring the construction bots.

"Okay to leave you two here?" Yin asked. "Yang wants to take the rover out to a loader for a few hours."

"No problem," Emma said.

Claude focused intently on the drill's progress. His malaise had disappeared. The excitement of hopping the suits across the Martian surface was over, but Emma smiled every time she looked at him.

She had never thought about rocks much, but rocks justified migrating to Mars for Claude. He was enjoying himself for the first time since they'd landed.

Emma moved to sit next to Claude and watch his pad. Without looking up he pointed out the depth bar, the chart where cutting samples would be logged, and the power consumption curves. Crisp, clear, and engaging.

I bet he was a good teacher, she thought. I wonder if he's still running that site for his old students.

***

The next morning, everyone crowded around to see them off. Liz waved as the airlock closed and Emma waved back like she was off for a holiday weekend.

Her stomach tingled right up into her chest and she couldn't wipe the grin off her face. She took several long, slow breaths and heard Claude do the same.

"I'm activating the GPS beacon. Governor, are you getting positive tracking from the satellites?" They were taking the rover with telepresent controls. Yin and Yang would get practice driving Rover One while they were gone.

"I'm tracking you, Emma."

Stupid machine can't appreciate what a milestone this is, Emma thought as she wriggled in her seat.

"Aren't you going to keep your hands on the controls?" Claude asked. "Governor hasn't been across the plain before. It could drive this rover right into a crater."

"It uses the rover's forward imagers for guidance. It'll stop if it needs me, the flexible human component." Emma grinned. "Engage route Claude-One."

The rover trundled away leaving ladder-like tracks in the sand.

Chapter Twenty-Six: Crater

THE METEOR STRIKE had been a near-miss. They were only going fifty kilometers northeast of Kamp to reach the crater, a hair's breadth compared to the size of Mars, but far enough to move off the deep sand and reach the first volcanic outcroppings on Peacock Mon's flank. Also far enough to confirm the satellite system orbiting above could track them and accurately beam microwaves to the rover's power receiver. Emma used GPS data to plot a route as smooth and level as possible. The trip wasn't intended to be thrilling, but she wriggled in her seat like a kid.

Claude stared intently through the cabin windows. He'd been inside the nederzetting his whole time on Mars aside from the short hop to Maintenance when, he admitted, he'd stared at the walkabout's feet. This was his first leisurely view of their new world.

As the rover cleared the modules, his head jerked towards Peacock Mons. The mountain rose in a gentle shadowed slope towards a peak a couple hundred kilometers away, higher than any mountain on Earth, ringed by cliffs like a delicate gold necklace. For a brief time, the surface blushed pink until the Sun rose high enough to color it burnt orange.

"I've spent way too much time living inside a glorified culvert," Claude said after a few moments gazing at the dead volcano. "Governor, are you listening?"

"Yes, Claude."

"Post this to all settlers. Let's ask MEX to design an observation bay for the nederzetting - something we can build with current resources, with windows so we can see Peacock Mons."

"Governor, log my 'yes' vote," Emma said. "Colony Mars picked an especially dull landscape for Kamp. We'll have to develop appreciation for rippled dunes and that hump of a mountain."

"The satellites provide excellent images of Peacock Mons, Emma," Governor said.

"It's not the same as seeing with your own eyes."

"Thank you, Emma. I will note that for reference purposes."

Rover Two trundled northeast towards a break in the ridge they would cross. It stopped occasionally so Emma could analyze some unexpected discontinuity, usually a small impact crater. She took the controls and maneuvered safely around each of these until Governor got the hang of it.

"Ancient." Claude said as Emma drove close enough to a shallow crater for him to see its floor. "See how the sand has coated the walls?"

Emma relaxed back in her seat and watched the scenery go by. Scattered chunks of dark rock increasingly protruded from the plain's rippled dunes. Around midmorning, she noticed the rover tilt slightly to one side. They were traversing a low ridge tiled with slabs of rock.

Claude pointed out fingers of something gray radiating towards them. "Ejecta - freshly exposed sand and chunks of dark rock not yet rusted red."

James would answer, yes professor. But Emma didn't say it out loud. This wasn't a time to be sad.

Emma paused the rover. The crater wasn't far ahead. It wouldn't have been hard to find from this distance, even without Governor and the satellites. A plume of dust drifted up and hung above the plain.

"Maybe we should leave the rover here. Go out and reconnoiter on foot," Emma said.

Claude frowned as he stood at his walkabout's access door. "It's like *becoming* a ship in a bottle."

"Once you're inside it's comfy as your favorite old chair." Emma smiled at the imager. They'd agreed to stream the trip live to MEX.

Emma pulled open the hatches where the walkabouts hung on the rover's hull. Grabbing two handholds, she hopped her feet up into the opening, bending her knees to slide into the suit's legs. She tucked her head, folded her elbows against her chest, sat up into the suit's torso, and stretched her arms into the sleeves.

"Ready Claude?"

Claude, less limber, lagged behind, but soon confirmed he was ready.

"Governor, open suit comms and seal us up." Motors whirred softly as Emma's walkabout pulled the access hatch closed at her back, the rover's docking clamps released, and the crane arm above the suit lowered her to the ground. The suit's tail extended automatically to form a stable tripod. The crane held her steady as the life support pack slid down and latched against the walkabout's back. With a gentle whoosh, the breathing air system activated, and the crane disengaged with a clunk.

Emma bounced from foot to foot and felt herself tilting backwards. The suit's tail steadied her. She kicked the surface sending up a cloud with the divot of sand.

"Claude, I'm going to try the rapid travel feature." She leaned forward and kicked off hard with both feet. Like pumping a swing back on Earth, she kicked harder each time her feet struck the ground, leaving a cloud of dust to mark each impact. Soon she was flying between kicks. Inside the suit, the whisper of the breathing air system never varied but the hum of motors cycled in time with her movements.

"This feels strange," she said for the benefit of the feed to Earth. "The suit does the work, but even so my legs are getting cramped. I must remember to learn to relax my muscles."

She stood up straight at the top of a jump and the suit landed on feet and tail, taking the shock of the sudden stop.

"Uff." Despite the walkabout's shock absorbers, the landing rattled her bones. "Governor, note that maneuver's only for an emergency stop."

Emma looked around for Rover Two. It was hard to judge distance on the sand, but the bright blue rover looked very far away with a small Claude moving deliberately at the back bed.

"Hey, Claude. Did you see me?"

"Yeah, you were flying. How's the suit doing?"

"Just great. Coming back, now. Governor, rapid travel." Emma leaned forward and kicked off, but this time she rode the suit like a horse, not pumping with each hop, and stood up little by little over a couple hops to make a more graceful stop.

"Claude, where'd you go?"

Claude came around from the other side of the rover, swinging both feet forward for each step while the tail supported the suit. He towed a box on sled runners.

"Just hiding so you don't run me over."

Emma laughed and led the way to the crater. The walkabouts were performing well and crossing the Martian sands was exhilarating. Emma felt sure Daan would accept the walkabouts for mountain climbing, and that her father would be pleased.

***

It took almost an hour to reach the edge of the crater since Claude was looking for bits of meteorite and stopped often to pick up rocks from the gray ejecta rays. He imaged each one carefully and noted the coordinates with Governor before dropping it in his box sled and moving on.

A pale cloud rose from the crater, fine as smoke, and wafted around the rim above their heads.

"That's extremely fine dust created by the impact," Claude said. "In this low gravity, it'll take a long time to settle completely."

"The ground slopes down into the crater," Emma said as they circled the crater. "The meteor must have hit at an angle from the north."

"A shallow angle," Claude said, following her down the slope. "Less than twenty degrees."

Emma took a few short hops across the rocky crater floor. It was a dozen hops long and half as wide.

"Don't hop too close to any of the walls," Claude said. At its highest point, the far wall was twice as tall as a walkabout. "The rock could collapse."

"So where's the meteorite?" Emma appraised the bare, gray crater floor through the light fog of dust. Gray striations splayed up the cliff on the far side like a frozen explosion.

"Gone, mostly. Vaporized. But Governor has the crater's dimensions, and if I've got any pieces of the meteorite, we can measure their density and calculate how big it must have been to create this crater. I'll show you how."

Emma grinned, even though he couldn't see her. He was still a good teacher.

"Let's bring the rover closer and deploy your drill," she said.

They hopped back on the path Emma plotted for the rover, leaving their footprints to mark the way.

"It's lunchtime," Claude said. "I'm hungry."

"Me, too. Time for a break."

The rover retrieved them easily, clamped them to the hatches, and opened the access doors.

"That's the best morning I've had in a long time," Emma said as she helped Claude slide out of his walkabout.

Emma turned to the cabin imager. "I hope you enjoyed our first walkabout romp on Mars. Please join us later for more surface activities. Governor, shut down the feed." Emma thought the morning had gone well. The Earth Scan sphere should be spinning happily.

Chapter Twenty-Seven: First Date

T HEY ATE LUNCH with the settlers back at Kamp. Liz gathered everyone in the north habitat and, while Governor drove the rover along the path they'd marked, Emma and Claude sat in the two front seats by a screen and imager. Emma grinned as she described the kangaroo-hop for rapid travel.

Claude finished his extra-sweet tea and plunked the cup down. "I'm really looking forward to this afternoon when we deploy the drill."

"Have any of you explorers looked at the weather forecast?" Ruby asked.

"It's a beautiful spring day here," Claude said. "I'd be working in short sleeves if I could breathe out there."

"I guess it's just a pilot thing. Ground pounders never think to look up. There's a front crossing Olympus Mons now."

"When's it supposed to pass us?" Emma asked.

"Three or four hours. The wind will pick up as it runs downslope to the Tharsis Plain, so it'll raise dust."

"Okay," Emma said. "That shouldn't cause us any trouble. With GPS guidance, Rover Two could bring us home in the dark if necessary."

The rover stopped with a slight sway and Emma switched off the video from Kamp.

"Before you start a feed to MEX..." Claude snagged his duffle bag from the seat behind him. "I thought we might take advantage of our privacy tonight. I brought a couple beers." He fished a pouch from his bag. "One for each of us. I appreciate gravity - I can pour my beer into a real glass - well, cup."

"I thought you drank the last of the beer for New Year's."

"This came in my gift box."

168

Emma laughed. "I have a tin of cheese and salami stashed in my bag."

"We can have a proper date - two kids out cruising," he said.

"It'll be the first date on Mars. MEX will hate to miss recording a video." And miss it, they will, she added to herself.

"Maybe we should leave a rover docked at Kamp all the time - for dates." Claude's mouth ticked up at one corner. A cute smile, Emma thought, as a fluttery sensation ran through her.

Before the silence dragged out, she cleared her throat. "Let's set up the inflatable. It'll just take a minute. I'll go out and you pressurize it before you join me."

The inflatable habitat was stowed on the back bed of the rover next to the drill. Robotic assist from the walkabout made it easy for Emma to carry it around to the rover's airlock. She pushed the inflatable's seal ring into the channel around the door, locked the clamps, and pulled packing straps loose. That took care of the outside work.

"Claude. Go ahead and pressurize."

She watched as a shudder ran through the inflatable. Air was flowing in.

The unit was cylindrical once inflated, a half-dozen paces across and not very tall. It struck Emma as an overly fragile structure to trust with her life, and the reflective coating didn't block radiation. Someone as persuasive as her father must have sold it to Colony Mars. She'd rather play with walkabouts.

"I'm going to try a turtle move," Emma said. "If this doesn't work, Claude, you'll have to drag me up when you get here." She hopped though the break in the crater rim, dropped the suit to its knees on the slope, and tipped over to one side. The walkabout slid a short distance, plowing up sand before it stopped.

"Governor, recover to standing position." She went limp and let the suit work. The walkabout jabbed its tail into the sand, rolled to its hands and knees, telescoped its arms, and stood up.

"That wasn't bad," Claude said as he hopped over to her. "Practically graceful. If you're done playing around, can we deploy the drill now? I want to get it secured in case Ruby's weather front blows up a lot of dust."

"Does Governor run these swarm-bots?" Emma asked as they rolled two drums to the bottom of the crater.

"Yes, there's a transceiver in the drum. Hey, look. My suit's got a fingernail." Claude pried open a panel with a thin edge on his walkabout's claw and activated the unit. "There's also an internal processor that runs the drill, tells the swarm how often to retain a sample, and which drawer to dump the cuttings." He slid each of the half-dozen drawers around the top of the drum in and out, confirming their operation while Emma unfolded a small power receiver.

Now that Claude's mind was occupied, he moved gracefully in the suit. Emma knew obsession could do that, could banish self-consciousness.

This was a great trip. Prospecting justified the walkabouts and that should quiet her father's critics. Besides, the swarm-bots were neat. She'd have to learn more about them.

"Now we add the anchors." Claude opened the second drum, a set of nested cylinders. They slotted each cylinder into a track on the drill unit.

He handed Emma a shovel. "Why haul weights from Earth when we've got an unlimited supply of ballast right here?"

There was no sand in the new crater, and shoveling loose rocks was hard. The walkabout joints didn't have a full human range of motion and Emma had trouble keeping the shovel level as she swung it to a cylinder. She began picking individual rocks from the floor and tossing them in. Despite the draft of cool air inside her suit, sweat trickled down her back.

They worked on silently until Emma noticed her helmet was clouding up. She increased the air circulation rate, but her helmet didn't clear. She pulled an arm into the suit's torso and touched the helmet. The fog wasn't inside.

"Hey, Claude. I'm getting a coating of something on my helmet."

"Me, too. It must be dust. Really fine, electrostatically charged dust," Claude said. "The front must be capping this dust plume, pushing it down. Look around."

Emma turned the walkabout in a circle. She was standing in fog.

"Hey guys, this is Ruby." The message filled Emma's helmet.

"Hey Ruby," Emma said, still distracted by her hazy vision.

"You know how I told you to watch the weather forecast?"

"Yeah."

"Well, I told you to watch the wrong weather. We've got a space weather alert now. A solar flare is rotating towards us and they expect the particle stream to hit in about five hours."

"Got it. Thanks."

"How bad is that?" Claude asked.

"These suits don't have much shielding," Emma said. "I don't fancy my guts dissolving from radiation. We need to get inside, under the rover's roof shield. Back inside the nederzetting would be even better."

"The ballast cylinders are nearly full. Let's finish them and go."

Emma bent the walkabout's knees and stretched its arms out, picking up the largest rocks handy to dump into a cylinder. They struggled back towards the murky shape of the rover, sliding on the loose gravelly slope, and stowed tools. The sky was ominously brown.

"Governor, dock us to the rover," Emma said. She heard the click as the crane snagged her suit and felt the walkabout compliantly go limp as it was lifted. The clamps jerked her slightly when they engaged. And nothing else happened.

"Governor, what's the delay?"

"The rover's seal to your suit isn't holding, Emma." Governor's voice was its usual soothing calm, but Emma felt her heart pounding.

"Standard procedure calls for me to re-clean the sealing surface and try again."

Emma felt the clamps nudge her forward, then pull back. And... nothing.

"Claude. You having any luck?"

"Same problem." His voice was strained.

"Governor, dangle me from the crane and I'll try to clean the seal manually." The walkabout used its tail to turn so Emma faced the seal. She wiped at it with the suit's claw, which didn't help.

"Governor, activate the electrostatic cleaning system."

Dust didn't leap off, just wiggled around on the seal, lining up with the magnetic field lines.

"Oh, hell."

Chapter Twenty-Eight: Flare

EMMA REOPENED the channel to Kamp. Yin and Yang offered to drive Rover One to them, but with the dust plume blanketing the ground, Emma feared its seals would fare no better. The transmission lag meant MEX would only now be realizing there was a problem, but no one expected any help from them.

"Can you crawl back in fast and slam the inner door shut so the leak doesn't deplete your air?" Yang asked. But Governor estimated the pressure drop would knock them out before they could get inside.

"Governor can bring the rover home," Emma said. "How about if we remove the inflatable and ride home on the bed." Rover Two's crane set them both down and they hopped around to the inflatable sealed against the airlock.

"It's no good," Emma said, panting after several tries. "The pressure inside has the seal swollen tight in the channel. MEX, you can tell the designers of this thing they did a good job."

"Maybe we can cut it off," Claude said.

"Look at the time," Emma said. "I don't think we should fool around anymore. These suits can travel faster than a rover. Let's leave everything and hop home.

"Just lean forward and try to relax, Claude. Governor, pilot these suits home. Rapid travel feature."

Emma kicked off and was beginning to relax when Claude gasped and swore.

"Claude, where are you? Are you alright?" The dust film was so thick on her helmet she couldn't see. Emma held her breath.

"Fine, yeah, I'm fine. Damn. Hit a soft spot or something and fell. I'm on my back, but all systems are nominal. Governor, get me upright."

He grunted as the suit rolled over and pushed itself up. "Okay. I'm taking off again."

Emma leaned forward and kicked off. Thump, thump, thump. She balanced in the stirrups and rode the suit. Without being able to see out her helmet, it was as boring as exercising in a habitat module except for the time ticking by until the flare hit.

"Hey, you lot, how's it going?" It was Yin, or maybe Yang calling.

"Swell," Emma said.

"Governor says you'll be here in twelve minutes. We need to talk about how to get you inside somewhere."

"Somewhere?" Claude asked. Emma didn't like the sound of that, either.

"Your dust cloud's floated across Kamp, too. We have the same airlock issue you had with Rover Two."

Claude took in deep breath, but Yin, or Yang, kept talking.

"Go to the maintenance bay. When you get there, the bots will haul you in through the roll-up door. The warehouse should be clean enough for the inside airlock to seal. The control room is shielded. You'll be fine."

"Will that work, Emma?" Claude sounded unhappy.

"It's a good plan. Yeah, it should work."

"Course it will," a Brit said. "It's brilliant."

Emma watched twelve minutes count down. With thirty seconds to go, the walkabout slowed its pace.

"Hey again," said Yin or Yang. "Go to the east corner of the bay door."

Emma stepped forward and stretched out her arms. A scraping sound reverberated through the suit.

"Display joint pressures." She scanned the data tables on her heads-up. "Damn."

"What's wrong?" Claude's question was sharp.

"Nothing for now. Just walk." Particles of dust had worked their way into the suit joints and probably scratched the solid lubricant pads, but that wouldn't stop them. She took another step and bumped into something. The bay's roll-up door was closed and she felt a thrill of nerves run through her. Which way was east?

She felt for seams in the door, pictured how they ran, and moved to her right till she bumped into Claude. "Guys, we're at the warehouse door."

"Now, lay down on your stomachs with your feet against the door."

After some grunting and maneuvering, they both said okay. The door scraped against her suit's feet and Emma jerked backwards. A moment later, she was inside, a beetle-bot holding her legs. It dropped her and swiped something across her helmet. See could see again.

"It worked. We're in the warehouse." Emma rolled the walkabout over and looked at Claude. He smiled at her through a clean patch on his own helmet.

"You go first, Claude."

The warehouse airlock was the same size as those at the nederzetting. He crawled in and slithered out of his suit.

"Okay, I'm in the habitat section. Governor, pump down the airlock."

Using the empty suit as a bot, the AI crawled it out to make room for Emma to creep in. Once the pressure equalized, Claude yanked open the inner door and helped her push back the walkabout's life support pack and climb out.

Half collapsed, she held herself up with her hands on her knees, and sneezed from the acrid dust hanging in the air.

"Mars has a big dust problem," Claude said solemnly.

"We did it." With a surge of defiant energy, Emma stood straight and hugged him. "The walkabouts did it. Daan, you there? You've got to try these things."

"That'll have to wait." Daan's sounded irritated. "Someone's got to pay attention to keeping us alive in here."

Claude interrupted Emma's frown.

175

"How long do we have to stay in Maintenance?" He turned, facing the closest imager.

"At least a few hours, mate." That was Yin.

"I'm hungry. Is there anything to eat?"

"Up top," Emma said, grinning again. "We can watch the solar flare from there, too."

***

Rover shielding wasn't as effective as meters-thick stone so, since no one was in danger, Liz insisted everyone stay put until the flare subsided. When Yang arrived in Rover One, Emma and Claude hopped in, leaving the walkabouts behind, and they headed home.

A crowd waited at the nederzetting airlock when they docked. Emma's upbeat mood collided with Melina's tears, and Claude returned her hug with surprise. "Melina, what's wrong?"

"You were almost killed."

"Not really," Emma said. "We got back in plenty of time..."

"It's Mars. Mars doesn't want us here." Melina's voice dropped to a whisper.

"That's silly. You're just upset." Claude patted her back.

"I've seen it," Melina said, pushing away from Claude and wiping her face. "I've seen something moving in the shadows." She spoke through tears. "I can never quite make it out, but it's a tulpa."

Claude mumbled something in confusion.

"You don't believe me. Emma, you saw it - in the Plaza. You said you saw something moving in the shadows, remember? Sanni's seen it too."

"I've had bad dreams," Sanni said, shaking her head. "Just bad dreams. Come on; let them shower."

Claude was sipping tea when Emma came down from the habitat's upper deck, and Liz was standing at the galley. "It's after supper. Did you eat at Maintenance? I could..."

Emma waved away the offer. "What was Melina talking about? What's a tulpa?" She accepted a cup Liz held out insistently.

"Melina's had a few bouts of... I guess I'd call it confusion," Liz said, shaking her head. "Sanni and Daan told me, but that's the first time I saw it for myself."

"What's a tulpa?"

"I looked it up. A tulpa is a sort of imaginary friend, conjured up in a person's mind. You picture some creature as you meditate and eventually it becomes real." She shook her head again.

"She's hallucinating?" Emma asked. "She wouldn't kill herself like Ingra, would she?"

"I told Governor to watch her and call us if anything odd happens. I put my medical code on that. She can't override it. But Governor can only monitor. It doesn't control the nederzetting doors."

"Can't you help her?"

"I asked her to talk to Governor's therapeutic psych program. I don't think we should do group meditations anymore - it might feed her delusion. If you meditate, don't mention it to Melina."

They sat silently for a few minutes.

"Where'd everyone else go?" Claude asked. He was still energized. "I thought we'd all be here to figure out how to retrieve Rover Two. And my drill rig."

"They wandered off. No one's very focused lately." Liz sighed. "MEX has lots of hypotheses but no explanation for what's happening to us. But, they are working on a way to clean the seals. They said, give them three days."

"See if Governor's receiving signals from Rover Two," Emma said to Claude. "You should be able to access the drill's telemetry, too."

"I left my pad in the rover," Claude said. "So if you don't mind, I'll use the habitat screen."

"I'm going to check on the garden," Liz said, taking her cup to the counter. She tilted her head to Emma, raised an eyebrow.

"Me, too," Emma said. "I haven't seen the latest batch of baby fish."

As they cycled the airlock to the fish module, Emma took a deep breath. The air smelled wonderful. "The humidity's high enough to make my hair curl."

"The module's still isolated from the Spine systems, to keep the heat in. I've got a couple extra fans set up to circulate air in the greenhouse and pumps for pond water. Close the door."

A slapping sound greeted them. The cat was batting a half-grown fish around the floor and it flopped vigorously.

"Hey," Liz said. "How'd you get in here?" Liz said. The cat froze wide-eyed for a moment, then grabbed the fish and streaked off through the open door to the garden.

"The cat's been following me in here every morning. He fell into the water once, so I try not to leave him alone. He'll pounce on anything that moves." She pointed to some tattered tomatoes fluttering by a fan.

"Yin and Yang are going to fabricate screens I can lay over the ponds. Thanks for coming with me, Emma. It's been hard to talk to the others. They're all sleepwalking."

Emma admired the thriving garden, then asked to borrow Liz' pad and entered her personal code. There was a message from her father and she opened it eagerly, but her smile faded. He was critical of the first abrupt stop she'd tried in the walkabout. He had other complaints about her test run of the suits and the rover. She closed the message without reading it through.

"Thanks, Liz." Emma jerked out the pad's plug and handed it back.

***

Rover Two remained stranded. Dragging the inflatable would destroy it, and MEX was reluctant to cut it off, which was the only way to get inside unless a walkabout could dock. Emma received several messages about the suit joints from her father's engineering staff. She was anxious to repair them.

"Not to worry, love," Yin said.

"We'll bring the walkabouts into the north docking module, so you can work in comfort," Yang said.

The smell of Martian dust stung Emma's nose when she opened the airlock door for the first walkabout. The vacuum system wasn't set up for the bulky suit so she couldn't clean it very well. She buried her nose in her elbow and directed Governor to crawl the suit through to the module.

MEX announced an upgrade to the electrostatic sealing system for the airlocks, but Emma couldn't modify what they had with parts on hand. Until the next transport was sent, they recommended cleaning the seals with microfiber clothes soaked in hydrogen peroxide.

"Just what we use in Maintenance now," Yin said. "Glad we have a research group to tell us these things."

"I'll have to rig a container of some sort that's easy to carry on the outside of a suit and won't freeze," Yang said.

Daan dragged a couple lighting strings into the dock where Governor dropped the walkabouts. He claimed he had to adjust the lights and stayed each morning to watch Emma repair the seals as he rambled on about mountains he'd climbed. Claude poked his head in once or twice, but didn't stay. Once when Emma realized Daan had been quiet for a while, she looked up and found him asleep in his chair. He was useless and never gave her a private moment with Claude.

All week Emma methodically disassembled the walkabout joints and polished out the scratches. Her pace was slow and, since the module only had one heater, she felt colder every sol. Finally she donned the thermal layer from a surface suit, but that meant she had to wear the utility pack too, which left her shoulders sore every evening. She had to use a couple replacement seals and her father reminded her she wasn't supposed to dip into those spares till long after Settler Four arrived. Close-up pictures she sent to Earth of the scratched lubricant pads brought more irritating messages from her father. Daan began asking if she was done with the extra lights each sol.

At least Claude was receiving data from his drill rig. As he'd hoped, the swarm-bots were into solid rock.

"It could be basalt. I need to retrieve my sample cuttings to know if it's lava from Peacock Mons or metal from the meteor," Claude said over supper one evening. "When can we go back?"

"I don't know yet," Emma said.

"You've been screwing around with those suits forever. This is my first chance to do what I came to Mars for. I want to go now." He glared at her.

"I'm working as fast as I can," Emma said.

"The rover's been sitting out there a long time."

"So what? You think someone's gonna steal it?" Emma glared back.

Her father insisted on a series of tests inside the docking module before releasing the walkabouts. Emma gritted her teeth, stretched each joint, and adjusted the tension after each trial, certain she already had the setting correct.

At night in her bunk, Emma pulled out her mother's holograph projectors. Right now her mother was probably at some art gallery opening or coffee house poetry slam, dressed in a colorful billowy blouse, wearing gaudy, dangling earrings, surrounded by friends. Her mother was always the life of the party. Emma bunched her eyebrows against the urge to cry. She'd never liked poetry anyway. She scrolled through the file of images.

The last image's metadata caught her eye. Medium - oil. Title - Family Vacation. Artist - Norman Rockwell. An old, antiquated artist was hardly her mother's style.

Oh no, she thought. It's got to be a corny tear-jerker. That *would* be her mom's style.

The hologram floated above the base, a family in an old fashioned car, boat tied on top, grumpy grandmother in the back, parents in the front, together. Kids and a dog hung out the windows, wild with excitement. She touched the caption's audio and heard her mother's voice.

"Your colony's your family now. I hope it'll be the family your father and I couldn't give you. I'm so proud you followed your dream. Enjoy your robots - just remember, it's people that make us happy. I miss you, dear."

Emma swallowed a silent laugh. She was right. It was corny. And it was a tear-jerker.

Chapter Twenty-Nine: Return

E MMA WAS NEEDLESSLY polishing a walkabout seal as Daan sat in his chair, examining his fingertips. when the message arrived - her father was finally satisfied with the repairs.

"Hey Daan. Wake up. You can have your damn lights back."

He looked confused.

"I'm done with the lights. The walkabouts are fully charged and pressurized. Want to try one?"

That broke Daan out of his stupor and he levered himself out of the chair.

The suits were lying on their bellies, which made entry easy. Emma got Daan settled inside one before she slid into the other.

"Run the checklist, Governor. Comms, life support, power..."

"What do I do first?" Daan asked.

"Crawl into the airlock on your hands and knees. Leave room to open the outer door. If you lay flat, I can crawl on top of you so we both fit at once."

They played outside for hours like kids in the snow.

"That was great," Daan said when they crawled back inside the docking module.

"Tomorrow I'll arrange with Yin and Yang to dock the suits to Rover One. Then we can retrieve Claude's drill and Rover Two."

"I'll be happy to help."

Emma smiled. It had been good to get outside again. Her headache was almost gone.

There were plenty of volunteers to retrieve the abandoned rover. Emma and Claude were going of course, and Yang offered to drive Rover One - he said he needed more practice driving.

Daan also joined them, the first step towards Olympus, he said. It was good to hear him talk about his old dream.

The easiest way to get the walkabouts attached to the rover was for Emma and Daan to maneuver out the north airlock and meet Claude and Yang in the rover. Getting them docked took a while, but eventually the crane hoisted Emma up into place and she felt a satisfying tug backwards as the suit engaged its clamps and the seal hissed closed.

Yang followed Rover Two's tracks, still visible despite the dust cloud that had chased Emma and Claude home.

Daan stared at Peacock Mons.

"It would be a long slog up the slope," he said. "But not much of a challenge until you get to the cliff at the caldera lip, I suppose."

"Sounds like you plan to try," Emma said. Daan smiled over his shoulder at her.

"I've focused on utilities for too long."

"You've got to focus on utilities, mate," Yang said. "That's what we need to keep expanding the nederzetting."

"You get to see Kamp's construction from the outside," Daan said. "Claude's right - too much time living inside a glorified culvert isn't good." He began alternating between the satellite views on his pad and staring out the window.

"You can climb to the peak if you want," Claude said. "I'd rather fly up."

The journey passed in relative quiet, each settler lost in thought.

They spotted Rover Two easily. Despite a film of dust muting its bright blue hull, it stood out against the reddish sand.

The dust had been so fine it wafted away without forming drifts. Yang circled the rover. The portable habitat was still attached to Rover Two's airlock and still fully inflated.

Claude hopped to a walkabout access hatch. "Governor, tell the drill swarm to return to storage configuration. Emma, are you coming with me?"

"You go with Claude," Emma said to Daan. "Get a feel for the walkabout doing real work. Tell me if it feels real enough to use when you climb Olympus."

"Damn," Claude said in a good natured way. "I'll have to wait for a new sand bunny to hop around before I get any help."

Claude led the way to the crater floor where the drill stood upright with a pile of cuttings dribbled down the sides. He folded up the power receiver while Daan dumped the ballast cylinders.

"All secure," Claude said when they'd loaded the drill on Rover Two's bed.

"You guys might as well retract the inflatable," Yang said over the suit channel. "You've got to go inside to do that, so might as well drive it home, too."

Emma sighed softly. She had hoped to ride home with one of them.

Claude and Daan hopped to the access hatches and extracted cleaning clothes from their tool pouches. By extending the suits' arms, they could reach the seals and wipe each one thoroughly.

"Here goes nothing," Claude said, maneuvering into docking position.

"Your suit is sealed to the rover, Claude. I am opening the suit's access," Governor said. "Daan, your suit is sealed to the rover. I am opening your suit's access."

Emma let out a cheer.

"I knew it would work," Yang said.

"Emma and I never did go into the inflatable," Claude said. "Want to come with me, Daan?" They donned the two surface suits hanging in the airlock as a precaution.

"Everything looks good," Daan said when they were inside the inflatable. "I'm taking off my helmet."

"Are you okay?" Emma could see Daan and Claude through the multi-layered plastic windows as vague shapes moving inside.

"Give the man a minute, love," Yang said. "I think I'll see what Yin packed for lunch while we wait."

"It's cold," Daan said. "I'm sick of being cold. I suppose there's a heating unit that goes with this thing?"

"No, just a circulation fan."

"That may be a mistake. If this is going to be a habitat, I don't want to wear a surface suit the whole time."

"Even with that foil roof, I feel naked to the radiation," Claude said. "This thing gives me the willies. I'm going back to the rover. Besides, I'm hungry."

"There's a man with his priorities straight," Yang said, returning to the seat next to Emma with a bowl of fish and chips in each hand.

***

When they returned to Kamp, Emma stored the walkabouts with their mules in the maintenance warehouse. Governor could operate an empty suit, so she left Governor to dock each suit to a mule and walk it back to its corner, dragging a power cable and dangling the suit. She'd have to wait for her first camping trip.

"I hate coming back here," Daan said as the rover approached the north docking module. "I felt more like myself on this trip, and I'm coming back to the same old problems."

"If I can spend half-time with my samples," Claude said, "I'll be happy stringing lights in the medical bay the rest of the sol. You, Melina, and Sanni can get some extra sleep."

Yang docked at the south habitat and, when Emma hopped through the airlock, she found Claude waiting for her. They trotted through the Plaza to the Spine.

"Hang on." Claude interrupted Emma's turn towards the north habitat. "I have something to show you."

"Go ahead," Yang said. "I'm hungry - hope someone's cooked supper." He hopped through the habitat airlock.

Mystified, Emma followed Claude into the fish module, on to the greenhouse, and stopped in surprise.

A table built from packing crates filled the center aisle. Claude had to hop up on a garden bed wall to walk around it. He faced her and swept a welcoming arm above the table. It was set for supper with a bowl of fish stew in the middle and Claude's pouches of beer.

"We never did get to our date. How about tonight?"

"This is great." Emma pulled a stool from under the table. "Who did all this?"

"Liz." Claude grinned as he picked up a ladle. "Allow me to serve."

I owe Liz for this, Emma thought as she poured the beer, holding the pouch carefully so not a drop spilled. She deserves a full report on our date.

***

The Settler Four mission would break Earth orbit in three months, October seventh on Earth, sol three oh six on Mars. Settler Four was called the Doctors' Mission because, in addition to vital but mundane supplies, doctors and medical equipment would arrive.

And a cryochamber of embryos.

The embryos would be housed in the new medical bay, so Liz encouraged Emma to spend her time installing utilities. She mentioned them often when Emma took time for a chat.

"Just think, Settler Four will bring two hundred new settlers for Mars," she said. "And if the viability tests go well, enough blastocytes will arrive with Settler Five to yield - assuming we can maintain an eighty-three point two percent success rate - to yield a population of two thousand in six or seven generations. A self-sustaining colony on Mars."

186

Emma shifted uncomfortably. She hadn't thought about the embryos lately. The S-5 mission would carry the only all-woman crew Colony Mars planned, to get a jump on filling Kamp with children.

Emma had never felt the need for children. When she was a little girl playing with dolls, her dolls didn't have babies. They built things and traveled to distant lands. But no babies.

Obviously a colony needed children to succeed, and of course more genetic diversity than four adults per transport could provide. It didn't make any sense to immigrate to Mars if you weren't going to raise children.

But there'd be no pregnancies until after S-5 arrived. There was time enough to worry about it then.

***

Daan, Melina, and Sanni managed to keep up with maintenance in the Spine and two habitat modules but had no time for the medical bay, so Emma and Claude installed utilities. It was surreal working in a puddle of light within a cold, dark, silent bay, so they talked as they worked. Claude especially. Emma developed an interest in rocks.

Claude spent most of the time talking about his samples. He was eager for the analytical instruments S-4 would bring, but made progress using old fashioned techniques like scratch tests, so Emma got a lesson in history as well as lithology. The new radiant heaters felt warm against her skin, but the stone benches and bay walls were still cold and sucked heat from the air.

From time to time Claude lapsed into silence, so Emma went over walkabout plans in her head. She agreed with Daan - she'd felt like herself on the crater trips. As soon as the nederzetting work-schedule allowed, she wanted to take a walkabout and one of the mules out for a test run. A mule would give her the option to stay out for three or four sols, sleeping under the dusty stars and traveling far on robotic feet.

As weeks dragged on Claude spoke less. Emma was cold and stiff every evening and her headaches returned, dull heavy sensations in her eyes and sinuses.

Utilities were nearly completed in Medical when Yin and Yang opened another new bay - another greenhouse. This bay attached directly to the Spine with no module in between. Its air ducts were built into the stone floor, which eliminated the sort of ventilation work the medical bay had needed. Even before fans were installed, cold flooded into the Spine. Heat and proper lighting would have to wait until S-4 arrived with more components, but Liz got started on the garden beds right away.

Emma helped harvest alfalfa to spread on the new beds of sand, carrying the sheaths into the cold bay after sweating in the warm greenhouse, trying not to trip over the raised beds visible only in light spilling in from the Spine. They'd dig the alfalfa into the raw sand later.

"I don't know what you're grinning at," she said to Yin at supper as she carried a baked potato to the table and sagged into a chair. "Every bay you open just dumps us back into the deep-freeze."

"We have more bays ready to open." He ignored her whine. "We're just waiting to build up the minimum required atmosphere."

"It's going faster than ever," Yang said. "Ruby's flying the stone blocks for us with that remote control jumpship of yours, as fast as we can manufacture hydrogen and O2 for fuel."

"I'll put up with the cold if I get to fly," Ruby said, a rare smile spreading over her brown face. Emma looked down at her own arms, nearly translucent white after so much time away from the Sun's warm rays.

"You weren't here when we lived in nothing but the ship modules," Daan said. "They were so cramped and claustrophobic we made building bays a priority."

Emma poked at her potato in annoyance. "Great, but no one can use your bays because you can't get heat or light installed."

"I'm allocating the components we have the best way I can," Daan stabbed his own potato. "I don't even have all the parts I should have from your knarr, thanks to the crash."

Ruby snapped back. "Like we crashed on purpose, just to annoy you? Who knew Yin and Yang would be so far ahead of schedule, anyway?"

"Hey, don't drag us into this," Yang said.

Emma and Daan both shot an angry look at him.

"Don't blame Yang," Ruby said. "Construction's gone without a hitch, which is more than I can say about the joints on your walkabouts."

"I have a walkabout ready for a camping trip - a couple nights out with a mule." Emma looked around angrily. "Trips are in our protocol from Colony Mars, you know."

"You can't possibly want to go back out there." Melina shuddered. Her shoulders collapsed forward as she hugged herself.

"Do what you want," Ruby said. "Just don't expect me to fly out to rescue you the minute you get into trouble."

"I'd think you'd be fine with any jumper flight. You seem to enjoy hauling construction blocks around while the rest of us work inside."

"I'm proving the remote-controlled ship is worthy. I've sent MEX the telemetry from all my flights. Oh, they'll fart around before they sign off, but that ship is ready to jump to orbit. There's no excuse to cancel the Settler Four mission and Daan's precious heaters."

"Stop bickering." Melina dragged herself out of her chair. "Come on Sanni. Bring the cat."

"Oh, Melina, don't leave." Liz put a hand to her mouth.

"I thought she was feeling better tonight," Sanni said with a sigh, pulling the cat out from under a chair and following Melina. Emma got up and slammed the airlock door closed behind them, shutting out the cold draft.

189

Chapter Thirty: Aloe

THERE WERE NO MORE lights or heaters available, so the new greenhouse bay stayed cold and dark. But the old alfalfa beds had to be turned over so Emma returned to the greenhouse to help Liz. Spading the old roots and stems into the sand felt good. It should tire her out and help her sleep.

"It's starting to look like healthy soil," Liz said when they finished the first bed.

Emma paused to admire their work, shifting the spading fork to ease her sore shoulders. Bits of chopped alfalfa stuck out of the sand here and there, water gave the sand a brown hue, and a worm wriggled away to hide. It did look something like proper soil.

"The next vegetables we plant here should do better than before." Liz consulted her pad, looking at the planting rotation schedule. "Potatoes here next, and alfalfa where the veggies were."

"Liz, Emma." Governor's voice sounded tinny over their pads. "Please open the airlock from the Spine. Someone wants to come in."

Puzzled, Emma hopped to the airlock. As soon as the door opened a crack, the cat slithered in and rubbed against her leg. She picked him up and, ignoring his attempt to wriggle free, carried him to Liz.

"Governor, you had me open a door for the cat?"

"Yes, Emma. He cannot open the door and needed your assistance."

"No point arguing with Governor over who's a settler," Liz said with a laugh. Emma dropped the cat. He leaped into the freshly turned soil and started to dig, scattering sand into the aisle.

"Hey, get out of there." Emma shooed him. The cat made a display of crouching in the bed with his ears back, and then leaped into the next bed.

"He uses his litter box, doesn't he?" she asked Liz.

"He's got the same germs we all have." She shrugged.

"Melina's been trying to keep him with her, but he likes it here."

"Of course he does. It's warm." Liz dropped a knife she was using to chop the dry alfalfa. "Let's take a break."

Emma flopped down on the stone edge of the bed. "I'm beat." She tossed her spading fork at the pile.

The fork hit Liz's knife and a spark flew. With a whoosh the pile erupted into flames higher than Emma's head. She shrieked as fire jumped to her arm.

Liz knocked her flat and scooped sand over her.

"What the hell!" Emma stared at the bed. The flames were gone. Liz stirred the smoldering ashes with the fork. A thread of orange ran along some crushed leaves. Emma grabbed a bucket by the closest fish pond and dumped water on the pile. A few fingerlings flopped on the wet sand.

"What the hell?" She was shaking and her heart pounded in her head.

Liz touched the side of her face. "Red as a sunburn. But it doesn't look too bad. I need to check your arm for burns."

"Dammit. What's the oxygen level in here?"

"I don't know. It must be high."

"I thought you were using a surface suit pack to take readings," Emma said.

"Yang needed it back, so I haven't checked in a while."

Emma winced as she lifted the blackened edge of her shirt.

"I'd replace your mystic crap with a couple good analytical meters."

"Hurry up. Let's get clean water on that arm right away."

***

Emma tossed her ruined shirt on the table. Most of the synthetic fibers had simply vaporized, but the edges were curled and melted. A thin line stuck painfully to her skin.

Liz wrapped her arm in wet towels. "How much does it hurt?"

"Not too bad." Emma grimaced.

"I'll get you some pain meds. Don't pull at those globs on your skin. Let them slough off on their own." She shook her head. "You'll have a scar there where the synthetics stuck."

"Pass me a dry towel, will you?" Emma draped it over her shoulders. "And, make me some tea? Please?" She gave Liz an exaggerated pouty look and they both laughed.

"Here." Liz set a jar of clear gel on the table. Emma wrinkled her nose at the oniony smell - something Liz made from the garden.

"I'm glad I brought a few aloe plants. Smear that on your face while I brew tea."

"What are you going to do about the oxygen level?" Emma wrinkled her nose as she dipped out some goo. "We burned all the packaging already."

"I could burn old plants as I cut them down." Liz paused with a cup in one hand. "I hate to lose the biomass, though."

"Yang can fill a cylinder with hydrogen," Emma said. "And rig up something like a Bunsen burner, something you could use routinely. Burning hydrogen will consume oxygen and leave you with water, which you need anyway."

"I don't want an explosion." Liz bunched her eyebrows together above a worried frown.

"Governor can model the reaction," Emma said. "Or MEX could run a test. Is Yang still bringing up carbon dioxide?"

"Yes, regularly. The plants are growing thirty percent faster than projected. I suppose that's why the oxygen built up. See, I *do* use science along with my mystic crap."

Ouch, Emma thought. "There's an air monitor on the habitat's life support system. Since we equalized the habitat with the Spine, it's redundant. I'll ask Sanni to help me move it to the greenhouse. Once I know the percentages in the greenhouse, Governor can calculate how much gas you'll need."

"Great, but first I need to finish bandaging your arm."

They were still alone in the north habitat, sipping tea, when the link beeped with an incoming message.

"Now what." Emma plugged her pad into the table's outlet.

"Malcolm." She frowned as she read the header and selected text-only.

I guess you know, after the jumpship crash, the doctors made me take medical leave. I remember watching the crash and waking up in hospital. I don't know how I got there. You should have talked to me in hospital.

I couldn't send you messages while I was on leave - you don't have me on your friends list. But you don't have to fix that now. I'm back in the control room today, so my access codes are enabled.

The jumpship shouldn't have crashed. No one should have been hurt. I warned you.

The Colony doctors are all against me, but I showed them. I passed the fitness tests.

I want to hear from you. Message me. Tell me how you are.

Emma opened MEX's shift schedule. Malcolm was listed as active, a controller for the GPS satellite system.

"Is something wrong?" Liz asked. "You look worried."

"No, it's nothing." Emma tapped out a text reply. *Glad you're feeling better. I'm fine, thanks. Things here are fine. I'm working now, so gotta go.* She read it over. It sounded polite and non-committal.

Malcolm wasn't coming to Mars and Emma wasn't directly involved with the satellites. She shouldn't have any settlement business with him. Good enough. She hit send.

***

"Well, guys. MEX did it." Yin watched an image from Collins Dock on the habitat screen. "Settler Four broke out of Earth orbit."

Liz had summoned them all for an early supper to watch the transport ship. She called it their cocktail hour and laid out a selection from the dwindling specialty foods, the dehydrated shrimp was gone but they still had some dried fruit ,along with a batch of bhang tea and toasted mealworms.

Yin ladled out a cup of tea for himself and settled into a chair contentedly. The screen switched to an animation, which was more exciting than the actual image. MEX enhanced the thruster burn into a flaming plume. But they couldn't do much to enhance a diagram projecting the ship's trajectory to the orbital transfer point.

Yang smiled with satisfaction. "We're going to get our next shipment of parts right on schedule."

"And more settlers," Liz said.

"Good, I need them. We're getting behind on preventative maintenance. And in the medical bay..." Daan leaned his head against a hand, gripping his hair. "I found a length of electrical conduit joined to a water pipe. It's a damn good thing the water's not hooked up yet. We need to go over the whole installation again."

Ruby snorted one of her mocking laughs.

"Geeze," Emma said. "Are you going out of your way to be stupid?"

She thought she was done with utilities for a while. It felt like a conspiracy to keep her from her walkabout trip. "Fix that one line and be done with it."

"It's a line you installed," Daan said angrily. "So you should fix it."

Emma glanced around for Claude. Surely he'd support her. But he wasn't in the habitat.

"Well, guys, maybe a fresh set of eyes will help." Ruby turned to Yin and Yang. "You don't have any blocks ready for me right now, so I suppose I'm stuck inside, too, don't you think?"

Emma swallowed the sour taste in her mouth.

They would spend weeks going, line by line, over the utility systems. Daan, who hadn't had time to work the

194

installation, had time to supervise and criticize now. In addition to the screwed up conduit, they corrected a few backwards valves and rewired some LED panels.

***

Three months dragged by until the Settler Four transport ship fired its mid-course correction. In the time-honored tradition of twice before, Liz declared a Kamp holiday. She brewed bhang tea and they all raised a cup.

"Go on Daan. Say it." Liz took him by the shoulders and turned him towards the imager.

"Aw, it's too late. A transmission takes so long to reach them."

"Send it. It's a tradition."

"Okay. Governor, send a message to the S-4 crew. Congratulations guys. You have 'slipped the surly bonds of Earth; And dance the skies on laughter-silvered wings.'"

The transmission lag precluded conversation, so after S-4 returned their thanks, Ruby terminated the feed.

Emma was too tired to eat the fish stew Liz simmered in the galley. Her eyes felt hot and achy. She ladled out a second cup of bhang to dull the ache and maybe give her an appetite. It was months since she'd been outside and thoughts of the walkabouts, hanging limply from their mules in the maintenance bay, haunted her. She hadn't heard from her father in weeks and her mother was busy at some retreat in the Rocky Mountains. Even Claude disappeared most afternoons. There was no one to talk to. Mars was a lonely place.

The mid-course celebration was winding down when Emma's pad beeped a message from Malcolm. He rambled about satellite systems for a few lines, then, *when Settler Four achieves orbit around Mars, what if the ship's disassembly failed? The ship could be refueled and I wrote a navigation program to bring it back to Earth - to bring you back to Earth.*

Talking about ship malfunctions gave Emma a funny feeling. It reminded her uncomfortably of the jumpship crash, of James and Luis buried on the frozen Tharsis Plain.

She slipped through the flap to her bunk to get a moment alone. There was a tap at the door and Liz poked her head in.

"Did you get bad news?" she asked. "You look upset."

"Oh, nothing. I got a message from Malcolm."

"I saw he was back on the MEX roster," Liz said, squeezing inside and closing the flap behind her.

"You were checking on Malcolm?" Emma looked up sharply.

"I keep in touch with MEX operations. I have friends there. Why are you so jumpy?"

"It's nothing, just, he's on again about how we should go back to Earth." Emma didn't mention he only talked about her going back.

"Maybe you should forward his messages to Filip Krast."

"No..." Emma gritted her teeth. "Malcolm was really upset when Ingra died. That's why he washed out from the S-4 crew. And he broke down when the jumper crashed - had to take a medical leave. He's getting back to work now. Besides, what harm can he do from Earth? Screw up a satellite map?"

Liz zipped the flap when she left and Emma flopped on the bunk, tears threatening to overflow. The privacy flap was utterly inadequate. She opened her mouth to breath, exhaling slowly. My eyes are tired, she thought. My eyes are sore and I'm so tired.

Chapter Thirty-One: Run

A FEW MORE WEEKS crawled by and Emma woke up not wanting to get out of her bunk. If she didn't leave on a walkabout soon, she'd be too discouraged to move. Expeditions were supposed to be endorsed by a settler vote, so Emma tried to convince the others to let her go walkabout.

"S-4 lands right before the storm season. That's ten weeks from now, and there's no time to do anything on the surface afterwards, once the storms close in. Besides, there are no utility components left to install, and you don't need me here right now."

"She's right about that," Daan said. "We've got nothing to do but sleep half the sols away. Well, all except Yin and Yang."

"I thought the extra sleep would do everyone good," Liz said. "I've talked to Noah, the S-4 psychologist, about our drop in productivity. He recommended more sleep and light exercise."

"Great, I'm ready to exercise," Emma said. "I want to take a walkabout out overnight with a mule. Alone, on my own." She sounded crabby, even to herself, but looked around defiantly.

"Emma should go," Claude said. "And I'd like to drop the drill out on the surface again while there's time."

"That, too," Emma said, happy to support him in turn. "Drilling is part of our exploration mission. Claude and Daan can take Rover Two and the other walkabout."

"You want to go alone?" Melina asked.

"Yes, that's the whole point of the walkabouts." Melina was going to object and Emma felt a flutter of panic. She just had to get away from everyone, get some real privacy.

"Whatever," Melina said. "It'll be quieter with fewer people around for a few sols. So I vote 'yes.'"

197

"I wouldn't mind catching up on sleep myself before Settler Four arrives," Ruby said.

MEX endorsed the trips, not that Ruby thought they should get a vote. Activity outside the nederzetting was popular with the public, so they planned a new infotainment based on the feeds.

Emma rode out to Maintenance with Yin and Yang the next sol. They dropped her at the bay and took the rover to join their construction squad. Emma stretched her shoulders, hoping to shake off the gloom she felt. Now that she was here, the trip seemed pointless. She should be excited, she knew, to take her first solo walkabout.

Be happy, she told herself, gritting her teeth. This is what you've waited for.

"Governor, send a private message to my father. Dad, I'm about to go outside for a solo camping trip. I hope you'll like what I've got planned. End. Okay, activate the live feed to MEX."

Emma plugged in her personal pad to check the video feed. The bay imager was focused on the two mules that squatted along the wall.

Each mule was a portable airlock barely big enough to sleep in, equipped with life support, a power receiver to recharge the walkabout, and multiple legs to follow the suit almost anywhere. The engineers called it a coffin early in the design, but her father banned the term and eventually someone started calling the units mules. They were even odder looking than a walkabout.

Each had an oblong cone at one end that reminded Emma of the tail of a turkey gobbler she'd seen once at a farm museum. The cone necked down to a short boxy body that would be coffin-like but for a window on either side. Instead of a turkey neck, a walkabout hung from the front docking port. The mules were enameled bright blue like the rovers, to stand out against the rust-colored sand in case a rescue by jumpship was needed. But they should never get lost since the suits communicated with Governor and orbiting GPS satellites.

"Governor, activate the beacons. Confirm comms with the mules and suits."

"Beacon signals are strong and clear, Emma."

"Activate the mules."

Each mule telescoped out four legs and rose up. The walkabouts' feet now dangled just above the floor. Governor confirmed the life support systems were operational.

"Send Johnny mule to the north nederzetting airlock." Governor would move the walkabout suit to Rover Two for Daan and Claude.

"Dock Molly over here by me." Molly obediently walked to the warehouse airlock, lifting each leg in a stiff prance. The mule backed in and retracted its legs to mate with the door. Its docking clamps connected.

"The seal is confirmed. Molly is ready for you to enter," Governor said.

Emma opened the airlock door to reveal the mule's access hatch, stenciled with a large yellow "M" for Molly.

Emma stripped out of her surface suit, tossed it inside, and pulled on her striped shirt and cargo pants. Next she heaved in her sack of supplies and crawled through. The mule was her camp, a hard-sided bivouac, or maybe more like a life support pod where she'd stretch out to sleep. She could sit up inside, but like a camping tent, it was too squat to stand in.

Emma provided a short tour of the mule's insides for her vid to Earth. Molly had sophisticated balance and travel algorithms, but was stupid otherwise. The intelligence was in the walkabout suit and through its connection to Governor.

Emma sealed the doors and slid feet-first into the walkabout.

"Molly. Undock airlock. Undock suit." The mule didn't have an extensive vocabulary.

She felt a gentle bump as the suit access swung shut behind her, the seal released, and clamps set her down on her feet. The suit's tail extended automatically.

Emma waited patiently for her life support pack to slide into place and felt the whoosh of cool air as the breathing system activated.

"Open suit comms. Does anyone read me?"

"Loud and clear. You ready to head out?" It was Yin, or maybe Yang. "Have a good time."

"I'm in the rover with Claude." That was Daan's voice. "We're ready to leave, too."

"Thanks everyone. Don't expect to hear from me until tonight. Governor, close all transmission links and open the warehouse door." Emma wanted privacy. MEX would just have to use animations instead of feeds from her helmet imager.

Emma kangaroo-walked out through the roll-up door. It felt natural in Martian gravity. As she turned towards Peacock Mons the suit beeped an incoming message alert from her personal account.

Emma swore. It was Malcolm.

She hesitated. This was supposed to be her walkabout time, a chance to get away from everything. She didn't want to deal with Malcolm.

She ignored the message and leaned forward. "Rapid travel."

Emma kicked off and the suit began to kangaroo-hop towards the mountain. The mule followed, kicking up a puff of dust with each prancing footfall.

***

It was a beautiful morning on the Tharsis Plain. Some lithologists, Claude had told her, classified the entire Tharsis bulge as a single super volcano, so Peacock Mons and its neighbors might be vents from the same underground magma chamber, rock frozen eons ago. She believed in the super volcano as she gazed over her shoulder. Thin clouds of ice crystals streaked the orange sky, streaming off the peak of the mountain. Peacock curved the horizon into a wide hump rising to a flattened peak. "Mountain" seemed a funny name for it.

Claude and Daan were traveling around the south flank to investigate a line of ridges mapped by the satellites. The ridges ran along the base of a small cliff which might have been formed by ancient glaciers. Better rock-hounding there, perhaps. The rover would trundle along under Governor's control twenty-four hours and thirty-nine minutes a sol, endlessly powered through the receiver on its roof. In two or three sols they'd deploy the drill somewhere along Claude's ridge. They had one walkabout and their surface suits - Claude claimed to get a better feel for his rock hammer through a surface suit. Maybe Daan would prefer a surface suit for climbing, too.

But Emma didn't care whether they used the walkabout, and she didn't want to run into them either. She headed north to a series of flat bottomed valleys between wide ridges of blocky stone. She could kangaroo-hop at top speed on the valley floors protected by the cliffs on either side.

Emma balanced on the stirrups in the suit's legs like a jockey.

Run, run, run, she thought. Run away.

I don't belong here, Emma thought as the walkabout picked up speed. No on needs me. Liz can handle the farming. Yin and Yang don't want my help with the construction bots. Everyone else is too tired to care. Even my father thinks my walkabout tests are stupid.

Run, run, run. The thumping jarred through her skull and drove other thoughts away as she tried to anticipate changes in the sand's texture, avoid protruding rocks, and keep the rounded mountain beyond her right shoulder. The Sun rose high in the dusty sky, banishing shadows from the dunes. Her legs and back began to ache and then throb. Emma gritted her teeth. Her stomach growled and she ignored it. She ran circles to let the mule catch up. It didn't matter, so long as she ran.

Finally she saw flat slabs of rock like giant, flaked cobbles, and slowed to a walk, feeling the change in surface texture through the suit's movements.

Emma walked slowly until a band of mottled darkness came into view. She turned her head side to side before her brain grasped the perspective. She was standing on a cliff looking across a shallow valley, only a few hops wide. The opposite wall was in shadows.

She sat back on her tail and scanned the dunes for the mule. There it was, a shiny blue cuboid on slender legs, moving doggedly towards her. It couldn't keep up when she used rapid travel mode, but it would find her.

Emma pulled her arms out of the suit sleeves, rubbed the tops of her thighs and hugged herself tightly in the narrow space between her chest and the suit's shell.

What am I doing here? I'm stubborn, stupid, an embarrassment. Dad pushed me to join Colony Mars to be rid of me.

Emma had never failed before. When she persevered, she always succeeded. Well, standing at the edge of a gray cliff and looking up at an orange sky didn't feel like success. She wished she had her mother's unreasoning optimism. Emma's throat closed around a hard, hot knot of pain. She watched the shadows creep towards her across the valley below until the mule caught up.

Emma leaned forward and jumped. The suit's tail stretched to touch down first. In less than a heart-beat, the suit adjusted the shock joints in its legs and held out its empty sleeves for balance. It wasn't a long drop, but with vertical rock higher than her head on both sides, Emma felt alone for the first time since she'd left Earth. No one could see her; there was no one to impress. The mule followed her leap, bounced a few times on the shock absorbers in its legs, and stood passively beside her.

"Molly, dock the suit," she said, not bothering to hide her ragged breathing. The mule shifted, grabbed the suit with its forward clamps, pushed the life support pack up with two slender haptic-tipped limbs, and hauled the suit into position. Emma willed herself to go limp and let the suit seal against the mule. The access hatch behind her opened and she shivered as the cool, dry air from the mule flowed around her. She leaned backwards, grabbed for handholds and levered herself out of the walkabout, lying on her back inside the mule, feet still inside the suit. She began to cry. She sobbed until she could hardly breathe and the shadow of the valley wall swept over the mule.

Chapter Thirty-Two: Wild

EMMA WOKE when the sunlight angled in through the mule's window. She felt terrible in some ways. Her mouth tasted awful, her back ached, and her eyes were full of grit. But she also felt light; the pressure in her head was gone. She was hungry. And she needed to pee.

The sanitary system was built into the walkabout's legs and arching her stiff back made her groan as she slid inside the suit. But even that felt normal. It hurt in a good way.

"I wonder how long I slept?" she said out loud and checked the mule's chronometer.

"Fifteen hours. Damn." But she smiled.

"No wonder I'm hungry." She dug into her supplies. Cold roasted potatoes tasted wonderful.

Liz must have done something special with these, she thought as she spooned out more wedges. Even the fish was tasty, not muddy but fresh and sweet.

"Governor, open comms to Kamp." She'd missed last night's check-in and knew they'd be worried. She paused as she shook out her shirt.

"Governor?" No response. Must be too close to the cliff to hit the satellite. But she frowned as she looked out. The cliff wasn't very high.

"Molly, my girl. We should get going." The mule didn't react; it had no conversation algorithms.

Emma slid into the walkabout.

"Molly, undock the suit." That was a command the mule understood. Emma tried Governor again.

"Show my position on the heads-up display." Still nothing. Humph.

Emma moved with a bouncy gait into full sunlight in the center of the valley. After a short walk she found a broken section of cliff face and clambered up on all-fours. She turned back to watch the mule slowly placing each foot, leveling its body, placing another foot.

I should be recording this, she thought, but the imager failed to engage. Humph again.

She tried to walk across the level stone blocks, but the suit veered to the left. The surface looked solid; she saw no reason for the suit to change direction. She was trying to start a diagnostic when the suit walked towards the cliff.

"No! Stop!" The suit walked to the edge. She tried to crouch for a jump, but the suit ignored her and stepped off into nothing. It hit a slope of sand, flipped forward, and slid down. Emma barely had time to brace herself. Even so she got a sharp bump on her head.

"What the hell."

The suit rolled on its side, righted itself, and proceeded at an angle across the valley. The opposite cliff was sheer and unbroken. The suit ran into it, staggered like a drunk, and continued walking, now moving parallel to the cliff wall, sometimes bouncing off a protruding chunk of rock.

Emma struggled with the suit for a while before giving up. It was ignoring her. She pulled her arms inside again and tapped at the panel in front of her chest.

The Kamp channel was dead. The beacon channel was dead, too. No one was tracking her. Emma found she could open status screens and tabbed through. The walkabout should be sending telemetry through the comm satellites to Governor, but showed no upload underway. There should be a GPS download every few seconds in fluttery bursts of signal, but the GPS chart showed a solid usage line across the top of the screen. The satellites were continuously downloading something to the suit. Emma tried to shut down the receiver, but the suit ignored internal input.

The suit-to-suit channel was dead, too. If the other suit was receiving the strange GPS download, Claude or Daan would be in the same trouble. But she couldn't help them until she regained control.

The suit lumbered along at a constant pace. Even though Emma tried to relax, her legs cramped and burned. The suit's motion only varied when it bumped into rock. The cliff's shadow spread across the floor of the valley.

Eventually the valley floor tilted upwards. She emerged on sand with the mule following. Ahead she saw a dark shadow farther upslope.

There shouldn't be any shadows. The sunlight was angled towards that slope. There must be an overhang.

The GPS usage line continued steady across the top of the screen. Maybe an overhang would block the incessant download.

She tapped the status panel and saw her link to the mule was still active.

"Molly, dock the suit." The mule obediently reached out. She felt the suit jerk backwards as its clamps engaged. The suit's legs kept moving, scooping out a depression until they no longer touched the sand. It swung its tail, searching for the ground.

The mule, standing sideways across the slope, tipped over. Inside, Emma fell against her shoulder. Still firmly connected, the walkabout suit and mule slid down the slope together. The mule began levering in one direction, then another, trying to regain its feet.

"Molly, it's night. Camp in the dark." She had no idea how the stupid mule would react, but "camp" was a standard command and she thought "dark" was defined somewhere in its program as a measure of lumens. The mule staggered and backed upslope towards the shadow, telescoping its rear legs to level its body. The walkabout suit hung above the ground, legs still pumping, tail carving a furrow in the sand. Emma twisted inside the suit but she couldn't see where the mule was going. She was panting with exertion when blackness swallowed her.

"Molly, stop." But the mule had already stopped. The suit went limp and Emma let out a thankful whimper. Looking straight out her helmet, she saw a thick crescent of light extending side to side, maybe sand, maybe sky. Now stable, the mule lifted Emma's life support pack, sealed itself to the suit, and opened the access doors.

Bruised and sore, Emma fumbled for handholds and dragged herself out of the suit. She laid still briefly, clasping her knees to her chest to ease her aching back. With a groan she rolled to look into the suit. The status line on the GPS chart lay flat at the bottom of the screen. There was no more download.

Gradually her heart rate slowed to normal.

Out the side windows were rough rock walls a few steps away.

"Molly, pivot front feet to the right, one step." That was successful.

"Repeat." Okay again.

"Repeat." The mule scraped its rear airlock door on something. Emma fumbled for a hand light and shined it out the window. She was in a cave, and her light disappeared into blackness.

***

A half-dozen times Emma started to *do something, anything*. But she stopped herself. She ate, she thought. She came up with a plan.

The walkabout's beacon was installed in the top of the life support pack. Being a safety requirement, it was one of the devices Colony Mars provided with a dedicated battery, and if she could detach it, she could turn it on manually. Emma slid back into the walkabout and tried to grab the suit's beacon, but it was out of reach. There was still the mule's beacon, but she'd have to undock the suit to reach it. A pale beam from the setting Sun fell on the suit's feet. She was afraid of the mule losing its footing in the cave, but more afraid of the suit going wild again. She gave Molly orders, one foot at a time, to walk a body-length deeper into the cave before she slid into the walkabout.

"Molly, undock the suit." Emma held her breath, but the suit stood still when the mule released the clamps. She wiggled the manipulator claws on the arms, shuffled the feet back and forth. So far, so good.

"Molly, kneel." Emma popped the beacon off the mule's front corner. It was no bigger than her fist, so hitting the manual switch with a claw took a few tries.

It should be signaling now, she thought as she turned to the cave mouth and paused, not wanting to risk a step closer to the opening.

"Here goes nothing," she said out loud. The suit responded as she sat, extending its tail for support. Emma tossed the beacon underhand, harder than she had intended. It lofted over the lip of the cave and disappeared into the twilight.

I've been missing all sol, Emma thought. Now Governor will receive a signal again. Figure an hour to run a jumpship checklist and Ruby will fly straight here.

She turned to look into the back of the cave. "I've got an hour to explore."

Emma swept her helmet light across the cave. It was as wide as the Plaza. Sand had drifted in, leveling the entrance, but farther back were blocks of jagged rock. Beyond that was darkness.

"Molly. Stay here."

Emma extended the walkabout's arms and knuckle-walked over the broken rocks. Once past the uneven surface, the cave extended left and right as far as she could see. The floor rounded up into walls and there were ridges running lengthwise, like melted shelves. Emma sat the walkabout on its tail and angled her light up. The roof was arched, and drips and curtains of rock hung on one side. The floor was clear to her left so she walked that way. Crystals in the wall sparkled and the cave snaked in wide curves first one way, then the other. It reminded her of something - a trip she'd taken once as a kid, when her parents still vacationed together. They'd gone to Hawaii, to Volcano National Park.

That was it, Emma realized. She was inside a lava tube, and it was a big one.

Chapter Thirty-Three: Rescue

EMMA WALKED on slowly, but the lava tube never varied. How far could it go? The center of the Peacock Mons volcano was two hundred kilometers away. That far? But rescue was her priority. After half an hour, she chose a flat section of wall and scratched her initials with the walkabout's claw tip. The first vandalism on Mars, she thought with satisfaction.

Then she walked back to the mule.

The tube continued in the other direction past the mule, out towards the plain, but there was a lot of broken rock in the way. Emma poked around the debris and selected a few fist-sized samples, a couple with sharp jagged edges and one covered in crystals. Half buried in the wall behind the mule were dark brown rocks, with dents and dimples all over, but smooth.

That looks different, Emma thought. I bet Claude would like some of those. She pried out small chunks to add to her pile.

"Better get ready for my rescue. Molly, dock the suit."

The mule's life support system interfaced with the suit's batteries, but Emma didn't want to deplete them. She shut down the walkabout, set all systems to minimal, and rolled up in a blanket. Her pad used little power, so she plugged it in and scrolled through the folders, looking for something to read. There were several unopened messages stored, including one from Malcolm.

She stared at his name in the metadata. What could he want?

Emma - you haven't called me - you've been bad, but I'll give you one last chance. Don't leave the settlement. The walkabouts will never be seen again. It's your fault I have to get rid of them. If anything bad happens, it's your fault.

A chill spread through her gut. Malcolm was a GPS controller and the walkabout went wild with a download from the GPS system. She sorted her old messages and opened the last one Malcolm had sent before the jumpship crash.

Don't let them disassemble the ship. I'll be back on shift after the weekend to convince people here.

The chill crawled from Emma's gut up to her chest. She shut off the pad and lay awake in the dark for a long time, staring out the window to the cave mouth, hoping to glimpse a moon racing through the sky.

When she woke, pink dawn light spread across the sand and a cloud of dust billowed into the cave.

"Emma, do you read me?" Ruby's voice came from her surface suit helmet.

Emma jumped up and banged her head on the mule's ceiling. "Yes. In a cave above the beacon."

Ruby's helmet appeared at the cave mouth. Yin scrambled up next to her, holding the beacon in one hand.

Emma shouted into her helmet. "Are Daan and Claude alright?"

"They're fine." Ruby hopped inside the cave and stood with her helmet against the window.

"Their walkabout. Did it go crazy?"

"Yeah. It tried to go tramping on its own. It's still thrashing around, docked to the rover. They're on the way back to Kamp."

"Why didn't you come looking for me after I missed my call-in?"

"We got an 'all's well' text," Yin said. He was peering into the deep shadows at the back of the cave. "So we thought, no worries."

"I didn't send a text."

"Liz didn't feel right about it," Ruby said. "When the other suit went off its trolley, it sent a travel log that claimed it was kilometers away while Claude swore it was attached to his rover. She had me flying crisscross patterns up this way yestersol, but I had to give it up at sunset."

"So how'd you find me?"

"Ruby did it," Yin said. "She dug into the satellite telemetry and found your beacon signal on a direct channel while the GPS system told us you were a hundred clicks away on a different heading."

"I think I know why." Emma told them about the nonstop GPS download and Malcolm's messages.

Anger laced Yin's voice. "Bloody rotter."

Ruby's channel clicked off and she stomped both feet, fists swinging. Her voice rasped when she finally spoke. "Rattle your dags, Emma, and let's get back to Kamp. Everyone's in a panic and my saying you're okay isn't enough for them."

"I'll come out in my surface suit." Emma rolled around trying to tuck her toes into the compression layer. She had to put the life support pack on the floor and lay on top of it to get her shoulders in the straps.

"Molly, shut down life support. Purge interior atmosphere." One nice thing about a stupid robot - it didn't argue. Emma's helmet muffled the whine of air escaping and in a minute the pressure was low enough for her to open the hatch door. Two pairs of hands hauled her out and set her on her feet. Yin tossed the mule's beacon inside.

"Hang on. I've got a present for Claude." Emma reached inside the mule for the supply sack and filled it with her rocks. "Governor, open a channel to the mule."

"Channel open, Emma."

It was a relief to hear Governor's mild voice again. Emma walked Molly out of the cave. Once clear, the suit's legs began pumping again.

"Governor," Ruby said. "Shut down the damn GPS satellites - EMP safe mode."

Jumper One wasn't far. Emma had never entered a jumpship from the surface before, so Yin went first. The vertical ladder was easy to climb, but she had to sidestep along a lip to the open airlock. Yin pulled her around the frame of the door while Ruby pushed.

Once the airlock cycled, Ruby slipped into the controls. "Give me a minute to open a channel to the mule and move it out of that cave."

Ruby hovered in a cloud of engine exhaust and snagged the mule with the ship's grapplers.

Yin yanked his harness tighter. "How did that bastard get into the walkabouts' controls?"

"Like the jumpship that crashed, betcha," Ruby said. "I'm gonna find out."

Emma shook her head. "It's funny. I feel good. Malcolm tried to kill me, and I feel great. I'm not depressed at all."

"Why would you be, love?" Yin asked.

"Lately I've been... Well, it doesn't matter. I hope Filip is on duty at MEX. I have to send him a message."

With Governor's help, she collected all Malcolm's messages and forwarded them with a report of the walkabout hijacking.

***

When Emma hopped through the airlock at Kamp, Melina tackled her with a hug. "I thought you were dead."

Emma rubbed her back and rocked gently side to side. Over Melina's shoulder, Liz sidled up to join the hug, followed by Yang and Sanni.

"It's Mars, isn't it?" Melina stepped back with tears running down her cheeks. "Mars wants us to leave."

"No." Emma shook her head. "Mars isn't the enemy, and our technology's not at fault. The walkabouts were sabotaged, just like Jumper Two."

"Quit blocking the door." Ruby's gruff words moved Emma towards the ladder.

"I could use a cup of tea," Emma said. "Let's open a comm link to Claude and Daan and I'll explain."

By the time they had Rover Two linked in, an MEX transmission arrived. They'd found the program that crashed Luis's jumpship in one of Malcolm's working folders, not even

213

encrypted. No one ever searched in a controller's offline files for the jumpship timer.

"I'm so sorry." Filip Krast sent a full audio-visual. "I've sent my resignation to the management board. If I'd searched more thoroughly... If I'd asked for follow-up psych exams..."

He hung his head. "Emma, the walkabout sabotage seems to have been aimed specifically at you. I've transmitted the programs as inactive text, so you can see for yourselves."

The modification to the GPS satellite was more complex, with false positioning overwriting the walkabouts' beacons, but had the same timer.

Ruby pointed to the display. "Look, there's a timer start but no stop. The suits would have walked forever. He was trying to kill you. I wish I had the bastard here. He was trying to kill us all."

MEX also found an incomplete program to shut down the orbiting power station.

Emma watched the list of file names scroll down. "Oh, shit."

"What?" Liz looked at the screen in alarm. "I'm not a programmer. What?"

"This file name is related to the S-4 transport ship," Emma said.

MEX confirmed her inference. With only a few weeks before S-4 entered Mars orbit, they'd have to search the entire orbital activity sequence for hidden commands.

"Murder and attempted murder." Emma was stunned. "I've got to send Filip a message - say I don't blame him."

"Well, I do!" Ruby's eyes flashed. "He should never have stopped looking for the timer that killed Luis. And James."

Emma bit her lip. How long had the signs been there, in Malcolm's messages? Why hadn't she forwarded them to Filip right away?

"There was no way you could have known about this." Liz seemed to be reading her thoughts. "Malcolm fooled the psych experts at Colony Mars. This is his crime and no one else's."

"But..." Melina was in tears again. "Why?"

Liz shook her head. "I doubt there's any answer that makes sense."

***

"This corks it for me." Ruby paced, circling the habitat, weaving among everyone sitting on chairs and boxes. Melina snatched the cat out of her path and hugged him tight. "I shut down all the feeds to MEX and suspended their access to Governor. I don't see how we can trust them for anything."

"But MEX found Malcolm's programs," Emma said. "They're helping us."

Ruby paused. "I say, every upload could be dodgy. We should terminate MEX's access to Governor once and for all."

"We can't do that," Yin said. "There must be fifty guys controlling the satellite systems alone."

"Operating around the clock," Yang said. "Not to mention analysts sifting through all Governor's telemetry. There's no way we can do their jobs."

Ruby's eyes flashed. "At the very least, we need to run full simulations on every transmission."

"Look how long it took you to find the jumpship timer, and that was just a few uploads."

"Governor could do it," Emma said. "The AI can run simulations at the speed of light if we create the right instructions."

"That still allows uploads to the AI." Ruby resumed pacing.

"How about if we do it at Phobos Base?" Emma asked. "Governor has redundant servers there. I can compartmentalize a directory to receive uploads from MEX and run the simulations. That would protect the servers in Kamp."

"None of us are sapience programmers," Yin said.

"We don't need to be". Emma turned to Ruby, eager to convince her. "Governor's already up and running. It has a mind in its own way. It's a settler, like us, and its priority is Kamp Kans. I've worked on smaller systems, like the one in the walkabouts. Those systems melded with Governor when we activated them, and I know how they're baselined. Human survival is a built-in priority."

Ruby stopped pacing, fists on hips. "That human survival thing didn't work very well in the walkabouts, did it? Or Luis's jumper."

"They got overwritten, bypassed somehow. That won't happen if Phobos Base runs your simulations. My father's company could make sure. He could send us custom programs to run from this end and no one at MEX ever has to see a copy."

"And how are we going to pay for that without going through MEX?"

Emma hated to admit it, but she wasn't sure how her father would react to an IOU. From Mars.

"I'll send a message to Miss Lambert."

"Who?" Ruby dropped her fists from her hips.

"Mademoiselle Lambert?" Claude asked over the rover's comm link.

"That crazy old bat who finances this thing?" Ruby swept an arm overhead.

"Yes. Mars is her dream. She'll protect it."

"But it still depends on the AI. How do we know Governor is loyal to us?"

"Governor, we're talking about you. Do you know that?"

"Yes, Emma. I am following the conversation."

"Don't you have anything to say about a fundamental change to your programming? About compartmentalizing your servers on Phobos?"

"No."

Ruby tossed her hands up.

The cat had been sitting in Melina's lap, snapping his head from side to side as they argued. Now in the lull, he jumped to the floor and pawed at a galley cabinet, crying his "feed me" meow.

"Melina, a settler requests your assistance," Governor said.

Emma snatched up the cat and held him out to Ruby. The cat hung in her hands, looking puzzled. "Governor thinks the cat's a settler. It bonded with a cat. Isn't that proof enough?"

She dropped the cat, plugged in her pad, and opened the MEX-to-Governor usage charts. They showed zero interaction since Ruby suspended the link.

"Governor, are you in contact with the settlers?"

"Yes, Emma. I have contact with all current settler transponders."

"Are you linked to MEX? On any level?"

"No Emma. I have suspended contact with MEX as Ruby directed."

"Are you missing any hierarchal command links?"

"No, Emma. I am not."

Emma returned their blank stares with a look of triumph.

"See? Governor doesn't care about MEX. It's on our side."

"How do we know there's not a back door?" Ruby jabbed her fists back into her sides.

"Now you're being paranoid."

Ruby's chin jutted out. "I may be paranoid. But Luis and James are dead."

"I'll ask my father to scan for back doors, too."

***

There were so many threads to follow.

Emma sent Filip her best wishes when his resignation was announced. She deleted all Malcolm's messages and didn't ask what happened to him. There were apparently a host of jurisdictional issues that she didn't have the patience to follow. As long as he couldn't hurt her, he was Earth's problem, and she didn't care how the Earth Scan reacted, either. Mars was her home now, and the settlers could trust each other at last.

Yin and Yang dragged the inert walkabouts into the docking module, and Emma spent her spare time refurbishing them.

Ruby studied the S-4 manifest to see if the cargo knarr carried enough servers to let Governor swallow the whole MEX satellite database. She was determined to break control ties with Earth.

As soon as Rover Two docked, Claude happily added Emma's lava tube rocks to his own collection and nothing could pry him loose from them. He spread rocks across tables in the Plaza, sneezing frequently as the irritating smell lingered, and dragged over portable lighting along with his optical microscope. Emma visited his makeshift workbench several times, absorbing his explanations of competing lithology theories and how the rocks would parse out the truth.

"He's like you right now," she told Liz. "Contented, doing what he came here to do."

MEX examined everything sent to Governor since Malcolm had joined the controller staff. Ruby monitored their work and gave them access to strip out programs Malcolm had planted in the GPS system. She locked them out again when they finished, and no one argued.

With the transport approaching Mars, the S-4 crew grew frantic for assurances they were safe. MEX went through the ship's AI line by line, and Ruby accepted text-only reports on their progress.

Liz was distracted by medical worries. Melina and Sanni could hardly function, but all she had to help them was Governor's psych program. She traded messages with Noah, the psychologist aboard S-4, in the hope he'd develop some treatment options. The text-only comms Ruby allowed hampered their discussions.

Liz quizzed Emma repeatedly about how going walkabout affected her. Emma confided her crying jag before Malcolm's hijacking, but said she felt unexpectedly optimistic holed-up in the lava tube. She'd been scared, but confident - her mind was clear, she could think, she could accomplish things. Exploring the tube was exhilarating and she wanted to go back.

"Noah suggested we administer adrenalin-mimics," Liz said. "The bioreactors S-4 is bringing could manufacture the drug, and I agree excitement perks us up, but long-term..." She shook her head. "We can't build a colony that way."

Emma never heard back from Mlle Lambert, but her father responded as quickly as the transmission lag allowed, saying 'anything for my girl.' He started a team designing manual overrides for the robots that Emma could build from Kamp's spare parts and sent her programming upgrades for Governor faster than she thought possible.

Emma used Governor's new capabilities to confirm Malcolm's code was gone from the GPS system and found no other intrusions. She set the AI to receive every upload from Earth at Phobos, even messages in plain text, and run the new scans before enabling access at Kamp.

Over supper one evening, Ruby announced she'd restored full communications.

"Wonderful," Liz said. "I've missed my family's videos."

Emma hadn't thought much about the messages everyone else must be missing from their families. She'd been okay with text versions from various acquaintances and even from her mother, and she'd saved her father's *'anything for my girl'* text - texts were normal from him.

***

MEX updates weren't the only file-types that returned to Kamp in the following week. Emma discussed the reopened exchange with Liz when they had a few moments together. "It's nice to access whatever we want from the Earth net again. Dad must have put every programmer he had to create the Phobos front-end so quickly."

Liz frowned. "But we're not taking advantage of the link. No one's watching their usual entertainments. Even Claude - he used to post to his lithology site all the time. Now he just hunkers over his rocks."

Each night in her bunk, Emma tried to rekindle the excitement she'd felt exploring the lava tube. Each night, the thrill receded farther away, and during the days, her headaches returned. Shared meals grew quieter until only Yin and Yang provided happy chatter. Even the Earth scan ball dimmed.

The settlers dragged themselves through their days again, but Emma didn't let the bleak mood stop her from building manual overrides. She worked in the Plaza close to Claude, though his impromptu lessons in lithology trailed off and stopped.

I know I can get these done, she thought. I've got grit.

Chapter Thirty-four: Hindsight

EMMA AND LIZ sat in the north habitat staring at spinach salad, poached fish, and a bowl of lukewarm beets. It was past supper time, but everyone was, once again, late. Sanni wandered in with a vacant look in her eyes. She dropped the cat on the table. He splayed out his legs and rested his chin to the tabletop.

"Hi Sanni. Has the cat been cheering you up?" Liz asked.

Sanni shrugged. "Melina's been in her bunk all afternoon. The other guys are coming, but they said not to wait on them for supper. I think I'll sleep, too."

Liz watched Sanni step into her bunk and close the flap.

"How's she and Melina doing?" Emma asked.

"Not good," Liz said.

Emma spooned out some beets. "Maybe Melina's right, maybe we don't belong on Mars. I loved robotics on Earth. I'm installing overrides in the rovers now, and that should feel great. But I'm..." She paused, reaching for the right word. "I don't know. I feel vague, disconnected."

"The colony will fail if we can't solve this psych problem," Liz had sudden, fierce tears in her eyes. "There's no joy. We can't live like this."

They heard the airlock in the docking module unlatch. Yin and Yang stepped in. Yin stopped at the table and slipped a finger under the cat's chin. "What's this little guy got to be tired about?"

"He's been with Melina and Sanni all sol," Liz said. "Just sensitive to their mood, I guess."

Yin snorted. "I love the furry git, don't get me wrong. But this cat's nothing but a mass of reflexes."

"Hasn't a sensitive bone in his body," Yang said as he brewed tea. "No way he cares about anyone's mood."

Liz looked up sharply. "That's true. He's never shown any sign of illness. Never any reduced activity. Not until now."

"Then what's wrong with him?" Emma stroked the cat's back.

"The cat's not the only settler who's still normal." Liz gazed at the two Brits. "You two work eighteen hours a sol. How come you guys are never tired?"

"We get tired," Yang said.

"It's a happy kind of tired," Yin said, handing Yang a couple cups.

"That, too," Liz said. "How come you're always happy?"

"We're doing exactly what we want to do."

"Colony Mars gave us the best erector set ever to play with. We're fine."

"I feel fine, too." Liz said it quietly, almost to herself. "Or more accurately, I feel normal."

She turned to Emma. "When's the last time you were happy?"

"It sounds strange, but... on walkabout," Emma said. "Even when Malcolm tried to kill me. After the first sol, I felt like myself again."

"It's following your passion that makes the difference," Yin said. "Even Ruby lightens up when she does a bit of flying."

Liz grabbed her pad and started tapping. Emma passed supper to Yin and Yang and they ate quietly.

Liz dropped her pad in annoyance. "It doesn't make sense. I entered all our symptoms into Governor, everybody's, as if we were one patient. Fatigue, confusion, depression, paranoia, hallucinations. I sent the file to MEX, to their medical AI, too, but it's going to say the same thing - I know it."

"And that was...?"

"The only diagnosis that fits all the symptoms is hypoxia." Liz looked around the table at three puzzled expressions. "Chronic low oxygen levels in the blood. But that doesn't make sense. Yin and Yang are fine."

"Yin and Yang spend more time at Maintenance than in the nederzetting," Emma said. "It has its own life support system. So do the rovers and the walkabouts, for that matter."

"So do the habitats," Liz countered.

"We equalize the atmosphere throughout the nederzetting. I could bring back the gauges for the upper level. You'll see - the habitat readings match the Spine."

Liz's eyes widened. She picked up her pad.

"Still doesn't make sense. The nederzetting atmosphere meets minimum standards." Emma took the pad from her and studied the tables.

"Barely! The pressure and oxygen are both at the bottom of acceptable." She slid along the time scale. "Levels go up a bit, then drop again... It does that a few times and never gets near Earth-standard."

Yang reached for the pad. "The bots transfer nitrogen and oxygen to the nederzetting as we harvest the gases. Yes, these increases match up."

"We open a new bay whenever Governor's calculations say there's enough air built up to support the added volume," Yin said.

"Here are the readings in Maintenance." Yang handed the pad back to Liz.

"Why is the atmosphere Earth standard there?"

"We top off Maintenance directly from the air harvesting system," Yin said.

"You recharge the surface suit packs and the rovers and jumpship at Maintenance, too, don't you?" Emma said.

Yang nodded. "That chart you're looking at shows levels at the Spine's main air return," he said. "That's the only place we have a sensor in the bays and the air always meets the minimum."

"Of course, pressure should be higher in the greenhouse," Yin added. "It's much warmer and you keep it closed off from the Spine. We haul in CO_2 for the plants and you have to run an airlock pump to get a door open, don't you? That means the pressure is higher."

"Yes," Liz said slowly. "And oxygen. I spend all my time in the garden and plants generate oxygen."

Emma stroked the side of her face, where her burns had fully healed. Yes, the greenhouse had a different oxygen concentration than the rest of the nederzetting.

"But, Liz, these measurements are from the Spine's recirculation system," Emma said. "You said 'oxygen in the blood.' Shouldn't you be measuring our blood levels?"

"Yes, I should. But I don't have the necessary medical equipment."

The four of them stared at each other in silence.

"Bloody hell. Have we caused all this trouble?" Yin said. "Are we opening bays so fast the air's too thin?"

"I don't know that," Liz said. "The composition meets our minimum spec..."

"It's easy enough to find out," Emma said. "We can use the habitat airlock to maintain a higher pressure in here, and everyone wear surface suits in the rest of the nederzetting."

Liz was already tapping at her pad. "We'll need everyone's cooperation. I'm posting the recommendation for a vote."

Emma fumbled her pad from a pocket and plugged it in. "I'm voting yes."

Yin and Yang quickly did the same. They paused again, watching Liz's post.

Daan voted yes.

"Majority," Yin said. He and Yang jumped up. "We're going back out to the robot squad. Top priority will be harvesting nitrogen and argon from now on - and electrolyzing oxygen."

The docking airlock had barely sealed behind them when Daan stepped in from the Spine. He closed the door deliberately and gave it an extra tug.

"I should have recognized the problem," he said. "I've done high altitude climbing and I know the symptoms. I once felt someone was following me in the Annapurna Range. Kept turning around and finding no one there." He collapsed into a chair. "Just like Melina's tulpa."

"The ocularity of hindsight," Emma said.

"We don't know for sure yet," Liz said. But she couldn't hide her excitement.

"I'm going to get a handful of mealworms for the cat," Emma said. "And mix up some powdered milk."

***

Yin and Yang pumped the maintenance control room's air into tanks and the beetle-bots hauled them to the north habitat, aiming to reach Earth's sea level conditions there as soon as possible.

Claude and Emma suited up to tend to life support chores in the Spine. Daan, Melina, and Sanni showed the worst symptoms, so Liz kept them in the habitat and took notes on their reactions. She recorded how long they spent in their bunks, asked them questions to gauge their mental state, and recorded what they ate and drank. In between she tracked the lively debate of her hypoxia hypothesis by Colony Mars experts.

"The experts on Earth think I'm nuts," Liz said at supper after the first full sol. "The minimums were thoroughly researched. They still think it's a psychological issue. They want to send us virtual reality headsets to simulate open earthly landscapes."

"Idiots," Ruby said.

Liz looked unsure. "But how could they be so wrong about something as basic as breathing air?"

Emma waved her fork. "Did they duplicate our diet, our living conditions? Run their tests in Mars gravity? Over time?"

"Noah's backing me up," Liz said. "He thinks hypoxia makes sense, that there could be an impact from low gravity on our circulatory systems."

"He's our new psychologist?" Ruby asked. "I like him already."

"The improved air is already working," Claude said. "My headache's gone."

"That could be because of your expectations," Liz said. "I'll have Governor analyze our comms to find out if our speech patterns show improvement."

"You can figure that out. I want to talk about a trip to Emma's lava tube," Claude said.

"I'd love to go back," Emma said.

"A trip up Olympus Mons would be better," Daan said. "That would create excitement on Earth, too."

"Prospecting is more useful right now," Emma said.

"Claude never got a chance to finish his work on the Peacock's southern flank, either. Maybe that should take priority."

"I thought you'd like the romance of climbing a mountain."

Ruby shook her head sharply. "Don't even talk about exploration until S-4 is safely on the ground."

"But storm season's approaching."

"Okay, so let's plan the first expedition for next spring."

It was a happy argument, since they were discussing exploration.

***

At the end of the week, Yang announced over breakfast that the north habitat hit Earth-sea-level conditions.

"I slept straight through last night," Sanni said, smiling.

Melina stepped out of her bunk with a puzzled expression. "What's going on? I've had the strangest dreams."

"Nice strange dreams?" Sanni asked, wrinkling her nose playfully.

"I can't remember. Hey, what smells so good?"

"I'm fixing stuffed squash for breakfast," Liz said. "Want some?"

"Yes, please. I'm starving. But I'm gonna shower first. I feel yucky." She bounced to the ladder, but paused to look around the module.

"Remember the clutter on Earth? So many empty events and meaningless things. It was suffocating. Life on Mars is minimalist, stripped to essentials. It's the right choice. How did I forget that? I'm lighter and freer than I was on Earth."

She heaved a contented sigh and climbed.

Yin thumped Liz's shoulder. "You solved it. Now we've got a fighting chance."

"We need to rethink our construction plans," Yang said. "No matter what we've been saying, Liz is right about radiation exposure. Yin and I need to worry more about mitigating risks on the surface, and now that atmosphere manufacturing will constrain construction, we have the time."

Yin's smile turned serious. "Ingra would understand. She'd be pleased."

Liz slumped in her chair.

Emma gave her arm a squeeze. "Hey, what's wrong?"

"Ingra," Liz said. "She was foggy from the thin air. She never had a chance to figure out what was happening to her. Even if she'd asked about the air, Colony Mars would have told her the pressures were fine."

Ruby nodded. "What you think you know that ain't so. That's what gets you into trouble."

Chapter Thirty-Five: Impact

THE ARGUMENT over which spring-time expedition to mount was still underway when MEX sent a message unlike any Kamp had received before.

"We have some bad news, guys," the new lead controller said. "It's best if you view the attached presentation. We're sending it to Kamp Kans and Settler Four's transport simultaneously. Then we can talk."

Emma tapped her pad. "I can't see the diagram very well on this little screen. What's it supposed to be?"

"Put it on the big screen." Ruby stood by the screen and cocked her head. "Well, that's a diagram of the solar system."

Emma could see planets orbiting in the ecliptic plane. Her eye jumped to Mars, circling the Sun with its Greek symbol trailing closely behind. A bright dot entered from above, tagged with a table of numbers too small to read. Its path hung on the diagram as a sparkling line. The dot angled into Mars and vanished. The animation paused for a moment, then reset and the sequence ran again.

"What the hell?" Emma muttered.

"That's an asteroid," Ruby said. "Show the time frame, Governor." An elapsed-time counter popped up in the lower left.

Emma watched the animation repeat.

"Colony Mars posted this to a fan site before we saw it, the ghouls," Ruby said as she looked at her own pad. "Governor, project the Earth Scan sphere." No one had looked at the Earth Scan in ages. When the image popped up near the ceiling it was a briskly spinning white sphere. "Turn the screen's audio on."

"...from the Near Earth Object tracking system. We have detected an asteroid coming from above the solar system's

228

ecliptic plane. The likelihood of a collision with Earth is zero. Normally there would be no public interest in such an object. This asteroid, however, will impact the planet Mars on April twenty seventh of this year. Our current projections indicate it will impact in the Noachis quadrangle of the planet's southern hemisphere with a kinetic energy of approximately one hundred million tons. This estimate will be revised as more data become available. The late detection of this asteroid demonstrates the need for increased funding to monitor outside the plane of the solar system..."

"Governor, pause. Claude, do you understand the kinetic energy number?" Emma asked.

He watched the screen wide-eyed. "If this asteroid hit Earth, it'd wipe out half a continent."

"Oh my god. Are we gonna die?"

"No, no, we're safe. Noachis is deep in the southern hemisphere on the other side of the planet. Mars has no forests to burn, no oceans to generate tsunamis, no tectonics. And no exposed life on the surface. But it'll kick up one hell of a dust cloud. Probably cover the entire planet for months."

He rubbed his chin thoughtfully. "Here's another expedition for next spring. I must get a piece of that asteroid to compare to the meteorite that hit in our backyard. They may have a common source."

"Forget about the rocks for a minute," Ruby said. "Will it kick up enough dust to make flying the jumper risky?"

Claude nodded. "Worse than any haboob we've ever seen."

"You'd think MEX would translate dates for us." Ruby always found something about MEX that annoyed her. "Governor, when is April twenty seven?"

"That Earth date corresponds to Sol four sixty-six."

"Governor, compare Settler Four's entry into orbit to the impact date."

"Settler Four will enter orbit in seven sols, fifty one hours and eleven minutes prior to impact."

"What?" Emma looked more closely at the animation. "Holy shit. Could it hit them?"

"I doubt it. That would be exceedingly bad luck," Claude said.

"This is already exceedingly bad luck."

"Fifty one hours should be enough time to land all the modules." Ruby said. "No problem."

"It gives me problems," Claude said. "When the walkabout went crazy, we left my drill rig out there, on Peacock's southern flank. And I still want to see Emma's lava tube. Those brownish rocks she brought back, they're metallic meteorite fragments. Ancient fragments."

"So what?" Ruby asked.

"Mars lacks Earth's geological processes, so we have lots of old craters and there should be meteorites lying around. But this is our first find - our first source of metal. And a global dust storm could bury everything."

"We've got GPS coordinates."

"Thanks to Malcolm's sabotage, we don't. Even the jumper's rescue trip was screwed up."

"There's a problem closer to home," Yang said. "A global haboob will shut down our atmosphere harvesting for a long time."

"We should pump as much air into the nederzetting as possible while we can," Yin said.

"If we're going to be stuck inside, I don't want to need a surface suit whenever I leave this module."

"Hey Kamp." They'd left the MEX link open and the Settler Four crew was monitoring.

Emma recognized Noah's voice. "We want to land, like Ruby says, not be marooned in orbit for god-knows how long. We enter orbit in less than a week."

"Ruby, you could refuel on Phobos," Yin said. "The bots there have full tanks and we'll be able to use the oxygen down here for the nederzetting."

Emma had only thought of Phobos Base for its servers that linked to Governor, but Yin and Yang kept track of the robotic construction squad there. Luis had landed the habitat module from Settler Three on Phobos before the crash. It was pressurized and ready for emergencies. The regolith on the moon wasn't as rich in water as on Mars, but the bots had been faithfully filling tanks with hydrogen and oxygen as they stacked construction blocks around the habitat for shielding.

"Okay, that takes care of space operations," Claude said. "How about surface operations? How about my drill and the lava tube?"

"I installed manual overrides in the rovers," Emma said. "I haven't gotten to the walkabouts yet, but I'd like to take a walkabout, so I can follow my own tracks."

"No override, no walkabout," Ruby said. Emma frowned, but Ruby folded her arms across her chest and fixed her with a steady gaze.

"Emma, I think Ruby's right on this." Liz gave her arm a squeeze. Emma sighed.

"Well, okay. If I take a rover to the lava tube, I can't go the route I used in the walkabout. I'll have to swing out to avoid the valleys and approach the tube from the north." She scrolled through satellite images on her pad as she talked. "I think I can find it if I line up with that funny outcropping I saw. It's a two sol trip each way."

"If you mark the lava tube so we don't lose it, Daan and I will take the other rover to retrieve the drill," Claude said. "We'll be back with two sols to spare."

Emma had been about to suggest Claude ride with her, but Daan was already nodding enthusiastically.

"I want to go," Melina said. Emma was so used to Melina and Sanni being zonked out that the sound of her voice was a surprise.

Emma was so used to Melina being zonked out that the sound of her voice, eager and strong, was a surprise. She looked at Melina as if it were the first time. At the halo of black curls, the curved nose below glowing eyes. How she sat on the edge of her chair, one hand on a knee, ready for anything.

Sanni was striking too. Her cheekbones were wide, something like Ruby's but her eyes were gray and her skin pale. She squared her shoulders and spoke in a rush. "Me, too. I

231

haven't set foot outside the nederzetting since we got here. It's about time I did."

"There's no reason they can't go," Liz said.

Emma smiled. "Then both of you, come with me."

Ruby turned to Liz. "I'll be working outside with Yin and Yang. Will you be okay in here alone?"

"Not alone," Liz said. "I've got Governor. And the cat."

Emma beamed. This was more like what she'd expected to find on Mars, settlers working together and solving problems. She pulled up a rover checklist on her pad and scrolled through the preparations.

***

Emma set out the next morning with Melina and Sanni. She won the coin toss, a simulation by Governor, and claimed Rover Two because its controls allowed the AI to drive on their search for the lava tube.

The pale red sky and rippled dunes weren't very scenic, but to their right loomed Peacock Mons, a burnished hump in the dawn light. Since Emma didn't need to monitor the controls, Sanni and Melina sat in the front seats. They deserved a good look at their world.

The second sol in early evening, after zigzagging in a search pattern most of the afternoon, Rover Two stopped on the level spot swept clean by Jumper One's exhaust.

"Let's get out here," Emma said after confirming their link to Governor. "I think I see footprints."

They suited up and stepped onto the surface. While Melina and Sanni played around getting used to the feel of their suits, Emma looked northeast. Poet's Mons was out there, the northern-most volcano in the chain, as broad and tall as Peacock, but the peak was hundreds of kilometers away.

She turned towards the Sun, low in the western sky. "We better hurry. It's getting dark."

In the slanting sunlight, footprints stood out clearly as deep divots in the sand between slabs of rock. They carried a beacon,

232

already mounted on a fabricated post, to the cave. Yin had made a long stake from some of their precious metal scraps. They took turns driving the stake deep into the sand with a sledge hammer and slid the post over the top.

"Test the beacon, Governor," Emma said, still breathing hard.

"I am activating the beacon," Governor said. "It is functioning properly. I am returning it to sleep mode now."

Melina stared into the cave entrance when they finished.

"We can't come this far and not go inside," Sanni said. "How about we spend all sol tomorrow exploring? We'll still get back to Kamp with a sol to spare."

The next morning they returned with hand lights. Emma agreed to sit inside the entrance, shielded by the rock, and relay communications while Melina and Sanni explored.

"I know the tube to the left is easy walking..." She stopped as Melina immediately turned right and clambered over the rocks. Emma grinned. Melina was a different person than she'd known.

Emma set her suit comms to relay and streamed images and audio live to Earth. The imagers captured walls of glittering crystal and curtains of frozen lava hanging from the ceiling. Melina and Sanni never reach an end. The tube was still wide when they turned around, carrying more rock samples for Claude.

Back inside Rover Two they doffed their suits and opened the Settler Four channel. The transport ship entered orbit flawlessly and Emma sent a welcome message, but she mostly talked about the lava tube.

"I wonder if Yin and Yang could fabricate blocks to seal the cave," Melina said. "I bet it would hold pressure."

"What a great addition it would make to Kamp," Sanni said. "We could live inside the native rock. Claude could do his lithology bare-handed."

"He'd like that," Emma said. "Governor, for now, take us home." The rover retraced its route while they slept.

***

Emma had all Governor's audio feeds open as the rover crossed Tharsis Plain, hoping to find someone to chat with.

"Hey guys, we've got a problem." It was Claude's voice from Rover One.

Emma answered his call. "Where are you, Claude? What's up?"

"We're still at the southern drill site. I got the rover... well, we're stuck."

"Stuck?"

"Yeah, it's my fault. I drove along a channel rim and the edge gave way."

Liz cut in. "Are you and Daan okay?"

"Oh, yeah, we're fine." Daan spoke this time. "But..."

"Tell me what the problem is." Irritation replaced Emma's worry.

"We slid halfway into a gorge. The rover tipped over on its side. The airlock's buried in the sand. Not that it matters. I don't see how we could tip this thing up on its tracks even if we could get outside."

"Oh shit."

"Excellent choice of phrase," Claude said. "The sanitary system was dumped on its side, too."

"I'm here." Ruby joined the conversation. "I can fly out and lift the rover."

"Wouldn't that use up tanks of fuel?"

"Yeah. So what? You want to stay out there?"

"But you need to get into orbit..."

"Let us try to help," Emma said. "Governor, divert to Claude and Daan."

Governor slowed Rover Two's approach to the ridges before sunrise the next sol. The skies were clear and Emma could pick out the brighter constellations.

"Let's take a look," Emma said, grabbing her surface suit. "Someone should stay inside the rover, as a precaution."

"I'll stay," Sanni said.

234

Emma and Melina slid down the broken rim of the gorge. They circled Rover One, testing slope stability, and finally approached carefully. The rover was lying partly on its roof with its airlock jammed into the sand. Emma waved to Claude and Daan inside. They'd spent an uncomfortable night.

Sanni maneuvered Rover Two to a wide patch of bare rock and Emma pulled a wire cable from its tool box. She and Melina slid back down the slope and climbed up the exposed tracks, looking for a place to secure the hook. The rover tottered and shifted.

"What the hell." Claude's voice boomed in her helmet.

Emma leaped from the rover and it settled back into the sand, now completely on its roof.

There was a strangled yelp, then, "Aw, shit. Be more careful out there."

"Can we get them out and come back for the rover later?" Melina asked as she hopped over to Emma.

"Guys, still listening? There's good news. You can get out the airlock now."

A short time later, Daan dropped to the sand.

"I want to pull the drill off the rover bed," Claude said as he carefully lowered a couple bulging sacks of samples.

Emma laughed. "I like you, Claude. You've got grit."

With a little effort they dropped the drill drums, rolled them to Rover Two, and secured them to the rear bed.

After two cycles of the airlock, they were all inside.

"We're on our way," Emma said. "Governor, take us home fast."

Chapter Thirty-Six: Settler Four

The next morning, the rover still raced across the Tharsis dunes.

"Attention, Rover Two occupants," Governor said. "I recommend you open the feed from Settler Four's transport ship. I also have a video you may choose to view of Jumpship One lifting off while you slept, followed by Jumpship Two mirroring its trajectory."

"Open a split-screen, Governor. I want to see the inside of the transport ship," Melina said.

Ruby was already docked and inside the transport's habitat module. She and the edgy crew were loading gear as fast as they could. They had to remove a bunk from the habitat and bolt it to Jumper One's cabin floor to accommodate the fifth person, but they were anxious to land and no one wanted to wait for a second trip.

Governor switched to the jumpship's imagers, but they missed the chance to watch the ship disassemble in orbit. Abundantly cautious, MEX wanted the jumper well out of the way before they blew the frangible nuts to separate the modules.

Imagers captured a good view as Ruby topped up her fuel tanks at Phobos Base. Emma had never watched the robot squad there in motion. Half-sized beetle-bots dragged tanks on skids to the jumpship. The habitat from S-3, her home on the journey to Mars, sat buried under fabricated stone blocks, its airlock peeking out at jumpship level. Sensors showed it remained intact, but Ruby didn't dock.

A satellite picked up Jumpship One again and watched it disappear over the curve of the planet in a spiraling descent orbit.

"Governor, do you have an image of the transport ship right now?" Emma asked. "A satellite view? Animation?"

"I love watching disassemblies," Claude said, sitting on the arm of Emma's chair and hugging her shoulder.

The transport ship popped up on the screen, still intact. Jumpship Two, under remote control, hung nearby.

"Governor," Emma said. "Display a live feed."

"This is the live feed."

"The ship should be floating apart by now. What's the delay?"

"MEX sent the command on schedule. I have no further information at this time."

Minor glitches were common and the crew was safe. There was no reason to worry yet, but Emma chewed on her lower lip.

***

Governor slowed the rover along the east side of the nederzetting, approaching the north dock. As the rover maneuvered Emma could see the top of Ruby's jumpship docked on the far side of the module.

"There're here." Melina was on her feet before the rover finished docking. "The New Four."

Emma exited the rover last and looked up the ladder towards the docking module's jumpship level.

I bet Ruby's still in the ship's cabin, she thought.

Sure enough, Ruby sat in the pilot's seat, arms folded across her chest, glaring at her screen.

"You're going to use Jumper Two's telepresent controls to bring the habitat down?" Emma took the copilot's seat. "I want to see how well it works."

"Well, it's not gonna work at all like this. I'm waiting for MEX." Ruby hugged herself tighter and scowled.

Emma gazed out the jumpship windows at rover tracks crisscrossing the orange sand, avoiding Ruby's scathing eyes.

The MEX lead's voice filled the cabin. "Yeah, we have another disassembly fail. I read the detonators as fired, so the

237

frangible nuts have fractured. But the connecting struts failed to unclamp. No indication of tampering with the program. Our controllers think it's just one of those things. Shouldn't take long to correct. Why don't you take a break and we'll call when we know more."

"Nitwits," Ruby said under her breath. "In a few hours the asteroid hits, and I can't land the whole ship in one piece. Governor, let me know if you see anything change or if MEX calls, okay?"

"I will do that, Ruby."

"Come on, Emma. We might as well join the party."

In the habitat, the new settlers were sitting around the table and everyone was talking at once.

William leaned too far sideways and toppled. Sanni caught him and propped him back in his chair.

"Sorry, I'm fine. Just dizzy for a moment," he said.

"That's a normal reaction to gravity," Grace said. "But I want anyone who notices any strange sensations to let me know."

"Well..." Hannah looked around the habitat uncertainly. "This is funny. It smells like fish in here."

Laughter reverberated off the walls and Melina struggled to keep hold of the wide-eyed cat.

New people, new partners on Mars. Emma wiped tears from her face as she gazed at the New Four. Hannah, whose soft, round hands would care for the colony's future children. William, his face tinged gray right now, but with intense eyes promising dedication to the fertility clinic he'd establish. Noah looked the part of a psychologist, with a wide forehead and calm expression. Emma thought he'd be easy to talk to. And Grace, delicate and birdlike but with a commanding voice. She was confidently giving orders in her field of space medicine despite her own weakness from the journey. With their arrival, the settlement's dynamics were about to change.

It didn't matter if she'd be stuck inside for weeks on end. There were new people to talk to, synchronous conversations without ten or twenty minute gaps between sentences. There were also more heaters and lights in the S-4 knarr, appliances for the Plaza galley, medical equipment, Claude's instruments, and more seeds. The transport might be in orbit, but even so, her world was expanding.

Liz pulled Emma through the crowd. "Come meet the rest of the settlers." She climbed the ladder to the life support level. Emma felt a cool breeze on her face as she reached the top.

Liz stood next to a stainless steel cylinder like a big, shiny beer keg. Frost glistened on the top and wisps of fog rippled across the deck. The cylinder was cooled with liquid nitrogen.

"Meet two hundred new settlers." Liz's face glowed. This chamber was the test batch of frozen embryos. Unconsciously, Emma's fingers rubbed the contraceptive chip on her arm. Colony Mars' plans didn't call for implanting these embryos, not yet. The test would prove the cryochamber's viability system. Emma smiled faintly. "The purpose of life?"

"The purpose of life," Liz said.

***

An alert tone woke Emma hours before dawn. She groped for her pad, hoping to see that, after hours of trying, MEX had unclamped the S-4 modules, but it was only her wake-up tone. Earlier than usual because this morning, the asteroid would hit Mars.

I would have slept through the impact, she thought as she fumbled for her shoes. Glad I set an alarm after last night's party.

Emma wrapped a blanket around her shoulders and slid her privacy flap open.

Over the heads of the crowd, an animation of the approaching asteroid played on the screen. In one corner was a bright patch of fuzz - one of the satellites must have an imager aimed at it. Where was Ruby?

They were short a bunk since the transport ship was still in orbit. Liz had moved the New Four to bunks in the south habitat with Yin and Yang. That meant Ruby should be in the north habitat, somewhere.

Emma tottered to the docking module, climbed the ladder, and entered the jumpship cabin.

Ruby glanced at her with a short nod, then back to her screen and a satellite image of the southern hemisphere in full sunlight.

"No luck, huh?" Emma felt the co-pilot's seat form snuggly around her as she flopped down. "The transport's safe in orbit, isn't it?"

"For a while." Ruby switched to a view of the transport, its modules still firmly joined. "The orbit's already decaying. Jumper Two's a robot now. Maybe it can grapple hold and boost the orbit even if Governor loses comms. I should..."

Robot. An idea jolted Emma. "How far is Jumper Two from Phobos Base right now?"

"Other side of the planet. Why?"

"How about the power station?" Emma felt her pulse quicken.

"S-4's approaching the power station." Ruby looked at her quizzically.

"The power station has onboard maintenance bots. They have tools - cutters and space torches."

Ruby's eyes widened. "I see what you mean." She quickly related the plan to Governor, asking for a maintenance bot to be ready.

Emma plugged in her pad and opened the feed from Jumper Two's forward imager. The closest bot was waiting. It was a small unit, so its weight wouldn't disrupt the power station's pinpoint aiming of microwaves as it crawled over the satellite. Slow and specialized, it had a limited operations range. It added collector panels, repaired micrometeor impacts - things like that.

"Did Governor tell it to grab the right tools..."

Too late. The bot stretched two of its limbs out to Jumper Two. Stars filled the imager's view as the jumper swung in an arc, towing the bot back to the transport in its grapplers.

Emma checked the space feed. "Here comes the asteroid. Boom." A smudge of orange dust bloomed and boiled outwards.

Emma craned her neck to look at Ruby's screen.

"Watch the storm, Emma, not me. Keep me posted."

Settler Four's transport filled the jumper's view and the little bot appeared, held in a grappler tip against one of the clamps.

"Is there a dust cloud from the impact?" Ruby focused on her screen.

"It's spreading fast. The forecast says..."

"On second thought, don't tell me." Ruby chewed her lip and reached for the transport with another of the jumper's grapplers. She hit too hard and the jumper rebounded instead.

"Let Governor handle it," Emma said sharply. "The AI gets feedback from both ships."

Ruby rapped her controls, let go, and sat back with a frustrated huff.

They watched as the jumpship clutched the transport with one grappler and swung the bot to the closest clamp. The image wobbled from shifting momentum.

Claude poked his head into the cabin. It sounded like the rest of the settlers clustered behind him.

"Governor will explain," Emma said tersely and turned back to Ruby. "Can't stop now."

The jumper moved the bot from clamp to clamp, cutting the modules loose.

"Which one should I bring down? Which module first?" Ruby asked.

"The knarr," Emma said immediately. "Governor, can that little bot survive a descent?"

"I do not have an analysis for that event. Stand by."

"Never mind. Cancel analysis. It's coming down." Emma leaned over to Ruby's screen and watched the little bot wrap all its limbs around the jumper's frame.

"Okay Governor. Bring the knarr down. Descent authorized." Ruby rapped Emma's shoulder. "Get out. I'm going up for the habitat."

"There's no time. Governor, how long before the cloud reaches Kamp?"

Ruby stared icily at a chart of cloud density versus time that Governor sent to her screen, the background shaded red well before she could get back to Kamp. "Well, damn."

"Let's concentrate on landing the knarr." Emma hopped out the open airlock still wrapped in her blanket. Yin and Yang waited for her. They had immediately understood the plan and summoned a loader and beetle-bot to the nederzetting.

A landing pad for the knarr had been ready for months at the end of the medical bay. Jumper Two set the module down, hovering on short bursts of thruster fire.

The bots nudged the knarr to align its airlock against the prepared end of the bay, and wriggled it to seat the seal.

Cheers echoed around her. Emma could hear Claude bemoaning lost data from the impact - he had no seismometers.

"Send the jumper to Maintenance," Yang called to Ruby. "There's still a beetle-bot there to refuel it."

Emma slipped back into the copilot seat to watch the space weather feed. The cloud, now a murky brown, hit the edge of sunrise on the Tharsis Plain. In just a minute...

"Too late." Ruby sat back into the pilot's seat as red lights began flashing. "The dust's too thick."

"We'd never have gotten the knarr down without Governor," Emma said quietly.

"Yeah, yeah. Don't rub it in." But Ruby's face glowed as she secured her controls.

"How's the power station's bot, Governor?"

"Its functions are nominal, but I will run a full diagnostic."

"Whatever protocol demands, Governor," Ruby said with a twisted smile.

"Did your construction bots make it back to Maintenance?" Emma asked Yang, who had slipped into the seat behind Ruby.

"No, only about halfway."

"Sorry. I hope they'll be alright."

"Oh, it'll take weeks to clean them thoroughly."

Emma turned to find Yin behind her, grinning.

"Just another sol on Mars," he said. "It all pays the same. Damn, I hate dust."

***

"Shouldn't the cloud get thinner as it spreads out?" Emma asked, watching a mosaic image of the entire planet on the habitat's main screen.

Claude shook his head.

"The cloud's getting thicker. It's absorbing sunlight and heating up. That whips up the wind and lofts more dust. More dust picks up more heat and generates more wind." He pointed to the latest thermal data in the lower right of the screen, a false color image of the planet turning from green to yellow to red.

"Those are rising temperatures at the top of the cloud. But the dust is so thick, surface temperature here at the nederzetting is falling. This cloud's dense enough to interfere with communications, too."

"Damn," Emma said, moving to the wall to plug in her pad. "I better warn my mother I'll be out of touch for a while."

By lunchtime, Governor's reception from MEX was breaking up. Soon it couldn't receive from the satellites orbiting overhead, either. That had never happened before.

"No point sitting here staring at a blank screen," Yin said. "I want to unload the knarr."

"I say, let's pull radiant heaters out first for the Plaza," Yang said.

"And move our kitchen to the Plaza. It's too crowded in here." Yin nodded in agreement.

"The knarr was shipped pressurized. We can cut into it now."

They all grabbed chisels and broke through to the knarr's airlock in a sol.

243

Emma stood at the open door and shivered. She'd hoped for something, maybe the smell of Earth. But only coldness tumbled out from a stack of boxes.

"Don't touch anything," Yin said. "Remember this module recently came down from space."

"Hand protection, everyone." Yang walked down the aisle tossing out pairs of gloves with long gauntlets.

The bay's bench tops were empty, so they spread cargo out, digging for what they wanted. The New Four sat on some boxes and watched. They helped occasionally, but mostly sat ashen faced in the unfamiliar gravity with incongruously cheerful grins.

"Governor, are you recording?" Emma asked when they paused for a break.

"Yes, Emma."

"I guess there's no harm sending the raw files to MEX," Ruby said. "Once the dust clears enough for comms, that is."

Chapter Thirty-Seven: English Breakfast

UNLOADING THE KNARR was a holiday. While they worked, the New Four shared the latest gossip from Colony Mars headquarters.

The bays grew brighter and warmer as they installed lights and heaters. Plaza's pond was warm enough for Liz to transfer duck weed and water bugs, preparing it for fish. She planted alfalfa in the new garden bays and had to chase the cat out more than once as he happily dug in the newly turned sand, scattering seeds.

Claude pulled up the knarr packing diagram and plotted a path to his spectrometer. It was a bench top model, its various sources and detectors enclosed in a gray box with blue panels here and there. Emma followed Claude through the short aisle he'd opened among the boxes to admire the instrument.

"That's too bulky for one person to carry. Here, let me slip past you." Emma squeezed by and a tingle jolted through her as she pushed against Claude's warm body. Her face flushed and he gave her a loopy grin.

She cleared her throat. "I think I can get on the other side... okay, lift. Where are we going with this thing?"

"Into the Plaza. There's too much going on in Medical."

They rolled a table close to Medical's door - good thing they're round, Emma thought - and set up Claude's spectrometer.

Yin and Yang were as happy installing the Plaza kitchen as they had been building bays. Settler Four's knarr included a cook top and oven with an assortment of pots and pans. They moved the habitat galleys to the kitchen and Yin announced their next breakfast would be served in the Plaza.

Emma and Liz carried all the beverage mixes to Plaza's cabinets. While Emma stirred coffee powder into a pot of hot water, Liz mixed orange flavored protein powder for the New Four. She'd insisted they all sit down and, newly returned to gravity, they didn't argue.

"Just what the doctor ordered." Liz set out cups.

"You probably know more about adjusting to Mars gravity than I do," Grace said, sipping her drink. She was modest about her specialty in space medicine. "There's nothing like firsthand experience."

Hannah, their pediatrician, tilted her head side to side. "I'm not dizzy anymore. I guess Mars gravity agrees with me."

"Have you tried the neurovestibular platform yet?" Grace asked. "I want to record how well you're sensing your body's positional orientation. And, I hate to start nagging, but I saw the flexion machines lying on the other side of the Plaza. I'd like to see those reinstalled, and get everyone back on an exercise schedule."

"That's for you space weaklings," Ruby said as she poured the bitter coffee.

"And for me, too," Daan said. "I don't know how much muscle and bone I'll need to climb Olympus."

"Mars medicine will be different from Earth medicine and from space medicine," Grace said, nodding. "Our children will discover what it means to be Martian."

"To be Homo rufus," Liz said.

Grace tilted her head, quizzically.

"One definition of a species is a group that's reproductively isolated. That's us on Mars - us and the embryos."

"Isolation means independence. That's a good thing." Ruby's chin jutted out.

Noah set his elbows on the table, steadying his arms as he sniffed at the protein drink. "No one knows how quickly we'll become independent or how Mars will change us. We're already a new kind of human community. I'll observe, like an anthropologist, really."

"I like Liz's idea." William said quietly. "On Earth I specialized in high risk obstetrics, so I've lost my share of babies."

Liz gave his shoulder a squeeze. From his face, he still mourned those losses.

He smiled up at Liz, laying a hand over hers. "Colony Mars screened every embryo for genetic strength. I'm going to spend the rest of my life with healthy, normal Homo rufus. But babies have to wait. I'll only be doing viability tests. Transplants will have to wait for Settler Five's med lab. There's always the old fashioned method, of course."

"I can wait another jaar," Liz said.

"And risk losing out on first-mother-on-Mars honors?" Melina grinned impishly. Sanni gave her shoulder a playful tap and Daan began studying this cup. "We've got a pediatric doctor now."

Emma's gaze wandered. A flash of caramel color caught her eye.

The cat pawed at banana leaves rustled by the ventilation system. Liz and Emma had transplanted several trees to large pots inside the Plaza. Melina snatched up the cat and distracted him with a handful of toasted mealworms.

"That cat is getting fat," Liz said. "How often do you feed him worms?"

"Everyone feeds him worms." Melina grinned and scattered a couple lunar cat toys from her pocket. The cat dashed off. "Something smells good."

"This still isn't a proper fry up," Yin said when he set pans on the serving bar.

"No eggs, no bacon," Yang said sadly. "Fried mealworms aren't the same at all."

"The baked fish is quite nice, though."

"Beans and roasted tomatoes too."

"And..." Yin tilted a pan towards Emma. "Hash brown potatoes for the American."

"You doctors better get the bioreactors set up," Ruby said, eagerly filling a plate. "We clearly need more cooking oil, and fast."

"Allow me..." Claude snatched up a plate, scooped out potatoes, and set it before Emma with a flourish. She smiled at him and speared an oily brown chuck.

***

For a few weeks they didn't worry about the storm raging around them, aside from Yang's occasional moan that digging out would be a miserable chore. But communications remained down.

"What will MEX do if they don't hear from us?" Emma asked over another of Yin and Yang's English breakfasts. "Could they postpone the next mission?"

"Not for now, I expect," Noah said. He had spent his last Earthside tour assigned to the steering committee at Colony Mars and thought he could guess their reaction. "Settler Five will only hit a potential launch-hold when it's time to transfer the settlers and live cargo to the ship."

"Even this storm can't last forever," Yang said. "The worst that can happen is a delay till the next launch window."

In her head, Emma was calculating her age in Earth years, figuring when she would be outside Colony Mars' optimum for childbearing.

Settler Five was the Kinderen Mission. In addition to the usual mundane supplies, they would bring the full cryo-bank of embryos, a major part of Colony Mars' master plan. The embryos were a diverse sampling of human genetics, donated by people whose ancestors came from all over Earth, and the four S-5 settlers were chosen for their desire to raise children on Mars. Once they arrived, Kamp Kans could theoretically resurrect humanity without further help from Earth.

"They won't launch a transport ship unless they know we're alive and well out here," Ruby said.

"They also need positive results from my viability tests," William said. "I'm feeling steady enough on my feet to start work. Anyone want to help move the cryogenic chamber to the medical bay after breakfast?"

"Too bad we can't raise the rabbit embryos," Liz said as she and Emma followed William to the north habitat. The chamber, connected to life support systems there, held two hundred human embryos and two hundred rabbit embryos. William would only monitor the human embryos. He'd defrost a few of the rabbit embryos each week and culture them until the conceptus stage. But that was as far as they'd develop.

"Without a rabbit momma to provide an implantation site, there'll be no little bunnies," William said. "Artificial wombs are way too complex and need way too much support equipment to haul to Mars."

Liz attached a hoist line to the chamber. "Unless someone invents a zero-g barnyard to send us adults, we'll need artificial wombs if we want mammals on Mars. If we could raise some creatures from every phylum on Earth, Mars would be the ark we hope for."

"Colony Mars will keep an eye on the latest research," William said. "Incubation equipment's improving all the time. Maybe that will happen if we get as far as Settler Mission Twenty."

Settler Mission Twenty, Emma thought. I'll be an old woman by then.

***

Emma and Liz were transferring a batch of baby fish to a growth pond and, as Liz netted the fingerlings to gently upend them into a bucket, Emma checked the water temperature.

"The temperature's dropped two degrees," she said. "I better check the other ponds."

She took readings throughout the greenhouse.

"All the ponds are down a little. I checked light levels, too, and they're dimmed by five percent."

Emma left Liz to tend the fish and went looking for Daan. He confirmed power levels were down everywhere.

William trailed after him, comparing the Spine to the mockup he'd trained on. As he noted, there wasn't much work for a pediatrician yet.

"I thought it was good news when the outside temperature rose a degree," Daan said. "Now I think microwaves from the power satellite are heating up the dust instead of reaching the receivers properly."

Emma glanced up at the arched ceiling. The thick blocks of striated rock shut out all sound of the storm. It could be a beautiful winter sol out there, but it wasn't. "I thought the microwaves are tuned to penetrate clouds."

"They are - or maybe, they were. The asteroid didn't kick up a normal storm. Maybe the cloud's particle size distribution is different. Maybe without Governor's feedback, the satellite's generator has drifted off-frequency. Or the beam's drifted off the receiver. There's no way to tell from down here."

Over the next few sols, power levels continued a slow decline while the temperature outside the nederzetting crept upwards.

Chapter Thirty-Eight: Power

DAAN WAS LATE sitting down to breakfast in the Plaza. He'd been checking power readings in the Spine.

"Our power levels are still dropping," he said as he reached for the coffee pot. "I'm afraid we need to reduce our usage."

"I bet I know what that means," Ruby said. "Cold and dark, I reckon."

"If I shut down some areas completely, we can keep a small area warm and bright. Right now, I can power a habitat module and a couple bays."

"Damn, we're going backwards."

Liz's eyes widened. "The fish module and greenhouse are our food sources, so they must have power."

"I'm still working on the walkabouts in the docking module and, Claude has his rocks set up in the Plaza," Emma said.

Daan shook his head.

"The Plaza's too big and open to other bays. Here's the plan. We'll close every interior airlock, which will isolate the medical bay, the fish module, and greenhouse. I'll give them and the north habitat full power and cut back everywhere else to minimal freeze protection, but no ventilation and no lights. No power to the south habitat, either." He turned apologetically to the New Four who bunked there with Yin and Yang.

"Wall to wall sleeping bags," Ruby said with a sigh.

"What about the alfalfa in the new garden bay?" Liz asked.

"I guess winter is coming."

"And I guess this is our last breakfast in my new Plaza kitchen," Yin said with a sigh.

Emma shared the group's stoic acceptance. This was only an inconvenience for now.

251

"We'll make it through the storm," Claude said.

He was sitting with Emma in her bunk, talking quietly while the others slept. Damn that worthless privacy flap, she thought.

The wake-tone sounded and the smell of frying fish seeped through the flap - meals were cooked in the galley again. They waited for the shuffling and grumbling outside to die down before stepping out.

The New Four accepted seats at the little central table and Emma sat on a packing crate, balancing her plate on her knees. The cat hopped from person to person, winding around their legs and meowing for bits of fish.

"I'm going to record temperatures throughout the nederzetting," Daan said as he got up. "The stone will hold heat for a while, and I'd like to keep track of the cool-down rates."

"Please check out the spot above the cryochamber in Medical," William said. "The wall feels warmer than anywhere else."

"There's a power receiver on the outside of the wall there." Daan frowned. "I'll take some readings. Maybe a radiant heater's just aimed poorly."

"Liz, we're not going to let the bananas in the Plaza freeze," Emma. "I've got an idea."

***

The banana pots were waist high and equally wide across, too heavy even in Mars gravity for Emma and Liz to lift. But inside a walkabout using its robotic assist, Emma could handle one by herself.

Liz held the flatbed steady while she heaved the pot up. The walkabout had to crawl on all-fours to follow Liz into the greenhouse where Emma could stand up again and deposit the pot in an aisle. They were back in the Plaza for their fourth pot when Governor sounded an alarm.

"The medical bay is losing pressure." Governor's calm, reasonable voice spoke in Emma's helmet. "William, leave the bay immediately."

Emma galloped around the Plaza fish pond to Medical's airlock.

"Is William still in there?" she asked inside her helmet. Noah, Grace, and Hannah were gasping as they tumbled through the door, so Governor replied.

"Yes, Emma. William is in the bay. He must leave immediately."

Emma dived through the airlock, slamming the door closed with her tail. Everything went dark, like she'd fallen into a pit.

Power must be out, you fool, she thought, pushing panic away.

"Helmet lights - on." She leaped across the empty module, yanked the next airlock open, and crawled in.

The door to the bay stood open so she crawled over the hatch frame into more darkness.

The bay was a confusing blur of smoke or steam, she couldn't tell. She slid one claw along the bench tops towards a dark moving shape. As she lumbered down the aisle, the shape fell.

She hooked onto William's shirt, but he jerked away, grabbing handles on the cryochamber. Emma swore and gathered a wad of shirt into the walkabout's claw. She tried to shove William into the airlock, but the cryochamber rolled away and he lunged for it.

Emma swore and threw William into the airlock.

"Where's the cryochamber, Governor?"

"I cannot see it. I have no visuals inside the bay, Emma."

She swept her tail across the floor. "I can't find it."

Emma spent precious seconds backing the suit carefully into the airlock to avoid crushing William. Dust swirled around her. Some must be coating the door seals. She held the door closed, telescoping the arms as far as they'd go so she could reach the other door with her tail. She rotated the handle but the door didn't budge.

Pressure in the module must be holding it closed, she thought.

She slammed her tail against the door and it crashed open.

By now, everyone was in the module. Still gripping the door to Medical, Emma twisted to open the walkabout's access hatch, and rolled out into Claude's arms.

"Are you alright?"

"Sure. Where's William?"

"They carried him to the habitat," Claude said.

"Is the airlock holding? Governor, is the pressure holding?"

"The medical bay is now at Mars surface pressure. The airlock is holding."

"Let's go." Claude grabbed Emma's hand and they jogged to the habitat.

Inside the habitat, William wore a medical gauntlet, and Grace tapped on her pad. Someone shoved a cup of tepid tea into his pale hands and he gripped it tightly.

"The cryochamber," he said as they came in. "I lost my grip on the chamber. Emma, did you get it out?" His voice was shrill.

"Governor couldn't see it..."

"You were already unconscious," Grace said. "You could have suffered permanent brain damage if she hadn't brought you out immediately."

"What happened?" Yang asked. "Tell me exactly what you saw."

"Dust tumbled down the wall, and then a banshee screeched." William sat wide-eyed and trembling.

"It must be the microwave beam from the power station," Daan said. "It's drifted off the receiver and heated the stone till a seam cracked."

"What if the beam keeps drifting? What if it breaches a bay we can't isolate?" Claude asked.

"I'll shut it down," Ruby said. She leaped to the airlock.

For a moment, everyone froze in shock.

Then vibrations spread through the floor as the jumpship blasted off.

"What's she doing?" Emma said. "She can't fly in a sand storm."

"If she keeps the engines firing at full, the nozzles will stay clear until she's out of the atmosphere," Yang said. "She can fly. She just can't land."

"But what good..."

The module went dark. Emma gasped at the blackness and a sudden sensation of falling. Even the perpetual hum of the ventilation system was gone. Someone fumbled in the darkness and a puddle of light appeared.

"I know what she did," Yang said, waving the hand light. "As soon as she was clear of the dust, Ruby shut down the power satellite."

"Well that's just great."

"We have to trust her to figure something out with MEX. It'll take half an hour or more for them to respond. We should sit tight."

William staggered to his feet. "Emma - the cryochamber!"

She grabbed a hand light. "Claude, help me back into the walkabout. Governor, what's the airlock pressure? Governor?"

Silence.

"Uh oh."

***

The medical bay was unimaginably black. Her helmet light barely illuminated the floor at her feet. Emma sucked in a startled breath. Something was moving. Pale dust sifting gently down the wall and overflowing the bench. Emma slid each foot slowly until she touched something. Aiming her light and bending low, she spotted the cryochamber, hooked a claw on its rim, and pulled it upright.

A gash ran through the chamber, its edges folded and torn.

"Can you see anything?" Claude's voice startled her.

"Hey. Is the power back?"

255

"No. I've got a surface suit. It has batteries. Lucky your channel is open."

"There's a crack in the wall, halfway up from the bench top. I'm bringing the chamber out, but it doesn't look good."

"Can you get a sample of the dust that drifted in?"

Emma swept her helmet light across the bench top and spotted some glassware. "I think so. Why?"

"Don't know exactly. Samples are always a good idea."

Emma scooped up sand in a beaker and carried the cryochamber to the airlock.

At the airlock, an eddy of dust followed her inside as she moved the chamber and beaker. She backed the suit into the airlock on its knees, braced against the hatch frame, and pulled the door as tightly closed as she could.

"Claude. You're on the pressure side of the airlock. Open the manual vent."

In a few minutes, Claude was helping her out of the walkabout. They left it braced against the bay door. Claude wiped the inner hatch rim with wet towels and the door seal held. They were safe for the time being.

They hauled the chamber to the habitat where William, still shaking, knelt to examine it. Frost on the surface had already sublimated away.

"One segment's breached," he said. "But the rest looks intact, if we can get power to it quickly."

Yin and Yang grabbed the handles. "It ran off the habitat's life support system before. We'll hook it back in."

"Why didn't you rescue the cryochamber instead of me?" William said to Emma as Yang muscled the chamber away. "All the embryos could have been lost. Maybe they are. Two hundred against one man."

"One man against could-bees." Emma stared at him through the shadows thrown by their hand lights.

"What?"

"They *could* become people, but they're only globs of cells. You're already a person, a sentient human being."

William shook his head. "You don't understand."

Emma pulled Liz into the shadows. "Did I do the right thing?"

"You did what you could." Liz hugged her. "Without you, William and the embryos would all be dead. Now he's alive and three of the segments may survive."

"What about Kamp Kans? Can William do viability studies now? Have I ruined our chance to be a permanent colony?"

Will we die alone on a barren planet?

Liz laughed softly and hugged her. "Someone will bring life to Mars, no matter what happens to us. When I say all life is precious, I'm usually talking in the abstract. You saved an actual life. That's enough."

Emma reached a hand to Liz and to Claude. Her adrenalin drained away, leaving her weak in the knees. Liz expected Emma to ensure success, but that was hard to believe as they stood in a puddle of light, the module growing cold around them.

Chapter Thirty-Nine: Data

E MMA LAY in her bunk, staring into perfect blackness.

The damaged cryochamber was in an airlock, against the outer door. That was the coldest spot in the nederzetting. William had it plugged in, waiting for power. A Martian night could freeze carbon dioxide into snow, but the chamber needed to be even colder. If the power was off for long, William feared he'd lose all the embryos.

Of course, the settlers would freeze to death before he'd know for sure.

The air was close and clammy. Emma couldn't tell in the dark if she was awake or dreaming.

A whoosh of ventilation startled her, deafening after the long silence.

She stumbled over sleeping bodies as the habitat lights flickered dimly.

Daan hopped to the Spine and returned with a report.

"Judging by these readings, someone switched the power station to a diffuse beam, so it won't cut into the bays. But that cuts intensity and the cloud's still interfering. We have about six percent of normal power available. Enough for the greenhouse or the habitat, but not both."

"We should power the greenhouse," Liz said. "Everything in the habitat can recover from cold, but if the plants die, we die. We can camp in there and shut down this module."

"I've got an idea," Claude said. "Governor, are you back?"

"I am running recovery diagnostics, Claude. Please wait."

"Good enough. Emma brought me a sample of the dust from this storm. Give me a couple hours to analyze it. Maybe we can figure out how to tune the satellite."

Claude grabbed a surface suit in the airlock before anyone could ask questions.

Emma followed him into the Spine. "You're thinking we can generate a signal to punch through this cloud?" Shivering, she pulled on the suit's thermal layer as he worked.

He sagged against his table, staring at his pad. "Damn. We didn't load the models I need into Governor. I can do the analyses, but I can't calculate the frequency to use."

"MEX could?"

"Sure, if we could get the data to them - the cloud's composition and particle size distribution."

"Run your analyses. I have an idea." Emma hopped down to the south docking module to retrieve more surface suit backpacks.

***

Hours later Claude helped Emma into the walkabout that stood, rigid, bracing the door to the medical bay, while Yin helped Yang into the other suit.

"I compared the sand from Medical to our usual dust drifts," Claude said as he fastened a backpack over Emma's arm. "The asteroid kicked up very different sand, rich in iridium and chromium. I wish I could do isotopic differentiation."

He handed Yin a roll of cable. "There's a heavy load of shocked quartz crystals and glass spherules. That changes the characteristics of the dust. If we can get these data to MEX, they can tune the satellites to cut through the cloud and give us communications and power back."

Yes, professor. Emma didn't say the words out loud. James would have said something like that and made it sound funny, have them all laughing. Instead she began the suit's checklist.

"What good will these packs do?" Daan asked as he held the next backpack.

Emma raised her arm and gave the pack a little shake. "I've modified the transceivers. They'll listen to the full width of the

259

spectrum. Once they pick up MEX, they'll relay the frequency to the receiver and get it talking to the satellites again."

"And this one is programmed to trigger Jumper Two to lift off and transmit Claude's data." Yang held up another backpack tagged with strips of cloth. "Install it on the robotic jumper, blast it up to Ruby, and everything will work out fine."

"I don't like this," Yin said as he checked that the cables would unspool easily. "Why can't I go with you?"

"Emma's the walkabout expert."

"Why can't I go with you in a surface suit?"

"The wind will drive dust into every crevice," Emma said. "That could short out the life support systems."

"Walkabouts..." Yang rapped his suit's claw against its side. "Are hard shelled. You can talk with me through a helmet."

Emma slid back into the walkabout braced against the door.

It took Yang some time to maneuver the walkabout into the airlock around Emma, but Claude got the door sealed behind them. Yang hit the air pump and Emma pushed open the bay-side door.

A drift of sand spread across the center of the bay, glittering like a pile of diamonds in their helmet lights.

They ripped benches away from the wall and shoveled sand until Yang found the crack. He slipped in the edge of a claw and began to wiggle the block. "Give me a minute. I know how these interlock."

Once the first block pulled out, sand flooded in around them, and Yang opened a hole big enough for the walkabouts. With more digging, he opened a path to the surface.

"Hey, Yin. We're going out," Yang said over the suit channel. "I don't know how long you'll receive me, once we move into the cloud."

Yang followed cables to the medical bay receiver and hung a backpack on its control box. Emma turned left and moved slowly along the bay, towing cables behind her. She couldn't see anything but heard the sand scouring her helmet. Flashes on swirls of dust were disorienting, so she turned her light off and concentrated on the heads-up display. Pressure and temperature were constant and life support chugged along.

Dad will be pleased to hear how well the suit's doing, Emma thought as she activated the recorder. "There's no loss of movement in the joints. Feedback from the claws is good..."

The drifts were so deep she reached down to keep one hand on the bay's wall. When the feel of the wall changed, she knew she'd reached the airlock module. "Yang, do you hear me? I'm at the Plaza, turning right."

"I hear you. The cable's paying out hunky-dory."

Emma worked her way along the nederzetting, calling out progress. She crept along the Spine to the north habitat, felt around the docked rover, circled the modules, and crossed the empty pad where Jumpship One once parked.

"Okay. I'm at the north receiver." She closed her eye, which seemed silly inside her dark helmet, but helped her concentrate.

"I'm attaching the pack." She opened her eyes and pushed her faceplate against the pack. "The transceiver's on. I can see the light. Are you reading me?"

Nothing.

Damn.

It took forever to get back. Emma was relieved when she finally heard Yang's voice crackling in her helmet. They rapped claws before continuing around the end of Medical towards the south receiver.

"Here comes the fun part," Yang said after she hung the next pack. He gripped a loop on a short strap, locked the suit's claw, and held the other end up to Emma's helmet. She grabbed it.

"We'll lose comms in a few minutes," Yin said over the helmet channel. "Be careful."

"I've got a cable tied off to the receiver. We'll follow it back," Yang said. "No worries."

Emma closed her eyes again as she stepped away from the nederzetting, into the storm, hanging on to her end of the strap.

"Right foot, left foot. Right, Left." Yang called out so Emma could keep in step. He aimed west of the maintenance bay as well as he could walking blind. After a very long time, the strap went slack. Emma felt a flash of fear before she realized he'd stopped.

"That's the end of the cable," he said. "Side step left." They moved towards Maintenance, she hoped.

"I ran into something. Brilliant. It's the side of the bay."

Emma heaved out her breath. They felt their way to the Maintenance airlock.

"I've tied the nederzetting cable to the airlock," Yang said. "Help me loose the second cable from my suit." He looped that through the airlock handle, too, and with Emma trailing on the strap, moved out into the storm.

They ran into the robotic jumpship and dug out the engines. Emma took the lifeline, the cable that would lead them back to Maintenance, and hooked it over a claw while Yang climbed up to install the last pack, the one carrying Claude's data.

"I activated the transmission," he said. "We've got ten minutes before the engines fire."

Right when they needed to hurry, the cable twisted in the wind and nearly slid out of Emma's claw. With her heart pounding in her ears, she slipped the loop to Yang over one arm and reeled herself hand-over-hand towards Maintenance.

When would the engines ignite? She hadn't started her suit's timer. The loose cable tangled around her feet, slowing her down.

The jumpship engines fired and Emma toppled forward. She rolled and twisted inside the suit, looking back. Dust swept past her and she saw a dark shape rising on pale blue engine exhaust.

"Yang, do you still have the strap?" Fear shot through her. She didn't feel any pull.

She scrambled backwards on all-fours, sweeping her tail back and forth, and bumped into him.

"That gave me collywobbles." He laughed shakily. "Uh, there's no reason to mention my little tumble to Yin."

Yang gripped her tail and Emma followed the cable to Maintenance. There they each locked a claw around the nederzetting cable and lumbered home.

The hole into Medical had drifted shut again. They dug their way in and rummaged through supplies on the benches. The hydrogen peroxide was frozen, but Yang found some microfiber cleaning cloths and wiped the airlock seal. "I don't think the seal's perfectly clean."

"Lay down in the airlock and we'll try."

Emma backed in, straddling him. She extended the suit's hands, braced against the frame and pulled the door closed.

"Governor, you there? Lock my suit joints."

"Claude, are you ready to open your door?"

"Ready."

The airlock pressurized quickly.

Yang banged against Emma's legs as he crawled through to the module.

Claude pushed her walkabout's pack up and dragged Emma out, leaving the suit braced against the door. "Hurry. I can hear air leaking."

They both sneezed violently as they crossed the module and closed the Plaza airlock behind them.

"There," Claude said, giving the last door an unnecessary push. "The Plaza pressure will hold that closed."

"Let's never do this again." Yin wrapped his arms around Yang.

"It was easy-peasy," Yang said, grunting in Yin's bear-hug.

Still sneezing, Emma spun towards Claude and hugged him. "Nothing to it." She sneezed again.

Claude returned her hug, swaying from foot to foot. "What about you risking your life? Any comment on that?"

"We're all risking our lives." Winning was exhilarating.

"My hero." He planted a kiss on her lips.

Chapter Forty: Winter

AFTER THE TRIUMPH of blasting Claude's data into space, it was hard to huddle in the greenhouse and wait.

The settlers took the cryochamber with them, plugged into an airlock outlet where the cold air rolling off its surface wouldn't damage any plants.

Any *more* plants, Emma thought. Frost had touched the greenhouse. Tomato and squash leaves drooped, sadly wilted. Dead leaves didn't bother the cat. He rolled through flattened squash vines as enthusiastically as ever. Liz said the banana corms should recover despite the limp, black leaves. "And potatoes in the ground are just fine. We won't starve for a while. I'll replant the gardens now, though. We're going to need more food."

Yin spent an entire morning carving a pattern of holes into the floor while Liz assembled handfuls of different seeds.

"I recognize this. It's Star Halma," Claude said when he examined Yin's work. "I haven't played this game since I was a kid."

"If you remember the rules, you can explain," Grace said as Liz handed her some seeds to use as playing pieces.

Liz sat next to William, cross-legged on the floor, while Yin and Yang perched on opposite bed walls, leaning down between their legs to reach the game board. Grace glanced to the far end of the bay, where Daan and Melina sat close together, their backs to the crowd. She left them alone.

"Emma? Sanni?"

"Oh, Chinese Checkers," Emma said as she looked at the board, the holes patterned as a six-pointed star. "You play, Sanni. The mealworms need feeding. Liz had them buried in blankets but they'll be hungry now. I'll harvest a batch for supper."

"Would you rather play?" William held his seeds out to Claude.

"No, no. I'm the referee. Ten seeds each and no cheating."

"I'll watch, too," Noah said. "It's great input for my psych evaluations." Yin gave him a good natured smack and everyone laughed.

While they set up the game, Claude followed Emma. "They're working awfully hard at being nonchalant. What do you think our chances are?"

"I worry about the CO_2 to oxygen balance. With so many plants dead and no way to adjust the mix, drowsiness or headaches will be the first symptom."

She took a deep breath and squared her shoulders. "If MEX receives your data, I'm pretty sure they can work out a frequency to cut through the storm."

"If?"

Emma avoided his eyes.

"How long can we survive in here?"

"I haven't asked Governor to estimate." She pressed her lips firmly together. "I can't think of anything else to do."

Claude hugged her close. "I have no regrets."

She hugged back, blinking at tears. Actually, she could think of one more thing to do, though she didn't say it out loud. Fewer people in the greenhouse would survive longer. Maybe long enough. It would be hard to decide when to leave, to step into the cold dark Spine. Not yet. Not now.

Everything depended on Ruby, if she was still alive somewhere in orbit. Because, without its link to Governor, if Ruby hadn't contacted the jumpship, it blasted straight past the satellites into space. Nowhere near where MEX would be listening for a signal.

The whole sol passed before the steady white-noise hum of comms began to crackle.

"Ruby to Kamp Kans. You guys still down there?"

Through a chorus of cheers, Daan answered. "We're here, we're fine. Where the hell are you?"

"Phobos Base. The habitat here is in perfect working order, thank goodness. I've been eating buckyball pasta and playing vid games, bored to tears, while MEX fiddled with Claude's data. Seems they got the comm frequency right."

Shortly after, Governor reported receiving transmissions directly from Earth and after a few diagnostic runs they were back to full power. Daan reset all the circuits in the Spine and the comforting whoosh and hum of the nederzetting returned.

They danced, they cried, and they terrified the cat.

Only William was somber as he studied newly downloaded messages. "There's fallout from the loss of that bank of embryos," he said. "I've got a folder of news stories. Here's one about donors demanding the return of embryos from Colony Mars' S-5 bank."

"No one can do that," Hannah said. "All identifying data's been stripped away."

"Really?" Sanni asked. "Surely they can reconstruct it."

"No way." Hannah shook her head. "Colony Mars guaranteed secrecy to ensure settlers use the full genetic diversity available, with no biases about race or ethnicity, not even subconsciously."

"It was specified in the donor contracts," William said. "But apparently that doesn't stop lawsuits." He scrolled through a list of articles. "Here's something. MEX flagged this vid."

He tapped the play icon.

"In a rare public statement," the announcer said, "reclusive financier Amelia Lambert issued the following statement regarding Colony Mars."

Emma shifted to watch over William's shoulder, but it was a thin, formally dressed lawyer and not Mlle Lambert who continued speaking.

"Mademoiselle Lambert extends her condolences for the loss of the embryos in a tragic accident on Mars. She wants the donor families to know that she, personally, has both a financial and genealogical stake in the colony. To demonstrate her commitment, Mademoiselle Lambert has arranged for ten clones to be created from her own somatic cells. These will be randomly placed in the primary cryogenic chambers, without identification, to take their place among the donated embryos traveling to Mars."

The lawyer looked up from his notes. "Mademoiselle Lambert said, she has always known humans would walk on Mars, but never expected to walk on Mars herself."

His eyes returned to the pad. "She believes that a permanent colony on Mars is the first step on humanity's voyage into the universe and has dedicated her life and her fortune to achieving this goal. You can help. Colony Mars now reopens donor applications for embryos to replace those lost on Mars."

"Savvy old woman," Ruby said in admiration. "I wonder what it cost to clone herself ten times?"

"I wonder how many thousand people have already applied to donate," Emma said. She stepped around to face William. "Does this balance the loss?"

"Every life is precious," he said. "My purpose here is to nurture life and I've lived to continue that mission, thanks to you."

"We give birth to a living world," Liz said, as if quoting something important. She snuggled into William's side.

Yang waved his pad. "Look, I found the revised launch schedule. They've shuffled the missions."

The S-5 Kinderen Mission with its two thousand embryos was delayed. Settler Six, *The Blacksmiths*, would launch in its place, now scheduled to leave Earth orbit in early December.

"Governor, translate that date. When the hell's early December?" Ruby asked.

Emma laughed at her snarl.

***

Later, alone in her own bunk, Emma set her personal messages on text to avoid disturbing anyone trying to sleep and scrolled through. There was nothing about Malcolm. There shouldn't be, of course, but she felt relieved. She wondered if he'd been prosecuted, but decided against searching for information. Let Earth take care of Earth's problems.

There were cheery updates on the arts circuit from her mother, one from each week, and a couple more files for the holograph pedestals. In recent messages the cheerfulness seemed forced. Her mother had been worried. Emma sent back a long reply, with stories about Ruby, the cat, and Claude. Her mother liked stories.

There was a message from her father, sent shortly after Ruby had blasted into orbit. Emma opened it, planning to send him a report on the walkabouts. His message started with a stiff greeting and she would have skipped straight to her reply, but the message was longer than usual and she began to read, then turned on the audio very low and held the pad to her ear.

"If you're seeing this message, then things turned out well. If you haven't viewed the statement Aunt Amelia issued, take a look. She's rescued me again by rescuing the colony - by rescuing you." He sounded oddly bitter. And who was Aunt Amelia?

"I never told you, I didn't want you to know... I was a failure. It's a good thing your mother never understood finances or she'd have left me long before she did."

He chuckled sadly. "When you were born, your great aunt contacted me and offered a deal. No one knows we're related... my mother's pregnancy was an embarrassment, I guess. Anyway, Amelia was the venture capitalist for my company - no one knows that, either. I worked every waking minute to

268

prove I could make it, that her money wasn't charity. And I succeeded. With the company, anyway.

"I promised Amelia I'd hand you a Colony Mars application, and I did. But I cried the day you left Earth. And now, maybe you'll never get this message and I'll never hear from you again." The message ended abruptly.

Emma lay in her bunk, staring at the ceiling. He cried? She couldn't picture that. He was gone so often when she was a child... trying to prove himself? That took grit.

What about Great Aunt Amelia? With a creeping certainty, Emma knew. Miss Lambert had never met with any settler crew but hers. The lawyer said something about her having a genealogical stake, even before the clones. Amelia Lambert.

Dammit. Emma's voyage to Mars was payment for her father's debt. She laughed silently until tears choked her. She probably should be furious, but it was too late to change how she felt. Her mom was right. People count.

"I love you, Dad."

***

The storm thrown up by the asteroid raged through the northern hemisphere winter, but there were gardens to replant, fish and mealworms to farm, equipment to maintain, and all the new components to install, so the settlers kept busy.

Yin and Yang planned to build a second layer of stone on top of the fractured medical bay to seal it. Once it was pressurized, they expected to salvage most of the equipment.

Emma talked with Ruby every sol she was stuck on Phobos Base, discussing upgrades to the jumpships. They even shared a couple video games using Governor to relay moves.

At last the cat was happy to spend his sols with Melina. Heaters warmed the new garden bay and everyone took turns helping Liz.

When the cloud's density tapered off near the surface, Yang started the beetle-bots digging out. They shifted sand from the maintenance bay doorway first, feeding it to the fabricator

269

inside to form construction blocks. As Yang said, there was no need to waste time getting back to construction.

"The bots are sweeping off Ruby's landing pad this sol," Yin said as he fried mealworms and potatoes one morning in a warm, bright Plaza kitchen. "The high clouds are thinning and she'll be able to land this sol."

"Surface opacity readings are way down," Yang said over a pot of beans. "We can take the rover out again."

"Alright," Claude said happily. "I'll get back to prospecting."

"Governor, send activation codes to the beacons at the lava tube and Rover One." Emma gripped Claude's hand as she talked.

"I have contact with both beacons, Emma."

"Yeah." Claude slapped the table with a grin. "Let's retrieve the rover I rolled into that south-flank channel."

"Yang and I will relinquish Rover Two to Emma and Claude for their trip," Yin said. "We can walk to Maintenance for a while." He heaved an exaggerated sigh.

"I've been talking to Ruby about your idea, Emma," Daan said. "To take a jumpship to the Olympus caldera rim. I can scope out a climbing route for later, but I think I'd like to learn something about the peak and not just haul my sorry body up and down."

"Bring back samples," Claude said.

Ruby's landing became a celebration. She even allowed Governor to stream the imagers live to MEX despite the indignity of being carried from the jumper. Her months on the tiny moon left her weak in Mars' gravity. Grace, with her space medicine expertise, fussed over her.

"I can't decide," Liz said. "Should we have an annual Doomsday Holiday on the sol the asteroid hit? The sol we regained contact with Earth? Or now, when Ruby came back safely?"

"How about all three sols?" Daan asked.

"Anyone want a vodka martini?" Liz asked. "Very dry, since all I've got is vodka."

But Grace held out a cup to Ruby.

"What's this?"

"Water. No alcohol for you. I'm going to get excellent data from your recovery."

Ruby groaned good-naturedly.

"It'll be easier to make glass from the sand the meteor kicked up," Yin said. "I'll have time to fabricate some proper martini glasses, since we're not opening another bay until the nederzetting is up to full Earth pressure."

"And maybe we'll fabricate some nice round windows," Yang said. "We received a design for Claude's observation bay."

***

Daan's exploration of the Olympus peak had to wait for Ruby to recover from space, but Emma and Claude spent the next few sols packing for their trip. Emma slid the cheese tin from her bag to show Claude. She'd show him her silky things later.

He grinned, tapping his personal duffle with a conspiratorial smile. He had to have beer with him.

The GPS satellites were online and Governor could drive the rover in light or dark, but it seemed proper to leave at dawn. A crowd wished them well as they hopped into the airlock. Emma sneezed in the lingering smell of the Martian surface.

"Ready to go exploring?" she asked.

"With you, I'm ready to go anywhere."

"Okay Governor. Start driving."

Their fingers intertwined as the rover lumbered across the Tharsis Plain.

\#\#\#

Thanks for reading. I hope you enjoyed my story. Check out more books in my "Colony *on Mars*" series. The stories are set in the same Mars colony as generations continue. Scan the QR code and keep reading. eBooks and paperbacks available.

Thanks! -- *Kate* --

Bonuses

Want more? These vignettes belong to the *Glory on Mars* story. There are no spoilers here, so read them as you run before you start reading the story, after you finish, or never. This is, after all, your book.

Bonus Contents

Mademoiselle Lambert

A T THE AGE of fifty-two Mlle Lambert began her life's work the day her father died. In a world where five hundred families owned half the wealth on Earth, her father had been the richest man on the planet. A wild sister escaped his grasp and disappeared years ago so now, as his sole heir, Amelia Lambert was the richest woman on Earth.

She moved out of his sprawling mansion and bought a modest Dutch apartment. There she incorporated *Interplanetary International*, which had only one employee - herself.

Immediately she awarded three contracts.

First, she hired a security firm to quietly and secretly remove all mention of her from the internet, especially pictures. Since her building was occupied by busy working people with little time to ponder over the quiet lady in apartment 6C. Amelia Lambert, like the Cheshire Cat, steadily disappeared.

Second she hired a law firm renowned for its honesty and discretion to be her agent. She messaged her instructions directly to the managing partner and he never met his client.

Her lawyer handled his first assignment satisfactorily - he engaged a maintenance firm for the apartment. Every Wednesday Mlle Lambert took her computer tablet and walked across a park to the public library. She passed through the lobby like a ghost and sat in the most secluded study carrel.

When the tablet detected her entering the library, it sent a message and a bonded crew was immediately dispatched. The crew cleaned the apartment, watered the plants, and restocked the kitchen. They removed trash, a week's accumulation of dirty dishes, and laundry. They replenished the drawers with clean plates and flatware, and hung new clothes exactly as their instructions dictated. Then, like house elves, they vanished, never seeing the face of their employer.

If the tablet failed to detect Mlle Lambert entering the library some Wednesday, it would message her lawyer and he would personally enter the apartment. If she was incapacitated but alive, there was a list of instructions. If she was not alive, the list was shorter.

Her third contract was the most unusual. Mlle Lambert hired the premiere company in the field of Artificial Intelligence. It dedicated servers scattered across four continents to her projects. The AI received a duplicate of everything she did, down to every key stroke. Slowly it learned her values, priorities, and idiosyncrasies. At some point in the future, when it had received no key strokes for a week, the AI would take over *Interplanetary International*. No one would know anything had changed, except for the cleaning crew who would notice, but never comment, that there were no more dirty dishes and no more laundry to be washed. They would continue to clean the apartment and water the plants. Forever.

Mlle Lambert grudgingly allotted a few hours a week to managing her father's estate, homes no longer lived in, art collections never viewed, jewels never worn - all the repositories beyond government fiat used to store wealth in the centuries before Bitcoin.

That left the bulk of her time for her opus. She had studied all her life in preparation - engineering, celestial mechanics, and every planetary mission over the past century. Mlle Lambert would colonize Mars.

She studied the institutions that shared her goal and determined which to support, which to acquire, and which projects to commission directly. She herself had no desire to journey to Mars. She disliked even her weekly walk to the library. But humanity would spread to the stars and Mars would be the stepping stone.

Flying Over Mars

There's an animation of flying by Olympus Mons: 46 seconds at youtube.com/watch?v=1BPNVtCgAbk.

You'll find a comparison of volcanoes on Mars to volcanoes on Earth: 2minutes 48 seconds at

youtube.com/watch?v=ySFpJ-clnzU.

These links worked when I published the book, but if they're broken, try searching with NASA Mars Olympus Mons for something interesting.

Surviving the Martian Surface

MARS' ATMOSPHERE was vanishingly thin, a hundred times thinner than Earth and ninety-five percent carbon dioxide. There was a bit of nitrogen, some trace gases, and way too little oxygen to do more than rust the rocks over eons. It was also bone-breaking cold most of the time. A summer afternoon on the Tharsis Plain might reach a comfortable twenty degrees Celsius but that same night would be minus seventy. A hundred fifty below wasn't impossible.

A surface suit would protect her skin and lungs. If it failed, she'd be dead in three or four minutes. Emma's capillaries would rupture through her skin and her lungs would desiccate and freeze without a suit. She shuttered to think of Ingra taking even a few steps away from the nederzetting unprotected.

Unfortunately, suits offered little protection against the radiation that bombarded Mars' surface in the absence of a global magnetic field. A major solar event could be fatal. Emma agreed with her father though, and not just because of his visionary rhetoric. Settlers couldn't cower inside the nederzetting forever.

Emma pulled off her shirt and pants and stuffed them into her duffle. Donning the suit was hard enough when gravity helped her maneuver, but in zero-g she braced her shoulders against the bunk wall and began to struggle with the inner compression layer. It hung from a shoulder ring and looked entirely too small.

Air pressure inside the helmet would protect her face, but the compression layer protected the rest of her body, pressing against her skin to keep those capillaries from bursting.

Emma had to accordion the fabric into her hands to get a leg started. She worked the fabric up, wriggled the suit over her butt, and pulled the ring past her hips. With a grimace she slipped a urine collection pad into the suit - she might be in the suit for hours. The pads were reusable. Yuck.

She scrunched up the sleeves and, slipping one arm at a time through the ring, got her hands to the ends. Finally she pulled the shoulder ring into position without dislocating a shoulder. The suit was tight across her chest. Pushing away a twinge of panic, she took several long, slow breaths before pulling on gloves and socks. Those were the parts of the suit that would wear out first and she had spares.

In contrast, the thermal layer glided easily over the compression layer and sealed up the front. Its outer side was tough to resist tears, while the inner side was a spongy material threaded with thin tubes carrying thermal fluid. Outer boots completed the suit. She left the outer gloves in a side pouch and pulled the life support backpack off its bracket.

She'd need the pack, even inside the ship. Already the tight fitting suit made her feel hot and a little light-headed. She shrugged into the backpack, snapped the quick-release buckles closed, and tightened the straps. All the pack systems ran to the suit through one bundled hose, providing air recycling and power. The pack was a rebreather - no way she could carry enough air if the suit released her breath each time she exhaled.

She pushed the connector into her shoulder ring and twisted it till it clicked. The air flow would start when she donned the helmet, but a side connection, twist-locked to a receptacle at the neck of the thermal layer, would regulate her temperature.

The surface suit was designated an essential use, so it ran on batteries. She heard a hum as the thermal system engaged. Emma left her bubble-like helmet stowed for now and floated into the center of the module, happy to rest for a few minutes.

Radiation on Mars

FOR AS LONG as there's been space flight, astronauts have faced radiation exposure. Energetic solar protons and galactic cosmic rays strike and tear DNA molecules, leading to diseases including cancer. Outside Earth's protective atmosphere and magnetic field, space is a hostile place.

Mars isn't much better, with only one percent Earth's atmosphere and no global magnetic field at all. A settler's exposure on the planet's highest peak would be eighty times Earth's average.

There are three ways to fight radiation: distance from the radiation source, exposure time, and shielding. Mars' distance from the Sun doesn't vary enough to make one season's solar radiation much less than another's, and cosmic radiation never varies. That leaves time and shielding to control.

Colony Mars' robotic squad fabricated stone many meters thick, so the nederzetting was as safe as Earth. But settlers couldn't huddle inside the bays forever. Cancer was a risk to accept and deal with.

Emma could monitor for cancer easily enough. In her personal bag, she carried a dozen capsules of graphene nanoparticles, biodegradable and harmless, each with a tiny magnetic core. Every twelve months, she'd swallow a capsule and wear the monitoring wrist band for a week. Nanoparticles would spread out through her blood and lymph systems, bind to cancerous cells, and mobilize into her blood. Passing through vessels under the thin skin on her wrist, any cancer-bound particles would alert the wrist band.

Cancer wasn't much of a problem on Earth anymore, and would be less of a problem on Mars once Settler Mission Five arrived. They'd bring hospital equipment, including a radiofrequency unit, and lots more nanoparticles. Spare parts would be included, because this unit was vital. It was the cure for cancers that they would all face.

The unit was a three meter long tube to saturate anyone lying inside with specific radio waves. A high dose of injected nanoparticles would grip every cancer cell - solid tumor or metastasized - and channel the waves in to kill cancer without damage to healthy cells. It was the Kanzius effect, the greatest medical advance since doctors figured out that germs cause infectious disease. A technology as important as anything in the life support systems.

All Emma had to do was avoid a really high-energy flare or solar mass ejection, where the radiation might burn her skin, blast her blood cells, and destroy her gut lining. But Earth monitored the Sun and could predict solar weather fairly well. Should be no worries.

Poetry

Hellas Crater
Largest impact crater seen,
The largest that we've found,
Could not exist on gaseous worlds,
It's gouged in rocky ground
The Hellas Basin's found on Mars,
From crater rim to dusty floor,
Nine thousand meters is its depth,
The height that airplanes soar.
The basin sits at antipode
To enormous shield volcanoes
That rise upon the Tharsis Bulge,
Punched right through the globe.
Dust emerges from its depths,
Storm after storm a' chasing,
Enveloping and planet wide,
It should be called Hell's Basin.

The Smell of Life
Methane can be made by life
Or hydrothermal systems,
By microbes in the regolith
Or from the rocks, if not them.
Methane doesn't last for long
Floating in the atmosphere.
Tens of decades, then it's gone,
Reacting in the sunlight there.
What Curiosity has found,
Unexpected and delighted,
A whiff arising from the ground
Has scientists excited.

281

It doesn't mean that there is life
Or that there was in past
It means we have a lot to learn
Before we'll know at last.
What difference would it make to us?
Bugs aren't likely to converse.
Even if they share our Sun,
Are we better off or worse?
I for one would thrill to know,
To find conclusive data.
Even if it pays no gold,
Life will always matter.

Olympus Mons

There's a nice pull back from a painting of a Martian shield volcano at: youtube.com/watch?v=QJZcFnzyrAw, 1 minute 28 seconds. This url links to a picture of Olympus Mons but any large shield volcano look like this. If the link is broken, try searching on Mars   Olympus   Mons for something else interesting.

Breeding a Colony

S HEILA'S PHONE hummed softly.

Drat, she thought, and hurried to her next assignment at Colony Mars headquarters. Today was the demographics lecture for Mission Five candidates. Finalists would be selected later in the week. This was no time to be late.

She paused as she entered the room, noting a buffet lunch on tables along the back. Mission candidates were seated at four round tables. Doctor De Smet stood near the door and gestured her to an empty seat.

She joined three candidates seated there, each one looking eager and nervous. Settlers would be selected from sixteen candidates roughly four years in advance of their launch date. Planners, engineers, and candidates for other missions often joined Sheila's group briefings. But today's topic was touchy and only Mission Five was invited.

Also unusual, only women were mission candidates today. Mission Five was the Kinderen Mission, the first settlers planned to become mothers on Mars - all women to give the colony a jump on growing its population.

Candidates were young, generally early twenties, though one girl was fourteen and present with written consent from her parents. Medical experts wanted families on Mars to be completed by the time a mother was thirty. Unlike on Earth, technologies to assist with later births would be limited.

Sheila was the last candidate to sit down. De Smet immediately joined Doctor Martin at the front of the room and called the meeting to order.

"Demographics," she said, projecting an image on the front wall.

"The quantifiable statistics of a population." Martin completed the thought. She and De Smet alternated like an endless relay race.

"Of course, the reproductive rights of all Mars settlers are completely protected."

"We're here to tell you about the choices you'll have."

"How different actions by you and your fellow settlers may influence the colony's success."

Martin tapped her pad, bringing up a list of the courses Colony Mars would provide Mission Five settlers over the next four years - pediatrics and obstetrics, child development and education, gardening and life-support maintenance. Next some word-charts describing how families would be structured around pairs of breeding women...

Sheila flinched at the academic jargon...

De Smet continued. "Elderly colonists (once some became available) would share child care and each child would have a father assigned. Colony Mars demographers have estimated that, to achieve a self-sustaining population able to survive mishaps..."

Sheila pressed her lips tightly together. There would, of course, be mishaps...

"The colony needs to establish a minimum of three independent habitats with two thousand settlers in total," De Smet said.

"Of course there is still debate," Martin said. "Some say there must be ten thousand humans living on Mars before the colony is truly established, but for either goal, the approach is the same. We believe the colony can succeed, even if Mission Five is the last mission to Mars." They both smiled with satisfaction.

"Is Colony Mars disbanding after our mission?" a worried voice called out.

"Heavens, no," Martin said. "We'll keep sending missions every twenty-six months for as long as possible. Forever. Well, as long as the money holds out."

Another candidate raised her hand. "Won't the colony be awfully inbred?"

"Ah! You lead me to my next point."

A map of the world popped up on the screen.

"In addition to four more settlers, Mission Five will carry three thousand cryo-preserved embryos in the blastocyst stage, donated by people originating from every continent, from every culture and ethnic group. Also a similar number of vials of cryo-preserved sperm. A deep genetic pool is available to the colony's women."

"And, of course, there are male settlers available. Less genetic range, but at least you can examine their phenotype."

A candidate giggled. "So I'll be able to choose my babies?" Any shyness among the women was evaporating.

"Well, no." De Smet frowned here. "You'll have full access to the genetic database, and all donations were rigorously screened for genetic disease. But any identifying data has been stripped away from individual donations."

"To ensure no discrimination, even subconsciously, against any ethnicity," Martin added. "To ensure the full range of genetics is utilized."

The room was quiet for a moment.

"Genetics are very important," Martin said, anxious to explain the wisdom of offering embryos with no individual data.

"Let me explain why three thousand is the right number of embryos." De Smet smiled proudly. "We discovered a natural experiment on human population dynamics. The volcanic Toba catastrophe destroyed most of our ancestors only a few tens of thousand years ago, putting the human race through a population bottleneck."

"The smallest population was probably less than two thousand individuals." Martin emphasized the number.

Sheila nodded. She'd scanned the mandatory background reading before coming.

"Of course," Martin said. "Colonists will make their own decisions, freely."

Laws defending reproductive rights were very strict and Colony Mars wanted to stay out of court, but the touchy subject of reproduction was vital to a successful human presence on

Mars. A Kinderen Mission obviously needed to discuss children.

"Our estimates for the colony assume women have a baby every two or three years between the ages of twenty and thirty-five."

Birthing half a dozen children in a lifetime had become rare on Earth. The candidates, however, murmured their enthusiasm. They would spend their days surrounded by children, obsessing over them. They'd been chosen for this.

"How long will it take? For a viable population?" Sheila called out the question, hoping to hurry the doctors along.

"Numbers." De Smet waved her hand vaguely. "It all depends on the assumptions you make."

"The computer model is available to you all," Martin said. "You can enter your own guesses about life expectancy, fertility rates, viability of embryos after decades of storage... With the technology you'll carry to Mars, your success rate, if you choose an embryo, should be eighty-three percent. A huge improvement over rates just a decade ago."

Sheila persisted. "Yes, but you have an estimate?"

"Between five and eight generations."

"A hundred to a hundred and fifty years."

"Of course, we can't say how you, the women of Mars, or your daughters will feel about our assumptions." She reeled off on another endorsement of reproductive rights.

Sheila ignored the litany. She and the other candidates made their decisions long ago, but apparently they were unusual. There must have been little evolutionary pressure favoring a desire for children because, before the modern age, women couldn't do much about it. Now technology gave them control over their own fertility. Since the late twentieth century, the average number of children per woman had been dropping, first in advanced countries like Singapore, Japan, and Italy, and later worldwide. Immigration masked the decline in some countries - North America didn't feel the effects for decades.

Doomsayers calculated that the human race would go extinct before the turn of the next millennium, "not with a bang, but a whimper." But birth rates leveled off. Unexplained bursts of fertility in various countries from time to time helped maintain the global population. Colony Mars needed to create one of those bursts and Mission Five candidates were selected for their exceptional interest in children.

"If a growing population is so important, why send any men to Mars at all?" the precocious fourteen year-old asked.

"Psychologists have demonstrated the value of fathers in society," De Smet said. "Not that every child needs a father, and of course you may structure families as you wish. But, societies where the male-to-female ratio is out of balance are negatively affected. We've studied China's one-child policy that led to excess men, or Russia after World War Two with excess women."

Martin tapped her pad and a pair of graphs with multiple lines zigzagging upwards popped up on the wall. "Nature gave us near-equal numbers of men and women during our reproductive years. It seems best to follow her lead. And there is more to consider than babies. As you can see, mixed-gender teams have higher workplace productivity and better emotional stability than either all-male or all-female teams. That's been demonstrated since early isolation studies. Once cross cultural differences in male to female relationships are adjusted for, of course. We think you'll find mixed-gender teams ease the tension that builds up in close quarters. Having men around will reduce your stress."

Based on the universal tittering, Sheila knew what sort of stress everyone was thinking about. They were all healthy young women, after all.

The fourteen year-old called out again. She was interested in cutting edge technologies. "Why not use artificial wombs to birth loads of babies?"

"Artificial wombs require too much support equipment," De Smet said, shaking her head. "Besides, someone has to raise those babies."

"Experts think a group of four to six children born within a year or two of each other will be optimum initially," Martin said with a smile. "A good match to the colony's food production and recreation space. And would provide a sufficient play and education group."

"Of course..." De Smet said.

Yes, yes, Sheila thought, while respecting everyone's reproductive rights. In a few minutes the doctors would leave the room. Sheila and the other candidates would mill about, grazing on the buffet and talking about populating Mars.

Learn More

Lots of people want to explore Mars. Visit some of these organizations:

mars-one.com/
exploremars.org/
marssociety.org/
planetary.org/
inspirationmars.org/
marsinitiative.org/
mars-sim.sourceforge.net/
solseed.org/
www.fit.edu/ and the recently established Buzz Aldrin
Space Institute at Florida Institute of Technology.
fit.edu/research/centers.php

Also enjoy:

astrobiology.nasa.gov/ask-an-astrobiologist/
and, of course,
mars.nasa.gov

Dunes of the Tharsis Plain were inspired by White Sands National Monument. Those dunes are bright white gypsum, not orange sand like Mars, but still inspirational.

About Kate Rauner

Kate Rauner, Hanover, New Mexico, USA

I write science fiction novels and science poetry, and serve as a volunteer firefighter. I am also a retired engineer and Cold War Warrior (honestly, that's what Congress called us) because I worked in America's nuclear weapons complex. Now living on the edge of the Southwest's Gila National Forest with my husband, cats, llamas, and dog, I'm well on my way to achieving my life-goal of becoming an eccentric old woman.

Visit me at KateRaunerAuthor.Wordpress.com or follow me on Facebook or Twitter @katerauner

Contact: kateraunerauthor.wordpress.com.

Scan now to find all Kate's books on Amazon.

Also by Kate

Visit Amazon for the complete series. Scan the QR code now, and I'll see you on Mars.

Born on Mars Book 2 - Mars-born settlers struggle to find the resources the colony needs to survive. Jake hopes to contact the second colony, settlers from the Earther lands of China and Africa who have ignored the colonists on the Tharsis Plain. Breaking through their silence may offer salvation or disaster.

Hermit on Mars Book 3 - The colony on Mars is thriving but Sig's life is falling apart, both in the robotics lab and with his partner. An urgent call from his mother - who lives in the Hermit's cavern, beyond the safety of the colony - seems like a chance to escape for a while. But life inside the colony bays hasn't prepared Sig for the rigors of a hostile Martian surface or for the strange society of the mkazzi - the miners who explore the mountains surrounding the cavern. Nothing works out the way Sig hopes as he struggles to save the cavern and his mother while regaining joy in his life

Water on Mars Book 4 - Bliss moves to Kamp Kans from her little burg at the best possible time to be alive on Mars. The colony is about to reach its population goal, cargo will arrive from Earth for the first time in generations, and she's going to build a waterfall inside a vast lava tube. So her team leader seems a bit crazy - what could possibly go wrong?

Storm on Mars Book 5 - Zeker swears trouble isn't his fault, but if something weird happens, he's close by. Neuroplasticity treatments may not have fixed his brain.

Receive news on all Kate's writing projects, plus book offers and free flash fiction - click now to join the Readers' Club at http://eepurl.com/bCpx1v or go to kateraunerauthor.wordpress.com and click on Follow Kate.

Titan - Fynn learns the Kin's secret when he's shoved into a stasis pod. He though he'd escaped his family's cult, but he's trapped on Saturn's moon Titan.

The award-winning story begun in *Titan* reaches its stunning conclusion.
Visit Amazon for the complete trilogy.
Scan the QR code now.

Collections of short poems in rhyme;
Inspired all by science;
Outward to the edge of time;
Or tied to earthly cadence.
Light and written all for fun,
There is no angst to hide.
You're invited now to sample one
Of my poems inside.
With a few
Haiku
Too.
Volume One includes *Platypusology*.
Volume Two includes *Because They're Big*
Volume Three includes *Desert Watermelon*
And many more

Thanks

My successes involve help from others - errors and inadequacies are my own.

I'm grateful to Critters.org. Critters is a site where authors freely share their expertise by critiquing each other's work. It's a wonderful resource.

Special thanks to @Jorkam on Wattpad, who caught numerous editing errors - always with kind words and good humor - and discussed technologies with me.

License Notes

Glory on Mars is authored by Kate Rauner and published by Kate Rauner at Smashwords. Copyright 2015 Kate Rauner.

Also available in electronic formats - check your favorite retailer or KateRaunerAuthor.WordPress.com for more information.

Cover by Kate Rauner, copyright 2019. Image of the Tharsis Quadrangle is from the United States Geological Survey (USGS) Astrogeology Research Program. Surface of Mars based on the authors own photographs. (No, not of Mars! Photos from the American southwest.) The robot is from the US government, DARPA at https://commons.wikimedia.org/wiki/File:Legged_Squad_Support_System_robot_prototype.jpg. Various free-use elements are included. Images have been cropped and color-adjusted.

Under End User License Agreement (02-2014), Typodermic Fonts Inc. retains title and all copyrights to the Title and Author Name Fonts https://www.1001fonts.com/nasalization-free-font.html#license and

https://www.1001fonts.com/neuropol-x-free-font.html#license

Connect With Kate

Visit me at KateRaunerAuthor.WordPress.com or follow me on Facebook or Twitter @katerauner

Contact Kate: Go to katераunerauthor.wordpress.com.

Made in the USA
Middletown, DE
06 December 2022

17203625R00170